erotic travel tales

Erotic
Travel Tales

EDITED BY MITZI SZERETO

CLEIS
PRESS

Published in the United States by Cleis Press Inc.,
P.O. Box 14684, San Francisco, California 94114.
Printed in the United States.
Cover design: Scott Idleman
Text design: Karen Quigg
Cleis Press logo art: Juana Alicia
First Edition.
10 9 8 7 6 5 4 3 2 1

"Season of Marriage" by Mary Anne Mohanraj first appeared in *Herotica 6* (Down There Press, 1999) and on Sulekha.com, 2000. "Bottomless on Bourbon" by Maxim Jakubowski first appeared in *Desires* (Altamira Press, 2000). "Wanna Buy a Bike?" by Alison Tyler first appeared in *Good Vibrations Magazine*.

CONTENTS

INTRODUCTION

FROM THE MOMENT I EMBARKED UPON *Erotic Travel Tales*, it became my primary goal to create an anthology that would be completely unique from any of the other anthologies offered for sale in bookstores. I cast a wide net in my search for writers, drawing them from both the playrooms of erotica and the groves of academia. I put out a call for submissions that reached as far east as China, as far south as Australia, as far north as Scandinavia. By collecting stories that take place in a variety of locations throughout the world, I felt it was equally important to hear from voices as wide-ranging. I am pleased, therefore, to have drawn into this anthology's embrace not only internationally known authors of erotica, but also novelists, filmmakers, bookshop proprietors, editors, poets, and university professors.

Erotic Travel Tales offers a taste of the exotic and the familiar, the known and the unknown. We visit Amsterdam, New York City, Toronto, and Taos, continuing west to Hawaii for a sexy romp at an eco-resort, journeying the remainder of the way across the sparkling sapphire of the Pacific to partake of most unusual table fare in Japan. We witness stolen pleasures and deceit in the Himalayas, and intimately observe an arranged marriage in Ceylon. We embark upon anonymous encounters in London's Soho, and travel back in time to the Egypt of the Victorian archeologists. We experience a woman's ecstasy in a cave ritual in Capri, and are party to the forbidden lust of a priest for a flamenco dancer in Spain. We search for lost love in Athens, and have a romp among the demimonde in Paris. We even get to learn what became of the ineffable beauty Tadzio in Thomas Mann's classic novella *Death in Venice*.

From reincarnation in coastal Australia to the sex clubs of New Orleans, from the incense-laden temples near Bombay to a young man's coming of age along Brighton's gloomy shores, each story in *Erotic Travel Tales* takes us on a journey of words — a journey of desire and frustration, joy and sadness, hope and despair. It feeds us a rich, sizzling ragout of human emotion and experience. Like real-life journeys, the fictional ones on these pages are not always easy to make, and may not come equipped with the proverbial storybook ending.

I hope that these erotic tales serve to satisfy your wander-lust…or perhaps to inspire it!

Mitzi Szereto
June 2001

Europa

❧

HELENA SETTIMANA

Her lips crept closer to the receiver, breath echoing back into her ear.

• • •

I want to *fuck* you. I want to fuck you across Europe like stampeding bulls: a humping Pamplona! I want to fuck you in a chintzy hotel with red velvet on the windows and a grimy carpet on the floor. London: pigeon shit on the window, pigeons on the sill. I'm wetter than the fog: listen! My pussy is drizzling for you: pink, red, and *alive* in a misty, gray-and-black world. It'll splatter the pavement — better watch your step!

• • •

Get me on a party boat in Amsterdam and let's laugh about this thing, together. Split my lips with your kisses. Screw me in the shadows lurking beside those red-lit windows. You'll smile when I cry out and bite your neck. I'll show the tourists my ass: my candy-pink, heart-shaped ass, your Valentine...if you want me to. No?... You always want me for yourself, you selfish man.

• • •

Give me Paris. *I know you can.* I'll sing songs by Piaf, in my best out-of-tune voice. I'll shout them down the Seine! Fuck the Eiffel Tower, that's too *common*. I want to do it in the Ste. Chapelle, underneath the painted stars, your cock brushing my lips. Just watch those pinched-faced priests turn white before they drive us from there. Let's shag ourselves ragged in the rear of a rocking, battered Citroen, and invite the *gendarmes* to run us out of town. It would be no great loss: I am bothered by the French and their sniffy attitudes, their stinking *pissoirs* and obnoxious, fluffy dogs.

• • •

Is it out? Is it in your hand? Yes? Oh, you make me so hot I could die from it! I love your cock...the way it weeps for me.

• • •

How about Roma? Could we go there, fleeing like fugitives? Could I get a room in a place with laundry hung in the courtyard, bronze bells ringing, calling the world to reflect and repent? Will it have a view of the Vatican and a crucifix over the door, watching us? Let's have Jesus watch you fuck me in the ass. Do you think he did that to Magdalene — *Yeshua Cristos* with his neatly snipped joint cramming the ass of that whore he supposedly married? In a sagging bed we'll make our own passion play. Make an altar of me that smells of bees and myrrh. You'll steal a candle, just because it's me with you, and anoint me with blood-colored wax. I'll welcome its warmth. Fuck me with it blazing, bleeding on my burning lips. I'll twist with the pleasure of it. I'm twisting now, twisting my nipple hard. You'll want to confess it all. The priest will never see me drawing the tears from your lap. Lap, lap, lap....

Do I shock you? But you know how I am....

I can't hear what you're saying.

Blaspheme? Me? *How hard is it? I know it's hard. Are you close, my love? Are you weeping?*

Do I scare you? I think the more frightened you are, the harder you get.

・・・

OK, then, take me to Venice: crumbling and sinking beneath the weight of our love. There the devout remember their dead and wait for their turn, so fuck me that I come alive, so that I know that I breathe. They say it is a city for lovers, but I think it is more like a morgue: a city of the drowned, the dead, and the waiting-to-die. Make my pulse quicken, show me blood so that I know that I am real. Pump the water from my heaving lungs. Are there fishes in my mouth? Do they swim to freedom from their sanctuary in my cunt? Are they in my hair, like Ophelia? My tits are like tiny coiled mollusks, and your tongue leaves rice-paper-colored wet trails of desire on my skin: snail's trails. We can boast of having been Atlanteans when Venice vanishes beneath the waves.

・・・

Mad? Of course I am mad. I am mad with love for you.

We'll have Saint Petersburg: that's where we can rest. I'll buy furs and black-market jewels and lie in seedy splendor in a wedding-cake house of pastel colors. The furs will be the color of my cunt. There in Saint Petersburg is where color lives, even in the dark of winter. Your breath will lie like a blanket on my face, colored like frost. You can dance for me and paw the ground and I can show you how Catherine loved. All I need is your hand and my imagination. Will you let me? I can go sidesaddle or astride. Then you can come in my mouth, snow-drifts on the red earth of my tongue. I'd suck you off right now, if only I could touch you....

You are there, aren't you? Let me hear you when you come.... That's it.... Say my name. Good.

3

You know what I like.... Oh Christ, baby, I have to go....
Later.... *I love you.*

• • •

Heat colored her face as she set down the receiver and turned to
the woman in the doorway.

"Who was on the phone?"

"Marc, in Brussels."

"And...?"

"And he wants me to go to Strasbourg tomorrow. There's
an emergency shareholders meeting he wants me to address.
We may bring the matter before Parliament, depending on how
convincing I am."

"He doesn't ask for much, does he?"

"When he says, jump, I ask 'How high?' Onto the plane I go."

"Yeah, I know: It's your job. And how long will you be gone?"

"I don't know...depends on whether he has any other jobs
for me once I get there. It's OK, hon, I can handle him. He's tough
on me, but I know what his weaknesses are. I'll manage. I'll call
you every night. We'll talk. That way you won't miss me much.
Honest."

vaporetto

ॐ

SIMON SHEPPARD

FIFTEEN YEARS HAD NOT BEEN PARTICULARLY KIND TO
Venice, nor to his memories of Venice. Nor to him.

The Hotel des Bains, for example. Tadzio remembered it
from his childhood as a grand and silent place. But these days,
breakfasts echoed to the sort of *nouveaux riches* American tourists
who bellowed "Good morning!" and clapped one another on the
back. And the hotel, for its part, responded with signs of incipient
decline. The carpets were tattered, the cherry-wood paneling no
longer polished to an impossible sheen. The once-perfect service
was now too often negligent or peremptory. But then, he thought,
perhaps every place seems grand and perfect when one is fourteen and beautiful. Impossibly beautiful, as he had been.

It was his own damned fault, anyway. When the Count
had suggested taking him on holiday to Venice, it was he himself
who'd insisted on the Hotel des Bains. The place was emblem-
atic, a reminder of a time before the Great War had ravaged
Europe. Before cholera killed his mother, before his drunk,

despondent father shot himself. Before things fell apart. A time when his beauty had drawn all eyes to him, a time when that beauty had been enough.

But the journey with the Count had been difficult from the first—missed connections, disappointing meals, difficulties with their lodgings. And then Venice, glittering Venice, had been unseasonably warm since their arrival several days ago. Beneath the fine facades that bespoke wealth and power, a fetid smell of garbage rose from the canals; tourist ladies in gondolas held scented handkerchiefs to their delicate noses. Both men's tempers had been short. Tadzio had had an argument with the Count that morning, one of many that had lately punctuated their time together. Jealousy, recrimination, reproach.

But, he reminded himself, if not for the Count, he might well be dead.

The estate Tadzio's father had left had been distressingly meager, most of his father's money having been gambled away or spent on whores. Tadzio, though quite unsuited for the world of work, soon discovered there was no shortage of older, wealthy gentlemen who would take an interest in him. At first, each of the men had been richer and more indulgent than the ones before. But as time went by and he drifted from man to man, his youthful softness hardened. He himself was often the one left behind, replaced by new boys who were younger and perhaps even prettier than he. Slipping toward the demimonde, he took up with a cocaine-sniffing painter. Tadzio himself began to use drugs. His once-shining looks became haggard, his attire disheveled. Even his health spiraled into decline. He no longer cared about the burden of beauty.

He'd first met the Count at a gallery opening; the painter's druggy canvases had become a minor sensation among Warsaw's cognoscenti. Tadzio was flying on cocaine, invulnerable. The Count, a well-known patron of the arts, had stared at him, as all the others had, but this time there was a difference. The Count's gaze was not merely voracious; it was tinged with pity. "My poor boy," he thought he heard the Count say. Suddenly Tadzio crumbled, tears in his eyes. His mother. He wanted his dead mother, the smell of her perfume, the warmth of her breast. The gleaming, lost purity of her pearls. Sobbing, he threw himself against the immaculately dressed nobleman. "My poor boy," the Count repeated. "Let me help you. Come home with me." Arm-in-arm they left the gallery, past the curious eyes of the crowd.

When Tadzio returned to the painter's atelier the next day, the artist flew into a rage, cutting Tadzio across the cheek with a letter opener, narrowly missing an eye. Bleeding, he'd run away, back to the Count. He and the painter never spoke again. Tadzio still bore the scar.

The Count had taken him to his country estate, locked him in a room where he'd had no access to drugs, and lovingly nursed him back to health, to sanity. When Tadzio regained his weight, the Count rewarded him with an expensive new wardrobe. When Tadzio regained his good manners, the Count took him to parties, and dinners at fine restaurants. When Tadzio, at last, had asked the man why he'd done all this for him, the Count replied, "Because everyone must care for something, take care of someone. And I could see beyond your troubles, see how good you truly are." The answer made Tadzio feel guilty, depressed, and strangely triumphant. He'd fooled another one.

As soon as Tadzio had gotten back on his feet, free of cocaine, no longer helpless and half-dead, strains inevitably began to show. The aging Count could see as well as anyone that Tadzio, once again so widely desired, might someday slip from his grasp. Gratitude went only so far.

And then the argument at the Hotel des Bains. He'd sworn to the Count that he'd always been faithful to him, and it had been true…very nearly. In the end, though, he'd run from the room, slamming the door, rushing red-faced down the corridor, past astonished chambermaids, down the stairway to the beach. The Lido was filled with ungainly bathers, noisy children, their stupid, indulgent parents, the rows of ugly little bathing-huts. He'd boarded a *vaporetto*, a noisy, public motorboat, not caring where it took him. Its route ran, via Piazza San Marco, up the

Grand Canal with its baroque display of riches, past the tourist gondolas, through a welter of floating trinket sellers and a miasma of festering trash.

He'd disembarked near the Ca' d'Oro. Half-blind with anger and remorse, he'd walked farther and farther away from the tourists' Venezia. Across the Laguna Morta, the cemetery of San Michele hovered in gray heat. The dead who were buried there, he'd once been told, were soon dug up for lack of space, their bones piled into a charnel house. In this stifling city where nothing changed for the better, only the dead were in motion.

His aimless path brought him at last to the winding, narrow maze of back alleys where the poor people lived. In the old days, he'd not even known they were there, the poor. So pampered had class and beauty kept him that the world itself seemed ever-rich and ever-giving. And Venice was most beneficent of all, that final gilded summer before disease robbed him of his mother, beautiful Mama with her strands of pearls.

Now he came to a little courtyard. On three sides stood laundry-draped tenements, their crumbling plaster peeling away, revealing the brick, crumbling too, beneath. The fourth side, the way he had come, held a little shrine of sorts, a marble memorial stone embedded in a wall, beside it a wooden cabinet that a long time ago had been painted green. Corinthian columns flanked a cross-shaped opening in the weathered wood. Behind the opening's green-painted metal grill hung a crucified Jesus, thin, naked, lovely, head indolently cocked to one shoulder, gilded loincloth draped provocatively low around his thighs.

Three ragged boys were kicking a ball around the courtyard. Sitting down upon a filthy stone bench, heedless of his white summer suit, he watched their innocent play. At one boy's kick, the ball went spiraling crazily toward the shrine. If not for the metal grillwork, the naked god would have been hit in the head. If he were living in a novel, he thought, all this would symbolize something.

"Carlo!" A man was standing in a doorway across the untidy little square, calling to one of the ragged boys. "Carlo!

Come here!" Was the man Carlo's big brother? His father? The shadowy doorway made it hard to tell.

Carlo glanced up briefly, but the boys continued their game. The man walked toward them, into the gray light of the humid afternoon. The man was thirty or so, swarthy, slightly stocky, with glossy black hair, a moustache, an Italian beak of a nose. The dark man noticed the stranger in his neighborhood, stared hard for a moment, then smiled. "Carlo! Come in. Your lunch is ready," the man said, but the man's eyes were not looking at Carlo.

The Italian's gaze did not discomfit him. Ever since he was a young boy in Poland, he'd been accustomed to the stares of strange men. Young men, old men, shop clerks, nobility—his beauty had drawn them all. And soon enough he'd learned to provoke them, those staring men. To pique their interest, teasing them with some unspoken promise. Long ago, behind his mother's back, his stolid governess beside him, he began to flirt outrageously. But even then, he understood that his apparent naiveté made it all seem somehow innocent, as though he were an unsullied thing of nature, quite unconscious of his own allure. There was, he still remembered, an old man in Venice, that long-ago summer at the Hotel des Bains, who would gaze at him across the dining room, or from a chaise longue on the Lido. Tadzio would sweep by the old man, his head held high, his heart beating wildly at the knowledge of the power that physical beauty conferred. He began to seduce, actually seduce, the pathetic old bird. A sidelong glance when he was at the beach playing with his friends. A perfect pose when he waded into the sea, his hip cocked suggestively, just so. The power that this gave him excited him, physically excited him, made him hard beneath his swimsuit. He'd had to plunge into the cold water to disguise his arousal. And still the old man stared, besotted by a purity, the purity of boys, that did not, in reality, exist.

"*Buon giorno,*" Tadzio said to the hawk-nosed man, who now had little Carlo beside him, gripping the boy around his skinny shoulders.

"That hurts, Papa," the boy said. They were father and son, then. The grip loosened slightly.

"Hello, *Signore*," said the man. "My name is Gianni." His free hand brushed the thigh of his well-worn trousers.

"Tadzio. My name is Tadzio."

What did this Gianni see, staring at him? A hapless stranger who'd lost his way? A rich tourist to be fleeced? An object of desire? All three?

An awkward silence fell. Then the dark man released his grip and said, "Carlo, go inside." The boy skittered off and disappeared into a doorway.

"What brings you here, *Signore?*"

"To Venice, you mean?"

"To this part of Venice, sir."

How could he explain? He decided to lie. "My wife is busy shopping. I decided to go for a walk."

"Ah, my wife is dead, *Signore.*"

"I'm sorry."

"It happened a long time ago, when Carlo was born." The hawk-nosed man shifted his weight onto one hip, began to rub his palms against his thighs. "There's only the two of us now. And life… life is hard, *Signore*. Work is not so easy to find." Ah, there it was!

"Are you hungry, *Signore?*" the stocky Gianni asked, an unreadable look on his face. "Would you like to share our lunch? It's not much, but…."

Rising from the bench, Tadzio said, "No thank you. My wife will be expecting me." He extended his hand. The man's grip was strong and calloused against Tadzio's smooth white skin.

He had to get out of there. Things had gone too far, lapsed into uncertainty, the crumbling maze that was Venice.

"*Signore?*" The man's quizzical smile broke through his reverie. Tadzio drew his hand away as if burned, then turned to go. He was already in the dark passageway leading from the square when he looked back. The dark, rough man was still standing there, still staring at him. Men's desires had led him to some strange places. And this place was as good as any.

He walked back to the man, stood motionless before him. Gianni smiled and his dark eyes moved down to Tadzio's white-clad crotch. "Come this way, *Signore*."

Will you demand money? Tadzio wanted to ask, but the words stuck in his throat. He followed the stocky Italian. Perhaps he was in danger. He didn't really care.

He followed Gianni into his house. He'd never been in a place like it. Even the cocaine-addicted painter's down-at-the-heels studio had had an arty, raffish elegance. But this Italian tenement had only an air of desperation and the smell of stale cabbage. Gianni led him upstairs, into a single shabby room. Little Carlo was sitting at an oilcloth-covered table, eating noodles in reddish sauce directly from a battered pot.

"This gentleman has come to visit us," Gianni said. The boy looked up, questioningly, but said nothing. Perhaps this was not the first time this had happened. The hawk-nosed man spooned out the food and handed Tadzio, now sitting uneasily at the table, a bowl. He took a bite. It tasted like poverty.

"Go out to play, *bambino*," Gianni told his son. The boy ran out, slamming the door behind him. They were alone. Gianni leaned over and ran his fingers over Tadzio's scar. The hawk-nosed man kissed him, tentatively, then fiercely, and dragged him from the table, across the pathetic room. Tadzio felt his cock swelling. He struggled out of his white linen jacket, then tore at the Italian's rough shirt. The man's chest, powerfully built and matted with hair, was so different from his own. They fell onto the room's single rickety bed. Clothes were strewn everywhere. Even erect, Gianni's dark, weighty cock was half-hidden by a long foreskin.

The Italian's piercing smell cut through the room's stale air. Tadzio pinned one muscular arm to the mattress and buried his face in the man's sweaty armpit. The honesty of the odor nearly made him gag. Hairy legs wrapped around Tadzio's waist. For a moment, Tadzio thought that Gianni was like the Count, that he wanted to be entered, but an exploratory touch was pushed away. The strong, hairy man wrestled around till Tadzio was pinned beneath him, legs spread askew. Reflexively, accepting the inevitable, Tadzio raised his legs. A single gob of spit and the Italian forced his way inside. The man's fucking was inexpert but enthusiastic. The bed groaned beneath his thrusts.

Tadzio looked up into the man's sweaty, triumphant face, smelled the garlic and tobacco on his breath. He shut his eyes and imagined the Count lunching at the Hotel des Bains, full of regret. And now Tadzio was so very distant from that once-perfect dining room, from the crisp white table linen, from the vacant velvet chair at the table for two.

It began to hurt. The fucking began to hurt. Tadzio clawed at the man's broad, hairy back, bit the man's lip until blood flowed. The Italian looked furious, then something else altogether, and his thrusts became even more brutal. Gianni's acrid sweat made Tadzio's pale skin gleam. A smell of shit arose. A guttural yell. Another. Gianni pumped one last time into Tadzio. And, as he shot his juices deep within the pale white ass, the leg of the bed shattered, with a sound of splintering wood, and they crashed to the floor. Startled, they stared at one another. And they both began to laugh at their own astonishment. And stared once again, perfect strangers.

Gianni's softening cock had slipped from inside. But Tadzio's was still hard, and he reached down to finish himself off. Gianni brushed the hand aside and, to Tadzio's amazement, bent over and kissed the hard flesh. A calloused hand worked up and down the shaft till climax was near, and then Gianni's soft lips swallowed him whole, and the end came.

Things were suddenly silent between them. Tadzio struggled up from the floor, wiped himself off as best he could. His suit, which the Count had given him, was tangled in a corner, soiled and wrinkled. Gianni still lay on the floor, a muscular hand cupped around his genitals for modesty's sake. A cheap crucifix hung on the wall above the bed, a tiny echo of the naked god in the courtyard outside. The sound of children, carefree for the moment, filled the air beyond the open window.

Tadzio was pulling his pants on when Gianni said, "*Signore,* I so much hate to ask this. It's not for myself, you understand, but for Carlo...." It was said gently, but behind the Italian's hard-eyed smile, Tadzio knew, was a threat. He reached into his pocket and pulled out a roll of *lire*.

Gianni held out his left hand, the one that wasn't on his dick. "For Carlo," he repeated as he took the cash. He looked down at the money in his hand. "So little, *Signore?*" he asked. "So little?"

mitsuko

کہ

ANN DULANEY

IN THE CONCRETIZED AND MISTY TOWN OF K——,
Hokkaido Prefecture, now some four or five decades in the past,
a man and his wife pursued a simple, traditional existence. He
worked as a clerk in an accounting office, sorting through
ledgers and making his notations in them with a careful script.
She maintained as comfortable a household as his modest salary
could provide, and she was a most excellent cook, able to turn
even the poorest vegetables and cuts of fish into sumptuous
treasures.

The man, whose name was Shoji, was soon to turn forty-
five years old. He was of meager frame, humble, unpretentious
to a fault, and generous too. He would give away house and
home to please a stranger. As for Mitsuko, his blushing bride
twenty-five years his junior, she endured the absence in him of
all aggressive ambition because he more than made up for it
in steadfastness and in the consistent appreciation of her many
natural gifts.

For two years they had been hoping for the blessing of a child, but as yet no embryo had found Mitsuko's womb hospitable, or so she would analogize. More probably, it was Shoji's spermatozoa that, like him, were too deferential to outpace their own brothers on the path to the prize and, once there, were far too polite to disturb the sleeping ovum.

Their little house shone with cleanliness, and every evening when Shoji returned in forced-smile dejection from the office, Mitsuko would reward him with artfully arranged flowers, a tray of delicate morsels for his palate, and a comforting shoulder massage. He would speak to her of his day, would tell her about the old woman he saw feeding birds in the park, or about the naughty boy leading a toy boat by a string who nearly ran him down. From these unrelated anecdotes, Mitsuko was able to glean that, for one more day at least, a promotion to junior manager was still not forthcoming.

Mitsuko successfully kept her disappointments to herself. Miraculously, she transformed vicissitude to the verisimilitude of being a model wife, with the same determination that transforms energy to matter and vice versa. She did not love her husband with any remarkable ardor, but she was faithful to him, and the noble consistency of her character dictated that she would be loyal unto him until the grave.

One day, Shoji rushed home and announced that the following evening his boss would come for dinner. The two clasped each other for joy, for that meant, surely, that Shoji's career was about to take a turn skyward. "Today," Shoji recounted, "when you brought me my umbrella, which I had foolishly forgotten—and in the heart of the rainy season, imagine!—my boss noticed you at my desk. He must have been thinking, 'Shoji-san left his umbrella at home in the heart of the rainy season: All his energies must be focused on work. Now that's real dedication!' I did not even have to beg him to come; he himself suggested it!"

Mitsuko blushed imperceptibly, and wondered what it all meant. At the office, she did not remember seeing Shoji's boss, whom she had never met and would not recognize; if indeed he had been nearby, Shoji had been, in all likelihood, too flustered to introduce them. So now this man would join them in their evening repast. Tomorrow! She would have to hurry to prepare.

As Shoji munched happily on his supper, and later retired with a cigarette to the comfortable leather chair—the one they never sat in because it had been so costly—Mitsuko fluttered about the house, dusting and straightening, in spite of the fact that their house was never less than immaculate. Mitsuko understood, however, that a psychological cleansing also needed to take place. It was a necessary process, a prerequisite, before she could admit a stranger, and one so prominent, into their home.

By the next evening, all preparations had been made. Mitsuko welcomed her husband and his boss into the house, which had been set festively with quiet music and fragrant orchids. Shoji was as giddy as a young boy, and he danced around and spoke crazily on inane topics. Shoji's boss, whose name was Miyataki, bowed deeply to her and presented her with a decorated parcel, no doubt a scarf or a fan or a little silk wallet, which she accepted graciously and well within the protocol of tradition. She hadn't expected him to be quite so imposing a figure, and when she accidentally caught his gaze, she felt the color flood her cheeks, and hurriedly cast her own gaze downward. Bowing profusely, she led the two men into the sitting area and ushered Mr. Miyataki into the expensive leather chair.

As Mitsuko offered the men cigarettes from a box made of teak, Mr. Miyataki verbalized his admiration of Mitsuko's necklace and earrings, which had been a wedding gift from her mother. She never removed them. Shoji, having always failed to comprehend their sentimental value and now in a rush to placate Mr. Miyataki, removed the jewels from her at once, pressing them into his boss's hands insistently: "Please, please, they are yours," he urged. "With my most humble compliments!"

Miyataki glanced at Mitsuko and saw that her face revealed not the slightest emotion whatsoever. A smirk played about his lips, and he understood quite well that this ill-made gesture on Shoji's part was not out of character, but what did Mitsuko think of it? What would happen if he were to simply pocket the jewelry, instead of finding a way to politely refuse it? Would she bear the insult with grace? He chose to accept it. He made only the slightest bow to Shoji from his seat, and then slipped Mitsuko's beautiful wedding necklace and earrings unceremoniously into his breast pocket.

Mitsuko's heart was burning with shame, and she was painfully aware of her naked earlobes and throat as she bent over the table and set to laying out the exquisitely prepared dishes for the two men to enjoy. Finally she motioned to them that the meal was ready, and then squatted a short distance away so that she might serve them efficiently without being intrusive.

Mr. Miyataki seemed a strange guest. He drank great quantities of sake, and she noted angrily that her husband, who was not so accustomed to the effects of the potent beverage, attempted to match his superior swallow for swallow. In addition, in what seemed to be calculated departures from decorum, Miyataki frequently caught Mitsuko's eye—ever so briefly!—usually when Shoji's attention was captured elsewhere, which made her shiver because his gaze could be so penetrating, and she was not unaware that his features were inarguably striking.

But what's more, he was not overly appreciative of her cooking or the courtesies she extended him. Disguised within the context of language that extended from ancient complimentary etiquette, Miyataki managed to insinuate every so often that something was lacking, that another sauce might have served this or that more eloquently, and so on. He seemed to deliberately test their hospitality in venturing so far from customary politeness. But to what end? Why had Miyataki come to their house? What did he really want from them?

Miyataki's comments, rather than rouse Shoji to defend his own honor or that of his wife, efficiently fueled Shoji's anxiety, and caused him to send Mitsuko scurrying for replacements and substitutions. Mitsuko realized that before long, the sake would have depleted itself, and there would be no further food items she could substitute. She saw her husband being played like a toy; she saw what a weak man he truly was. But what was worse, she saw her husband's chances at promotion slipping through her own graceful fingers.

The situation, although on the surface a quite calm, exceptionally amicable exchange of pleasantries, was fast becoming desperate. Shoji's head was beginning to list, and Mr. Miyataki's smug dissatisfaction was clearly growing. Soon, the situation would be beyond rescue. Her husband would never ask for or demand his own promotion, but willingly placed all dependence on circumstance — on *her* — to carry the day.

Mitsuko placed a lacquered tray of fresh salmon before Mr. Miyataki. These cuts had been quite dear, and she knew if they did not please him, nothing would. He considered them, frowning slightly. "Won't you please try?" Mitsuko asked reverently. Shoji, red-faced, was heard to comment, "My dear, clearly Mr. Miyataki would prefer something else. Surely there is something else to offer him?" Nothing else, she thought, disconsolately. I have nothing else to offer. The situation is hopelessly compromised. They would always be poor; they would never enjoy comfort.

She still crouched quite close to Mr. Miyataki. The look in her husband's face was one of desperation. She herself could feel how her brow had furrowed, could feel how her knees trembled. Miyataki, the only one bathed in true calm, the only one who seemed masterful and in control, looked boldly at her again, his dark eyes sparkling with something between amusement and expectation.

She was a woman of great honor, but Mitsuko knew if she did not do everything in her power to please Shoji's boss, Shoji would always blame her, and rightly so, for all subsequent misfortune. She laid the tray of salmon on the table thoughtfully.

"Perhaps I do have something else Mr. Miyataki might care to try?" she asked as she began to slip nimble fingertips into the silk folds of her kimono.

There was a pregnant moment of silence, and she hesitated. Mr. Miyataki, understanding all at once what her intentions might be, broke the silence, and even included a measure of warmth in his tone: "Ah! Might you be suggesting some home-made delicacy? Indeed, I am intrigued," he told her confidently, winking at Shoji.

Shoji crouched nearby, not yet fully grasping what was happening. Mitsuko shrugged her shoulders carefully, coaxing the kimono to drop with grace about her slender, pale arms. Black nipples, like a pair of demure, flirtatious eyes—a contrast to the expression of her true eyes, which stared emotionless and defiant away from the two men—peeked over the lip of sleek, embroidered fabric. A few subtle motions more and Mitsuko was able to lay the garment altogether to one side, now serving Mr. Miyataki clothed only by her white slippers and the little black crested wave that shrouded the center of her body. For the first time, Mr. Miyataki appeared genuinely pleased. His demeanor toward her also became noticeably tender.

Shoji's eyes blinked once, then twice. The sake in his belly and a calculated gesture from Miyataki told him to relax, so he kept silent. What was Mitsuko up to? Well, whatever it was, it made Mr. Miyataki happy. Maybe hope existed after all.

Mr. Miyataki, who had been kneeling at the little table, now took the opportunity to reorganize himself. He lay down on his side, rearranging his long limbs, supporting himself on one crooked elbow, and looked up at her in anticipation.

Mitsuko assumed a most immodest pose then, one in which she reclined before him, her spine rounding, her legs splayed outward, affording him a view of her that no one, her husband included, had seen since her own infancy. But Miyataki's pleasure was quite evident. A silent smile and a keenness about his eyes informed her that she should continue with this method of service.

Mitsuko lifted a pair of chopsticks into her fingertips and secured a piece of the expensive salmon. Using the fingertips of her free hand, she drew apart the curtains to her womb, exposing herself fully. Her next action was to place the morsel on the threshold of her womanly opening, thus imbuing the flesh of the fish with her own subtle aroma and flavor. This she next placed before the parted lips of Mr. Miyataki.

Miyataki held out his tongue and accepted the salmon into his mouth, drawing his lips poignantly over the lacquered chopsticks, unwilling to sacrifice the smallest trace of the delicacy. A deep-throated purr emanated from him at the successful delivery of this bit of sustenance. "Quite excellent!" he congratulated her.

Mitsuko's body relaxed slightly, in obvious relief. Her husband grinned at her, also significantly relieved and brimming with spousal pride. "Another, if you please?" Miyataki requested.

Wielding the chopsticks, Mitsuko fed Mr. Miyataki morsel after morsel in this fashion, placing each bite of food into her natural *jus* before offering it to him. Each bite produced from her more of the precious extract, and the activity itself became increasingly enjoyable for them both. Shoji, too, watched them hungrily, and once in a while Mitsuko would treat him to a sample, although they both understood that the vast majority of preferential courtesy must continue to be extended toward Mr. Miyataki.

Before much longer, Mitsuko's body had come to produce so much liquid, that food items slipped easily inside her: quail eggs, small fruits, rice cakes. She would let them marinate just inside her body, warming them to a suitable temperature, and then she would give birth to these tender bites, reveling in a sense of pleasure of her own, enjoying both the tactile sensation as well as the look of rapture emblazoned on the face of Mr. Miyataki.

After some time, Mr. Miyataki decided he could no longer tolerate waiting for Mitsuko to expel the food from her body before she fed it to him. He took to placing bites of food inside her himself, and then, positioning his lips directly over her, sucked the little treasures into his own mouth. This seemed to give them both such exquisite and almost unbearable delectation that Mitsuko's body began to quiver from head to toe. Like a good homemaker, she rejoiced in the pleasure she was able to offer her dinner guest, but also, Mr. Miyataki's lips and tongue were skillful, as any general manager's should be.

Shoji regarded them both with unbridled admiration and took to making his own suggestions, albeit ones that fell on four deaf ears: *Oh, try a lychee! Try a chestnut! Try these noodles! Try them in combination!*

But when Mitsuko reached for a bowl of bright black cherries, that was when Mr. Miyataki called an abrupt halt to the operation. He sat back on his haunches and opened his trousers, drawing out what had become by then a most ominous instrument. He took it in both his hands, one palm enclosing the tip of the bulging tool, the other stroking it methodically. A consummate professional, in just a few moments he had artfully produced a fine spirit of his own.

His hand encapsulating the milky liquor, he smilingly applied it like a paste to the outer surface of Mitsuko's seat of femininity. "Cherries are my favorite of all treats," he told her. "And they must be specially prepared to be properly relished." Mitsuko dutifully held her legs apart for him and reclined on both elbows, becoming ever more dreamy, her muscles ever more active, as the deep red gems were inserted into her.

Her breath came in sharp, shallow gasps as she fought to contain her pleasure. But now Mr. Miyataki's familiar lips were at their appointed position, and the pleasure mounted beyond her control. Mr. Miyataki, seeming to sense the close of the meal was too quickly approaching, and not wishing for the comfortable evening to end, withdrew his mouth, probing her opening with only the slender tip of his tongue. Mitsuko, hovering on the edge of what might have been the most vertiginous drop of her life, found herself being safely lowered to earth by means of one fluffy cloudlet at a time: Mr. Miyataki eked the pleasure from her so gradually that, as each cherry emerged from her quivering womb, he was able to chew it completely and expel the stone, often pausing to utter a word or two of appreciation—"Delicious! Excellent! Superb!"—before the next ruby appeared at her entrance. He delivered her of them so slowly that even the candles on the table seemed to lose their stature. Shoji found time to steal a glance at his watch and saw that it was getting quite late. Mitsuko, no longer able to keep silent, found that the last few cherries accompanied a long and steady, high-pitched, almost operatic tone that culminated in its own extinguishment in the fierce clenching of her abdomen.

For a long time afterward, all she saw were pinpricks of light behind her eyelids. At last, she opened her eyes and drew her knees together as modesty returned. She reached for her kimono and drew it about her. The tea service! But Shoji and Mr. Miyataki were already on their feet, shaking hands and bowing to one another. Mr. Miyataki was preparing to leave. Mitsuko jumped to her feet and found the simple act of walking to the door unexpectedly difficult. She bowed to Mr. Miyataki as respectfully as she could in her condition, and he told her that it had been a remarkable evening. He patted his breast pocket reverently, the pocket containing her wedding jewelry, and added his wish that they meet again, stating that the meal she prepared in his honor had been quite superior and extremely satisfying, and, finally, that he had high hopes that her husband would soon enjoy a greater degree of success at work.

Mitsuko and Shoji rejoiced. Indeed, within the week, Shoji was promoted to Junior Manager. In tribute to not only that wonderful event but also the kingly generosity of Mr. Miyataki, the twin boys Mitsuko was successfully delivered of later that year bore a respectful and complimentary resemblance to their father's patron. Regrettably, however, Mitsuko's cooking never quite regained the same heights.

And what of the contents of the gift Mr. Miyataki presented to her on their first meeting? Was it a fan, a scarf, or a silk wallet? Indeed not. The decorated parcel contained a fine set of jewelry, perhaps not so terribly valuable, but certainly very pretty: a necklace and matching earrings of coral and pearl to replace the ones that had been sacrificed — gems that Mitsuko wore with fierce, glowing pride. She let it be known unequivocally, whenever anyone asked about them, that she would never remove them.

coming round the mountain

꩜

TABITHA FLYTE

CALLUM WAS SICK, REALLY SICK, BUT THE WAY CHELLE said it, as she burst into my hut just before sunrise, suggested that it was an inconvenience more than anything else.

The guides brought us hot chai, and Chelle and I sat wrapped up in our rugs, supping the hot liquid, mulling over the dilemma. She said disdainfully that Callum had altitude sickness. *Why?* she asked, *does it always happen to me?* I wanted to say that it wasn't exactly happening to her, but I was guilty myself. I couldn't help thinking that maybe I had brought it on them—I had been wishing so hard that she would get sick, or collapse over the mountain edge. Well, maybe the gods had been listening after all but had misheard the name.

Last night, I couldn't sleep. The air was thick with the plaintive wail of mountain wolves, but I thought I heard them having sex. I pictured them in the adjacent hut, him on top of her.

Him groaning fast, white buttocks pumping. Her nipples, hard as a rockface, in his mouth. I tried to block it out, as we had a heavy day's walking ahead, but I grew hot and wet. I tried to imagine that it was the handsome guides with their weather-beaten faces and shy smiles who were making love to me, but my fantasies just boomeranged back to him, bloody Callum.

"I don't know what to do," Chelle whined.

"I don't think you have a choice, do you?" I responded. "The only solution is to take him down, lower, where the air is less thin, where he can breathe."

"But it's so fantastic here," Chelle said, and she looked around the hut contentedly. Outside, the guides were making rice and smoking roll-ups, contemplating the day's walking instead. I knew that she didn't want to descend. Chelle had decided that she would "do" the Himalayas, and it would take more than Callum's illness to stop her.

Yesterday, I had hovered toward the back of the group, watching them march up the trail together. The stones crunched beneath our feet, and occasionally they paused to admire a small wildflower or insect. Ahead lay the white-capped mountains that we were all there to see. They were magnificent and brooding, but I was distracted by Chelle's backside, which swayed in front of me, like a baby elephant's. Did Callum like her arse? Did he cup his fingers around her buttocks at night, massaging away the pains of walking the allotted ten kilometers a day? She had been bitten on the calf, and a trickle of blood faintly dribbled a line down. Even though it must have made the walk two times harder for both of them, they insisted on holding hands. I felt my loneliness amplified a thousand times more, and as we ascended I found myself asking in rhythm to our footsteps, *What am I doing here…what am I doing here?*

• • •

We had met in Kathmandu. I was looking for adventure—yes, to discover myself. I was bored with my jobs, my friends, my *suburban existence*. My family, naturally, had disapproved.

My mother said, "This is life—accept it." My father said, "You only want mountains, not the valleys," and I shouted back, "What do *you* know?"

At the hostel, I met a Frenchwoman, Amanda. We went out, marveling at the buffalos wandering the streets, weaving between motorbikes, old taxis, and rickshaws. We gazed at the temples and shrines. Some buildings contained exquisite wooden engravings of bodies entwined, making love, hands and tongues everywhere. Later, I found out that they were scenes from the *Kama Sutra*. At the time, though, I didn't know what they were. They made me feel quite strange.

It was early evening and we were walking back to the hostel when I saw the most amazing sight of all. It was his face that held me: the lips, a slightly darker patch above, and a row of sensual teeth that seemed to be designed to dig into the neck of some lucky victim. He had dark blond hair, marking him out as a foreigner like us, and it was tousled superbly in the way that even people who insist on smooth hair would approve of. Then I saw he was with a woman. She was a slim but heavy girl in a fleece jacket, shorts, and trainers. She too had dark blonde hair, but whereas his was radiant and alive, hers was dull and made her skin look tired.

I hoped they were together in the way travelers hook up, like Amanda and me. Travelers can't be choosers: Anyone who shares a language, or even has the same color passport, is a potential friend. But then as I watched, she tucked him under her arm, the scolding way women only use with men they have bullied for years. I would never have put them together. It had nothing to do with their looks, which, to be fair, were on a par, but more the way that they looked. He had a softness—not feminine, but a male softness, inquiring and gentle; she seemed hard, full of severity and judgment. Maybe it was a yin-and-yang thing, maybe it was the age-old adage about opposites attracting, but from where I was standing it seemed like an obscenity.

She went into a shop and he waited outside. I guess he must have seen us, me, looking at him. He smiled and I smiled back. He mouthed a *Hello,* and that was all the excuse I needed to walk over there, with Amanda trailing behind me.

I can't remember the words he said, for I was too caught up watching his body move and wondering what it would feel like on my skin. As we stood there, some little street kids bolted by, chasing a football and he grabbed my arm to stop them careening into me. I felt waves rush through my body. I wanted to fuck him more than I had ever wanted to fuck anyone before. If he had asked me then to perform any depravity, commit any sin, anything that involved him and me, I would have agreed.

The woman emerged from the shop, holding a paper bag. I stared at him beseechingly and he hesitated.

"Come on, then," she said impatiently.

"She's from England," he said to her.

She looked at us, for just a second too long, and then maybe she decided we passed.

"Hi," she said. "English people, wow!"

She stuck out a plump pink hand and I had a sudden vision of pig's knuckles.

"Chelle," she said. "What are your names?"

I learned that his name was Callum. *Callum, Callum...*the word swiveled around dizzily in my head.

As we commenced the tourist's conversation—*Where had we been? How long had we spent there? Where were we going next?* — I stared at Callum's feet in their brown leather sandals. He had slim, tan legs, a heavier torso. Now that we were close, I hardly dared look at his face. He had cheekbones of suffering and romance, eyebrows of strength, and all this was topped off by a mouth that showed such sensual promise. He smiled at me, and for a split second he was between my legs, his face stained with my juices, and he was diving down on me, nuzzling my thighs. I had to shake myself away from the thought.

He likes me, I decided. I wondered how we could get rid of Chelle; maybe she had followed him. His eyes, shining on me, gave me confidence.

"So how come you two are in Nepal?" I asked him. We stood side-by-side. She responded, banging on about the mountains, about her never getting an opportunity like this again, begging her boss for one month's holiday, having a very high-powered job, etc.

"We're on honeymoon," he added, and I felt an avalanche of sorrow cascade down my heart.

• • •

They needed two more people to join them on a trek. Amanda and I looked at each other and then agreed. To cement the deal, we decided to eat together. Chelle wanted to go to a place that her guidebook recommended. I didn't know then, but Chelle only went to places that her guidebook recommended. It was a restaurant on the roof of the hostel, and it took us a full twenty minutes to find it. Although I didn't admit it, the choice was excellent. It was a balmy evening and the stars seemed to blink benevolently.

"The sky is so much more beautiful here than at home," said Chelle, and I was annoyed because that was exactly what I was thinking.

The tables were small and Callum's legs were long. We banged knees, and every time I felt the swell of his leg against mine, I had to draw in my breath, for my heart was beating so strongly. He was next to her, and sometimes their hands disappeared. To accommodate his long legs, I opened mine so that his leg pressed against my inner thigh. It was a pleasing arrangement. I could feel heat radiating from my knees, emanating, wrapping around him.

Callum and I didn't speak much. Chelle rattled on and on. Occasionally, she would look to Callum for agreement and he would nod enthusiastically, though I don't know if he was keeping up any better than I was. I wanted his knee to go further up me. I could almost pretend it was right up me, pressed against my pussy.

On the way back, Chelle and Amanda walked ahead, their conversation propelling them fast through the streets while we dawdled. The mountains made a haunting backdrop, and I couldn't help pretending we were in some kind of movie. I could easily have pretended that it was just the two of us, but he started talking about Chelle, about what a great girl she was.

"And how come you married?" I asked. I had to know. Phrased like that, I knew it sounded bad, but Callum didn't look surprised or offended, though his answer, to my mind at least, was less than satisfactory.

"Been together seven years, and I thought, I'm never going to meet anyone else—I mean, anyone better than her...."

We had lost them. One moment, they were ahead of us, the next there were only old men with sticks and women in saris rushing home with bags of fruit.

"I'm afraid," I interrupted.

"Don't worry, I'm with you," he said. I could tell from his voice that he was smiling.

"That's what I'm afraid of."

I wondered if he knew how close he had come to masturbating me with his knee in the restaurant.

He took my hand, and I felt my body rushing out—every fiber, every nerve, every part of me seeming to rush toward him, pleading *Touch. Touch me.*

"You're shaking," he said, and covered my hand with his, sandwiching me.

He must have felt it too. It was like a magic spell.

I felt as if I was melting, my whole body liquefied. I couldn't look at him—I wanted our bodies to meet, trembling. I felt a sliver of wetness run down my leg.

"I'm sure I've met you before," he ventured.

"It's possible." I thought of the idea of reincarnation. He moved toward me, saying, "I feel...."

"Oy, over here!"

They had found us. Under a streetlight, Amanda and Chelle were encircled by a halo of gold light. Callum and I were still in the darkness.

"There you are," barked Chelle impatiently, and took Callum's arm.

"I was just saying, I feel like I've known Ella for ages," Callum said swiftly, and it was such an obvious cover-up that I was thrilled—so there *was* something to cover up.

"That's traveling for you," said Chelle complacently. I hated her. "You get to know people so quickly."

We walked back to our respective hostels silently. It seemed even Chelle had run out of things to say. When we parted, he leant forward and kissed me on the cheek. I was unprepared and I tilted my head ever so slightly, but the result was that his lips fell on the corner of my mouth.

"Goodnight, Ella," he said, and it was as though he was breathing fire into me.

" 'Night, Callum."

And then Chelle kissed the air next to my cheek, and I obediently pecked the air next to hers.

. . .

"Look, I'll…I'll take him down. One of the guides will come with us. We'll meet you at the bottom…if you want. I'm not bothered about going on—I've seen enough mountains to last me a lifetime."

I was thinking, A chance to be alone with Callum! Even a sick Callum was better than nothing! We had been on the trek for five days now, and Callum had studiously ignored me. Well, not ignored exactly, but he certainly made sure he was never alone with me.

"You want to turn back now?" Chelle queried suspiciously. "But we've nearly made it to the higher peaks."

"Actually, I'm worried I'll get sick too. It's too cold for me." I held out my hands. "I have poor circulation!"

She took them. "Huh, they're freezing. Still, you know what they say about cold hands?"

"Ahh, yes, cold hands equals warm heart," I laughed. *And other places too.*

"The guides will lend you more clothes if you ask," she suggested. Typical—she wouldn't mind letting the guides freeze to death.

"No, I think this is the best solution...."

So it was decided.

When I told the other members of the group, they compli-mented me; how kind I was, how thoughtful. Only Amanda didn't say anything, and I knew she had guessed my real reason. She looked at me a little strangely, and when later it came to goodbye, she whispered into my ear, "Don't get hurt."

"I won't. I've got a great guide, the best equipment," I said confidently, but she said, "I don't mean that."

I knew exactly what she meant, but I didn't listen.

• • •

The guide packed up Callum and we started walking down. Callum leaned hard on the guide's shoulder, and I carried our bags. We trod down the stone paths, barely pausing to enjoy the views. The guide was fantastic. Sometimes it looked as though Callum would roll away down the slope, as he seemed to be sleepwalking, but the guide held him at all times. I just kept thinking how it was far easier going down than it was going up.

I know it was probably wrong; Callum was very ill, which was a terrible piece of misfortune, especially on his honeymoon, but I don't remember when I ever felt happier to be alive.

• • •

Late that afternoon, after we had walked for maybe five or six hours, we set up a two-person tent. The guide set up his own a few yards away. It was snowing ever so lightly, and before I went in, I caught some snowflakes on my cheeks.

Callum was delirious. I didn't know what he could see with those rolling eyes. He was so handsome, even midfever; his face was drenched with petals of sweat. His cheekbones pro-truded even more, now that his excess flesh was receding. Why couldn't it have been Chelle who got sick? We could have been striding at the top of the mountain now, hand in hand. No, he would have stopped for her; she didn't stop for him.

The guide had given us a sheepskin rug to cover ourselves with. It felt fantastic against my skin. He said he would get us some food, and said we were to relax. He opined that Chelle was very "tough," and he laughed loudly so I did too.

Callum groaned. He wasn't sleeping, he was in and out of consciousness; light and dark, noise and quiet, external and internal worlds were bewilderingly colliding. Was it the beating of his heart, or the shuffling of the guide, or perhaps wild animals outside that I could hear? It was light outside, but dark in the tent. I moved around like a shadow.

"Callum?" I whispered. I pushed the rogue hair off his forehead. The style was unfamiliar. Usually, his fringe dangled dark and low, ominous like a heavy cloud.

He gripped my hand. His palm was sweaty, almost greased, but it was somehow torturously arousing. I could barely move for fear of giving myself away. He needed me. He loved me.

I put my right hand to his dry lips. His lids fluttered close. He smiled.

He murmured something, and I leaned close, my ear hovering over that sensuous mouth:

"What, Callum?"

This time I heard:

"Chelle." A smile fluttered to his lips, as mine withered and died.

Oh God, he thought I was her.

"No," I said lamely, "I'm not Chelle," but he carried on, as if I hadn't spoken.

"If I die...."

"You're not going to die," I whispered. "Honest, Cal." That's what she called him. Cal, not Callum.

"I feel so hot. There's a fire inside me."

"Me too," I said, although mine was slightly different.

"I'm glad we came though...I didn't want to...but now you're here, looking after me. I know how much you love me...."

"Cal," I interrupted. I sopped his forehead with a flannel. He was sweating like a trouper.

"Lie next to me," he said.

I moved under his arm. He didn't smell bad, but he did smell strong. I pulled off his T-shirt, and he sighed relief. I worked the flannel over his chest, stumbling over his rosy nipples. The color of them was the healthiest thing about him. I moved my hand over his flat belly. It wasn't hard, but not soft either. He couldn't afford to lose any more weight.

"I'm so hot still...."

I decided to undo his trousers. They came off easily. He managed to help a little by raising his legs. He was just wearing his underwear now. I couldn't stop looking at him, wanting him.

"Chelle," he murmured approvingly as I toyed with the tiny buttons of his boxer shorts.

He needs a good wash, I told myself unconvincingly, *he needs to be cleaned.* I trailed the makeshift flannel over his damp skin down, down, to the line of sweet hair. I pulled down his shorts to his knees and took my first look at his cock. Beautiful. And then as I was watching and waiting, his penis unraveled and stalked me out, a one-eyed worm rising up to look at the world. My friend.

"Whoops," he said, embarrassed. I moved the flannel around to caress his balls, and he seemed to relax. He parted his legs more, and I felt that familiar surge of power you get when a helpless man presents his cock to you. He was mine, all mine, and after so long dreaming about him, there was no way I could let this erection go to waste. Every erection counts when your time together is limited.

"Oh, Callum," I sighed—correcting myself quickly: "I mean, Cal."

I kissed his dry lips. I couldn't resist. No one would know. Even he would never know—but he would love it. I kissed him harder, snaking my tongue into his mouth. His mouth was wet and obedient; I wanted to climb on in. At the same time I was fumbling for that hardening cock with my hands.

"Chelle, what are you doing?" he murmured.

His penis was rigid. I couldn't believe how hard he was, and my pussy dampened appreciatively. I lowered down to him, where the air was less thin, and where we could breathe. I took his lovely cock in my mouth, and I played with its perfect head with my tongue.

"Fucking hell, Chelle," he said, "what did I do to deserve this?"

So she only gave him blowjobs when he was a good boy! I thought, priding myself on my generosity. She obviously didn't enjoy it much herself! I sucked like a woman possessed. I *was* a woman possessed; I formed a tunnel with my lips and passed him in and out. I was a better suck, a better fuck, than she. The idea got me going—spurred me on. I'm the best, oh yes. He couldn't stop groaning, his hands were reaching for my hair, pressing me on.

I put my fingers to myself. At the same time, I straddled the rug, feeling its hot skin stir inside me, as if a thousand wild animals were taking me. I fingered myself.

"Chelle, don't stop, baby, I love you."

Even the deceit aroused me. The big fucking con, the cheating was bad, yes it was bad, and that's why it felt so good. Only, it wasn't wrong, it was no sin, because we were loving it, weren't we? He, me…and as for her, what the mouth doesn't get to suck on, the heart doesn't grieve for. I bent over him, my arse up in the air, worshiping his cock, and as I sucked him, I pleasured myself. Soft, light, easy strokes. He was another woman's man, but for now, he was mine. I was greedy for him.

I deserved it. *We* deserved it.

As he shuddered, a thousand ancient shudders, he was whispering, "Thank you, thank you," but I stayed silent because I knew he thought I was someone else.

And then he rolled over to avoid the wet patch. I tied on my sarong and went out to write postcards home.

• • •

Later, I fed him rice mixed with water. He only ate a little. Afterward, I had to help him with a bottle to pee in. He apologized and cried a little, berating himself for being useless, and I told him that he wasn't, and that I loved him. I said that he would be better soon, and would be able to take care of me.

Outside, I watched the sun go to rest over Annapurna. I had stopped looking at the view; I had simply got used to its beauty, perhaps like the way a married couple look at each other. I thought of him and us. Another time, another place. In a next life. I thought of the taste of his cock and his snow-white come.

The guide saw me smiling to myself and he grinned at me.

"He is a lucky man," he said, and I wondered, *Oh God, what does he know?*

I tore up the postcards. How could I send them lies about my adventures, my traveling, when I had found what I was looking for? And it wasn't a place, it wasn't even myself, it was Callum.

• • •

"Chelle, sleep next to me," Callum requested. "I'm getting cold."

That was progress. He was coming out of the fever, just as the guide said he would. I uneasily took off my clothes. I climbed in naked. I pressed against him, my hands around his stomach, keeping his warmth. I copied his breathing, and soon I fell asleep.

I woke up in pitch darkness. It was so thorough a darkness, it was almost unlike any I had ever experienced before. Lost. I couldn't see my own arm, my watch. But I wasn't afraid. I pressed myself against him. The rug felt wonderful, pure heaven, against my skin, and I thought that I might slip it between my legs and masturbate myself asleep again. It seemed a nice thing to do, while he was sleeping next to me, but then I sensed that he too was awake.

His hand tightened around my waist, sending erotic messages down me. I couldn't see him, but I fumbled toward his outline. We kissed. Lips on lips, a slip of tongue, a sliver of tooth. I stroked his forehead. In the blackness, we needed to feel for each other. His cock was stirring against my thigh. His pubic hair tickled me there. I felt the rigidity of his shaft, and his fingers, which had so excited me when he touched my hand, trailed toward the top of my legs. I steered him in, I gripped him tight, and showed him how I liked it. We were too far gone now to stop. Besides, I told my guilty conscience, he thought I was she, so who was I hurting?

I got on top of him, took care of him like a proper nurse. Healing him, working my medicine, I would either kill him or bring him back to life. We were fucking on the roof of the world.

He couldn't see me, and I couldn't see him. We were just bodies in motion, fucking together. The pace, the heat, the silence, and there was just him and me in the blackness, moving fast. I ground into him, and he poked up into me, gripping me down ferociously, filling me up, catching a pace, a rhythm.

He held my tits tight with the rug in his hand, and my nipples were firmly teased and controlled by his fingers. Then he was barking up into me, as I rode down on him, firm in the saddle, howling a hot, sweet orgasm.

I thought he would fall asleep straight away but he didn't. We lay panting in the darkness. Callum didn't say anything, and I was frightened that if I did I would disturb the spell. We were suspended in a magical balloon, and I was scared that if he knew what was going on—who I really was—it would pop.

I don't know how long we lay there but soon, sooner really than I was ready for it, he rolled on top of me. I don't know where he got the energy. Although he had rammed me sufficiently, and I didn't know if I could come again, I opened my legs gratefully. Callum wanted me! I felt his shaft slip through the gateway of my parted thighs.

"Chelle," he murmured as he drove inside my hole.

"Cal," I said, uncertainly.

He was moving inside me, weaving figures of eight in my pussy. I just let him do it to me. I deserved it. I curled my legs over him, and felt my clit press against him. Ah, the joy.

"You've never been this wet before," he said, as he soared in and out.

I maintained a diplomatic silence. Pulling him closer inside me, I thought: *Oh God, he's inside me again!*

"And the way your cunt is moving, Jesus, I can't believe… what an incredible cunt you've got!"

All the better to suck the juice out of you, my dear.

He hoisted up my buttocks with one hand, and we started moving in time, but against each other. I used to prefer fucking with the lights on, as the eyes are a sexual organ too, but the sense of touch was so much amplified in the darkness, and, I confess, I contorted my face and rubbed my clit and breasts with much more abandon, for he didn't know what I was doing.

This time, I, we, couldn't hold back. A silence had borne me through the last few times, and this time, I was myself; I wasn't fucking him as Chelle, but as me. I couldn't, wouldn't, hold back.

"Callum," I implored, "fuck me, fuck me!"

"Jesus, Chelle, you've never been so good before." I squeezed his arse, dragging his cock up into me, more and more.

"Give it to me, harder, oh yes, Callum, oh yes."

"You're so wild, what's going on?"

His incomprehension—OK, his stupidity—was music to my ears. I was so much better than she was. I was the best he had ever had—that's what he was unwittingly telling me. I mashed against him, jerking like only wild animals do.

"Screw me, harder, Callum, I need your fucking cock, I need it in my cunt, I need your fuck, I do."

"Oh God, Chelle, you're amazing, you're amazing."

"You are, you're the best…."

I wanted him so much, each and every fucking part of him. I wanted to squeeze him dry. I rammed him into me, and then I searched for that private place, that tiny hole, and even as he protested, I inserted a finger. I felt him tense and then relax.

"Jesus, Chelle," he groaned, "what are you doing?"

"Shhhh," I said, and then "yes." My finger was locked up him, secure, and triumphant. He rubbed harder, faster against my clit, and I had to bite my lips to stop myself from howling.

"Fuck, I'm not going to last long," he warned.

Nor was I. Paradise never does. And this was paradise: this darkness, this sensation overload, this communion. Complete abandonment, I gave myself up to it. I was contracting, tightening out of control. We twisted and writhed together, and then when I felt his strokes speed up, and the tension mount, I rose up meeting him, gasping his name, coming all over each other, gasping how much we loved each other.

• • •

In the morning, the light poured through the tent flaps and I could hear the guide potter around outside. Callum sat up, gulped down his water, and then looked at me. I covered myself with the rug, remembering the way I had teased myself with it before.

"I had such a strange dream last night…" he said uncertainly.

"Did you?" I asked ambivalently.

"It was just a dream." Then he said, more strongly, "You know, it seemed so real, but it was only a dream."

I nodded. As I stared down into the valley, I knew exactly what he was trying to say.

moonburn

Mitzi Szereto

SHE RARELY GOES OUT IN THE DAYTIME. This is not because she doesn't like the sun, but because she likes the moon better. It seems wiser and more economical to store up her erotic energy for the night rather than squandering it by day. Besides, pretty much anyone can be out during the day; there's nothing particularly special about baring your flesh to the sun. And, if anything, she is *special*.

One might expect her to look pale and sickly from this self-imposed retreat from natural light, but it's exactly the opposite. Her skin possesses a rich, shimmering glow similar to the kind earned from an expensive Mediterranean tan, although this glow comes from her exposure to the moon and cannot be compared to any identifiable shade of summer bronze. Even her hair appears to have been created from the night—as if the darkness has been pulled from the sky, then combed into silky filaments to frame her face and cascade like silvery-black water down her gracefully arched spine.

She is neither young nor old. It would even be difficult to say whether she can be defined as beautiful, since nobody bothers to focus on her face. The knee-length khaki duster that doesn't quite conceal her customary uniform of seduction remains unbelted and open in the front, placing on deliberate display a pair of long, black-stockinged legs with diamond-patterned seams snaking up the calves, which stay shapely from so much nocturnal walking. Midway up the thighs the tops of these stockings terminate in the hooks of a red garter belt, the elastic straps forming a lacy frame for the meticulously manicured crossroads of her vulva. She likes the feeling of being closely trimmed. It enhances the subtlest sensation while retaining an element of mystery that a complete divestment of hair would have sacrificed.

With every step, her rounded breasts undulate proudly against an out-thrust rib cage, the dainty, peach-colored nipples pointing an invitation at passersby approaching head-on. The extravagantly tall heels on which she somehow manages to balance her slight weight look like weapons designed to be driven into an unsuspecting foot (and have on occasion served this purpose). As these sadistically spiked heels sound their call-to-arms against the luridly lighted sidewalks that make up her battleground, their wearer's clitoris swells with need, stiffening to a nipple-like point in the cool night air. Fortunately the khaki coat performs its intended function of cloaking both her naked-ness and her desire from those walking behind or passing to the sides. After all, she doesn't wish to cause a stir.

The streets, sidewalks, and doorways of Soho are filled with people, particularly at night when those seeking to burrow into the sexual underbelly of London emerge from their lairs. Hence there is never a shortage of prospects for anonymous encounters—and that suits her just fine, since she prefers quan-tity as well as variety. A dread-locked young busker strumming a cheap out-of-tune guitar and singing an off-key Beatles melody can be as satisfying as the proper middle-aged businessman skulking guiltily from a gentlemen's club, his enjoyment of the evening's high-priced entertainment stiffly evident in his custom-made trousers, which still retain the pert imprint of the aerobicized buttocks of a lap dancer. Hopefully he can brush away this sexual stigmata before returning home to his sharp-eyed Missus.

Although summertime is best for these urban peregrinations, she doesn't curtail her activities in compliance with the fickle English weather. Obviously lust cannot be put away in a closet like a pair of rubber boots, only to be taken out when it rains. It's just that in the milder months of summer the city offers the greatest variety of people. American students with their shabby backpacks bursting with traveler's checks and condoms, foreign tourists on the lookout for forbidden adventure, staid and tweedy Englishmen stepping out on their wives—the possibilities seem endless, as are the manner of the encounters. If you ask her whether she has a favorite, she couldn't say. Each experience has something to offer—a pleasure to be tasted and savored for that particular moment, then set aside as the next pleasure moves in to replace it. And she wouldn't have it any other way.

He tells her that he performs as a mime in Covent Garden, a stepping-stone to what he believes will be the professional stages of the West End. His hopeful young face is painted in the mime's traditional whiteface, with a sorrowful, down-turned mouth edged in black and matching eyebrows in a state of perpetual surprise. Yet even with this theatrical and comical camouflage she can see that he's very good looking. He smells of greasepaint and the more subtle and tantalizing scents of youthful male sweat and budget cologne. This excites her and prompts her to rub her pulsing clitoris against his blue-jeaned thigh, creating a distinctive wet spot on the fabric. The rough, American-made denim provides a satisfactory surface on which to pleasure herself, and she thrusts her tongue between the mime's eagerly parted lips, sighing her climax into his throat.

By now, the young busker's green-flecked pupils have become dilated with desire, and he leads her hand toward the cylindrical bulge straining the front of his jeans. His movements are clumsy as he stuffs her slender fingers inside his unbuttoned fly, his desperation for relief nearly thwarting him from his goal. She will not need to work very hard, for no sooner does she grasp the spongy head of her partner's prick and proceed to squeeze it than a warm, creamy liquid fills her palm. She wipes the familiar stickiness away on the white cotton handkerchief she keeps ready for such eventualities in the pocket of her duster, her clitoris still fused like a melting flower against the young man's denimed thigh. A pair of fingers finds their way inside the slippery channel of her vagina, and they search about with fledgling urgency, making moist smacking sounds in the traffic-choked evening.

"Come home with me and let me fuck you!" the mime cries hoarsely into her ear, sucking the lobe in meaningful invitation.

But she never goes home with anyone. There is never any reason to.

With the night still in its infancy and the moon yet to reach its zenith, she tosses back her head and shakes out the tangles from her dark tresses. They shine silver-black as they catch the waxing London moonlight, providing a striking contrast to the glowing petal of pink protruding from her precisely trimmed pubic mound. Touching the mime's expectant face, she kisses him a kind farewell, allowing her tongue to lap over his lips to taste his fleeting youth before she continues on her way. She knows better than to drag out these things, since that can lead to something more involved.

The forlorn young busker will be left alone with his fantasies of *what might have been* throbbing in his jeans, the only evidence of his encounter with the dark-haired woman in the khaki coat drying to a perfumed powder on his fingers. Within minutes he will be a memory, as a man several years his senior, attired in a handsomely cut three-piece suit and swinging an expensive black-leather briefcase, advances toward her, his expression one of dreamy distraction. She has seen his type before. With the emergence of so many gentlemen's clubs in the area, it is not uncommon to find up-and-coming executives and their high-powered bosses wandering the streets of Soho long after the office has closed. As the man's footfalls bring him nearer, she checks to make certain her coat remains open in the front, exposing her nakedness and her need to their fullest. Never yet has this startling image failed to entice a man — or, for that matter, a *woman* — into her sexual sphere. Although the more timid of these Soho pedestrians might pause only long enough for a whimsical exploration with their fingers, the bolder of her male and female quarry have no compunction about giving free reign to their genitals, or their tongues.

In the darkened doorway of an Indian restaurant whose staff and patrons have gone home hours ago, the rear flap of her duster will be flung up to expose her garter-striped buttocks so that the man in the three-piece suit can bend her over and fit the desire-slickened head of his prick into her hindmost entrance. She prefers to take it this way, finding it a less vulnerable thoroughfare than the traditional one, which can easily become sore in the span of a busy evening. The louder the grunts made by the well-dressed businessman stationed at her protruding buttocks, the more vigorously she cries "Harder!" as people pass along the sidewalk, either unaware of this hindward coupling transpiring a few feet away or too jaded by the sexual excesses of Soho life to care.

Still lodged firmly inside her, the man pulls her disarranged figure into the narrow alleyway that runs alongside the shuttered restaurant, his need for privacy undoubtedly stronger than her own. Here the guttural sounds of masculine lust emanating from his throat will be drowned out by music from an adjacent nightclub, the thunderous pounding matching his strokes beat for beat. Grabbing the rusted iron bars lining the littered alley to support herself, she hikes a spike-heeled foot up onto the man's briefcase in order to be penetrated more effectively, his amused snort of "Darling, you'll never walk again!" urging her toward greater abandon, at which point she grasps her ankles and bites her moon-burnished lower lip, waiting for the inevitable *filling*. With each eviscerating thrust, her sharp heel scrapes across the fine, buttery black leather of the briefcase like

the tip of a knife. She smiles at the damage she has unintention-
ally inflicted upon the innocent and very expensive case. Every
time its owner looks at it, he will remember her.

The likelihood of this alleyway encounter's going unno-
ticed is not to be, however. For no sooner does the gentleman in
the three-piece suit clench his teeth in climax than a male figure
of markedly rougher exterior pauses at the mouth of the alley to
light a cigarette and be treated to a performance he concludes is
considerably more up-market than the one for which he has just
paid good money. His rugged features twist themselves into a
lewd grin as he witnesses the other man's shudders, the grin
changing to a raucous chuckle as the stealthily hidden target to
which his better-dressed counterpart has been aiming his strokes
makes itself apparent on withdrawal. The newcomer steps forward so that he will be seen by his rival. Although not above
using force to get what he wants, he has found that his rough-
hewn appearance is usually a sufficient form of persuasion.

Stuffing himself back into his custom-tailored Savile Row
trousers, the man in the now-rumpled business suit makes a
hasty and undignified exit through the far end of the grimy Soho
alleyway, but not before pulling his lacerated briefcase out from
beneath the dangerously spiked heel of the woman whose pos-
terior has just squeezed a lifetime of come out of him. He would
not have minded sticking around for another go, only he doesn't
want any trouble. And the unshaven brute with the cigarette
smoldering between his thick fingers definitely looks like *trouble*.

With his partially smoked cigarette clamped between his
lips, the newcomer moves into his predecessor's place, forcing
the khaki-coated woman's ankles farther apart with a mud-caked
work boot. He acts quickly before the moment is lost, his razor
stubble scraping her silky neck as he wedges himself against her
buttocks. In his world it's rare to find a woman willing to volun-
teer herself so freely in this fashion, and he fully intends to take
advantage of his windfall. However, he must first bow to tradition, the hot, slippery opening his fingers meet when they search
between her thighs proving too irresistible a lure for his prick.

By now her lower half has turned liquid, the rigorous activity she just indulged in prompting this wetness to spatter her nylon stocking tops. Therefore she doesn't even flinch when her new partner launches the entire length of himself into her vagina. Nor, for that matter, does *he* flinch when she jabs a spiked heel onto the toe of his work boot at the moment of her climax.

"We'll have to do this again sometime," he replies afterward, zipping up his dampened fly. She offers him an empty smile, knowing such a scenario is unlikely to take place a second time. She takes a deep drag from his freshly lighted cigarette, the acrid rush of smoke to her lungs steadying her and readying her to move on. He had been exceptionally rough when taking her in the rear, dragging out the process longer than she's accustomed to. She could tell it was a treat for him—although that's often the case with the men she meets, which might explain why they appear so reluctant to let her go after they have finished. She touches her neck where the man's facial stubble has scraped it raw, hoping this one won't get it into his head to follow her. This has happened in the past with others, especially these rough types who are used to getting their way.

To be on the safe side, she takes a circuitous route past the pubs and strip clubs and thinly disguised bordellos of the neighborhood, the juices from her two alleyway lovers trickling down the insides of her thighs and fusing her buttocks together. Certain she has not been followed, she pauses in the shadow of a doorway, using the handkerchief in the pocket of her coat to wipe herself clean. She has already forgotten the men whose fluids stain the crumpled white square of cotton, although the image of a muddied work boot forcing her feet apart will abruptly reawaken her passion and keep her walking these moonlit sidewalks for a little while longer.

As she rounds another Soho corner, she collides with a pair of pillowy lips as red and glossy as those of her vagina after a busy night of anonymous couplings. Eyes lined black with kohl stare unflinchingly into hers, seeming to have the ability to see inside her. Their exotic owner might be a dancer in one of the clubs, or a woman stood up by her date, or a prostitute. She might even be herself: a kindred spirit prowling the night in search of nameless, faceless pleasure. But none of this matters when their lips meet and her tongue melts like caramel in the other woman's mouth. Her clitoris still burns from its encounter with the young mime's blue-jeaned thigh and its ruder chafing by her work-booted lover, who kneaded it relentlessly between his coarse fingers until she climaxed twice in his hand, gracing his palm with a wet and fragrant souvenir of his big night out in Soho.

The fleshy fire surging from her closely groomed vulval lips is momentarily cooled by the saliva-moistened softness of the other's mouth, only to flare up again as two shiny red lips wrap covetously around it. With the ankles of her spike-tipped legs gripped so that they remain flush to the pavement and widely splayed, she finds herself held captive by the kohl-eyed stranger's painted mouth, which sucks the syrupy wetness from her like liquid siphoned through a small opening. Her ecstasy will be swift in coming and when it does come, it leaves her plea-surer's lips even glossier than before. When she glances down to admire herself—something she likes to do after an erotic encounter—she is greeted by a clitoris glowing bright red with lipstick. She shivers with pleasure, this altered landscape almost as pleasing as the act that brought it about.

"Can I see you again?" asks the woman, the kohl having streaked beneath one eye.

The only response is the sound of a khaki duster snapping sharply in the night breeze as she walks away from the kneeling figure of her female lover. She doesn't mean to be rude: There is simply no other way.

Her body still humming with sexual electricity, she debates whether to continue with these nocturnal wanderings or belt up both her coat and her nudity against the misty elements. A damp chill has begun to blow in off the river and a watery sun is due to replace the moon in a few hours. Perhaps the time has come to go home.

What the hell, there's always tomorrow night.

Journey of
My Hands

✲

GERARD WOZEK

Journal Entry: April 29

They say it's easy to rub a Frenchman the wrong way—
but not when you're offering up massages for little more than
the price of a McDonald's Happy Meal and a deluxe French-
vanilla shake. I haven't been able to make my rent payments by
only teaching conversational English part time to Parisian businessmen, so I've posted a provocative "position wanted" ad in
a gay French/English newsletter: *Male to Male Masseur eases
your tensions with his adept methods, will travel to your home, 120
francs for half an hour.* I've decided that in addition to appeasing
my surly Gallic landlord and supporting a voracious writing
habit, it will provide an amazing opportunity to see Paris from
the inside out.

I don't care if I have to wear ostrich feathers and imperson-
ate Edith Piaf in her final concert before sweating over a 300-pound

sous-chef who lives in the Seventh Arrondissement or yield to the caprice of an Algerian barber who has me jostle his testicles on the tip of my tongue while he slowly shaves my neck. I come from durable stock—at least, that's what I'll keep telling myself.

• • •

Journal Entry: May 10

Yesterday, before arriving at Dr. Trigano's ultrabaroque flat in the Madeleine district, I was instructed to bring along a particularly exotic brand of Haitian rosemary oil—a cold-pressed syrup that I could only purchase at the morning market near St. Sulpice. "You'll find it at a rustic-looking stall covered with papier-mâché rosebuds and crystal beads," instructed the kind voice of the physician on the telephone. So, before my appointment, I jostled around long tables of flypapered cheese rounds and fish-netted wine bottles, iced wheel-carts topped with fresh salmon and vegetables, makeshift altars with plastic-globed Madonnas and rosaries, until finally I arrived at the tropical medicine stand with the sought-after unguent.

Dr. Trigano, who turned out to be a toadyish man in his late fifties, was delighted with the amber-colored oil, but I was astonished to discover that it wasn't to be used for his massage. Uncapping the flute-necked bottle, the doctor sniffed the sprig floating in the center and exuberantly declared, "It's perfect for sizzling the plantains with!"

Seated on a stool in his silver-chromed kitchen, he began preparation for an elaborate meal: turkey quail eggs, bacon-rolled melon balls, roasted walnuts in wild mushroom sauce, perfumed Thai rice, shish kebabs à la Martinique, fried bananas, glazed oranges, *foie gras* from the pricey Fauchon *supermarché*, and a caramelized rice pudding for dessert. It turned out that the surgeon from the Marie Curie Institute was a closet chef who loved to try out his developing culinary skills on strangers. I left his lush home with neatly boxed leftovers and a tip of 500 francs for my buoyant conversation. At the foyer, we briskly shook each other's hand, which was the only part of the doctor's anatomy I was requested to touch during the whole encounter.

. . .

Journal Entry: May 21

Pino, an Austrian jet pilot who lives at 5 rue Christine in the oh-so-opulent St. Germain neighborhood, craves to be read to. His refurbished apartment was once the address of the notorious literary couple Gertrude Stein and Alice B. Toklas, before they were kicked out of their first residence on the rue de Fleurus.

My client offered me a hazelnut *pastis* and shelled pistachios from a carved wooden cup once coveted by Ms. Stein herself. Setting up a copy of Gertie's infamous *Autobiography* on a music stand, the dashing young Pino pointed out the passages I was to recite, while I was instructed to vigorously rub his shoulder blades. "With feeling," he murmured as I pounded his back muscles into *crème brûlée*. "Remember, you're doing it for Alice.... That's right, call me Ahhhhh-leeeece!"

My later afternoon appointment turned out to be much less eccentric. Antoine lives near the Japanese Gardens on the rue des Abondances. He answered the door wearing taffy-like pink slippers and a genuine Issey Miyake peignoir, the color of champagne ice, which he had bought at Bon Marché. During our brief self-introductions he periodically rubbed his teeth with licorice seeds that he plucked out of a tiny Limoges snuff box. On our way upstairs to his salon, he pointed toward his collection of Art Deco statuary and framed photographs done by Man Ray and Brassaï. "You have to watch out for imitations," he scolded. "Those antiques vampires that line the Place des Vosges in the Marais will try to gouge you with fakes!"

When we finally approached our session, he lay down atop layers of organdy silk pillows and, with Jacques Brel playing in the background, I was coached to slowly drip a warmed jar of Marriage Frères tea-jelly over his back. Then, straddled over a genuine fur-tufted toilet seat originally used by Marie Antoinette, he requested that I squeeze an infusion of scented rosewater into his rectum while he vigorously beat his engorged cock to orgasm. Later, when I got home, with the lyrics to "Ne Me Quitte Pas" still burnished into my memory, I tried to peel the tea-jam's honey-like residue off my fingernails. Still heady from the scent of jasmine and spunk, I plunged onto my pull-out sofa and fell asleep thinking of the handsome garçon I happened to spy coming out of a jack-off *toilette* on the rue du Roi de Sicile. Maybe I'll lurk around there tomorrow....

• • •

Journal Entry: May 25

If nothing else, being a masseur has turned me into a walking *Plan de Paris*. I've received a goodly number of requests from French residents asking for directions, which surely must mean that I've arrived. The other day on the Metro, going to a client, I raced past the transit stop for the Louvre. I realized that in the many weeks I've lived in Paris I still haven't had a chance to see the *Mona Lisa*.

I looked out the window of that speeding train and thought I saw my mummified fingers in a display case for that famous Paris museum. I imagined tourists and residents alike, huddled close to the window, gaping at the mummified remnant of a man's journey across the skins of Paris. I shut my eyes, scraped the callus on my forefinger, and hung onto my knapsack filled with baby lotions, dildos, condoms, and paddles, as the train barreled toward the next client.

• • •

Journal Entry: June 1

Last night I covered my once-cheerless one-room studio in the Fifteenth Arrondissement with posters from *Pierre et Gilles* along with frames from my growing collection of *Tintin* comics. I turned my hardcover volumes of Herman Hesse and mounds of my Gibert Jeune student journals into makeshift end tables. Over my bricked-up fireplace, I hung a Louis XIV mirror, stained and pocked from excess moisture and age. I strung up cheap Christmas lights I found in a bin at the Monoprix over the two terrace door windows that look out onto a monotonous row of iron window grids, cracked geranium boxes, and the vagrant man who sleeps underneath a mammoth orange-and-blue umbrella.

Then, before I went to bed, I watched a well-groomed gentleman across the way examining his half-dressed body in the reflection cast over the surfaces of his windowpane. He slowly rubbed the bulge in his athletic briefs, then gingerly took out his erection. I watched him touch his clavicle, move his left hand across his right arm, and as he squeezed his hard nipples his lips began to purse. The way his glass pane was tilted open, it seemed as though the lights of the Tour Eiffel were superimposed over his forehead, as though he were a Las Vegas dancer wearing a surreal headdress or a Daliesque figure morphing into a cityscape. His fingers were gliding along the wet shaft of his cock, and my own hand moved in sympathetic rhythm, my eyes following the actions of his wrist, his right hand covering his bulbous crown. Together we came, our chests heaving, our hot breath merging across the narrow, cobbled street. (Did he see me? It seemed he viewed only himself. Am I always so invisible?) He moved away from the sill, and I fell asleep to the singing of the homeless man, whose muffled words swirled into the concavity of his bumbershoot roof.

· · ·

Journal Entry: June 22

Massaging all of gay France, I have now learned the expression for condom (*preservatif*) and found out where I can post my card on the message boards of the trendiest club bars. Yesterday I called the office and quit my day job teaching English, raised my service fee for massages, and clipped my fingernails (although Jean, the naval officer from Lyon who is now a regular, likes them long so that I can scratch his shoulders with them).

Last Sunday, it felt good to give my hands a break. I went to the Billy Wilder festival at the cinema near the Trocadéro, then listened to old Dusty Springfield CDs at the Virgin Megastore on the Champs-Elysées. The handsome men filtering out of the Beaubourg *toilettes* made me gape, wishing I could follow them.

Right before dusk I sat in the Jardins du Luxembourg in the heart of the Left Bank and stared at the bronze replica of the Statue of Liberty. I looked across the row of chairs past the *pétanque* bowlers and over toward the fountain, where I noticed someone had left a toy sailboat meandering in the octagonal water basin at the center of the park. The little ship was lopsided and kept rocking back and forth. I thought to myself, All some-one has to do is turn the fountain showers back on and the least little trickle will sink that ship in a heartbeat.

• • •

Journal Entry: August 13

Zeinhold sings show tunes at Le Pompadour, a sullen little cabaret near rue Montmartre that caters mostly to a geriatric crowd. Widows from World War II still throw their lacey handkerchiefs onstage when Zeinhold sings "The Legionnaire" or mentions the name Charles de Gaulle. When I met him after his singing engagement, we didn't go back to his apartment for his regular rubdown, but instead he took me down into the sewers of Paris.

Official tour guides were leading what appeared to be mostly Americans on their jaunt through the sooty *égouts* of the ancient city here, but Zeinhold knew of a staircase that led away from the paying gawkers. Amid the underground piping, twisting phone wires, traffic light cables, and the city's ancient pneumatic postal network, Zeinhold undid his bowtie and slipped off his ruffled shirt. "Robbers pulled off a bank heist and escaped through here," my half-clothed, semiregular client remarked between heavy, deep breaths. "Thrilling, eh?"

Stretched out on the floor of a narrow tunnel, his small frame was motionless as I let the tips of my fingers glide over his shoulders, then down to his sweaty boxers. (Actually, it reminded me of a blowjob I once had in the Catacombs.) As I yanked his silk underwear off, he flipped over to reveal his hot wand, its tip twinkling ooze in the muted light. As my fingers and wet tongue-licks quickly worked him into a froth, he began to sing what sounded like an old Maurice Chevalier standard. The French lyrics echoed off the cylindrical walls, and I started to imagine that I was Leslie Caron on some Hollywood back lot and everyone was calling me *Gigi;* but I couldn't get my cues right, because I kept forgetting lines, forgetting why I had ever come to Paris in the first place.

· · ·

Journal Entry: September 9

Last night I dreamt I made love to Tintin. It was an erotic comic book come to life. I arrived at Tintin's apartment on the rue Coustou and entered, only to find pictures of Captain Haddock and Professor Calculus in various stages of undress. (Captain Haddock appeared to be uncut!) Snowy was gently snoring underneath Tintin's matchbox bed frame as he lithely slipped off his ubiquitous blue sweater and brown knickerbockers. "How old are you, exactly?" I asked him.

"Somewhere between fourteen and four hundred," he giggled as he spread himself out on the bed sheets. I straddled his back and gently kissed a small birthmark just above one buttock. He reached over to grab the end of an opium hookah, and I could vaguely smell the Vaseline used to keep his orange pompadour so stiff. "Just don't tell Johnny Quest or Hadji," he cautioned. "They might not want to engage in our ménage anymore."

Just then Babar the Elephant sauntered through an armoire in the dining room. He slipped his soft gray trunk between my legs and lifted me away from that scene, through a window and out over the spire of the Eiffel Tower. When I looked down I saw a gaggle of Madeline look-alikes with their mouths wide open, waving at me in astonishment. As I flew up over the crowned head of the elephant, I somersaulted over cloud-banks…until I woke up.

· · ·

Journal Entry: September 20

I've started to let the telephone ring and not answer. If it's a regular client, he knows now to ring twice, hang up, and try calling back. The only thing I'm able to count on lately has been stiff neck muscles, cramping fingers, and a recurrent callus on my left hand. And, of course, that male voice on the other end of the line that says, "I saw your ad in the paper and I'm interested in treating myself to your *mains*."

Usually, though, when I hear that ring, I just pretend that it's some handsome botanical expert from the Luxembourg Gardens phoning, some beautiful gardener, rough-hewn and tanned, with toned arms and gentle eyes. We meet at a table by the Medici Fountain and he smells like dried sweat and plumflowers, and his hands are still caked with peat moss and red clay. He gently reaches over me from behind like the marble lovers, Acis and Galatea, who are flirting in the pond water, and just when no one is looking he bites my ear lobe. We dash behind the fountain wall and peek at our swollen rods under the bas-relief of Leda and the Swan.

Two nights ago I turned my make-believe lover into an epic poem in my new Gibert Jeune notebook, but that can't make the rent, so when the phone rang at ten o'clock, I answered. Dr. Trigano was requesting my services for the sixth time, and he knew better than to call me so late, but his voice had a palpable urgency to it. When I arrived at his *palais*, I was met with the aroma of cinnamon tea lights floating in an oversized crystal soup-tureen instead of the usual smoke from meats broiling in the kitchen. A perfume of chocolate vapor permeated the air as well, as though a dessert fondue was coming to a boil. He quickly ushered me into the formal dining room where his lion-clawed table was set with a candelabrum poised at the rim of one end and a pillow-tufted quilt spread across its wide oak boards.

He slipped off his silky pajama bottoms and lay down atop the wide table completely naked. I was then instructed to dress the physician as though he was a turkey being made up for an

American Thanksgiving feast. Borrowing a technique for making truffles memorized from when I subscribed to *Martha Stewart,* I began to line his navel and chest with dried apricots and figs. I drizzled a warmed spigot of maple syrup over his legs and thighs, placed caramel pecan clusters in his eye sockets, and squirted a pastry bag of cookie dough around the base of his scrotum. As my hand rubbed the sticky syrup over the doctor's rising shaft, he dusted himself with powdered sugar—and quickly came in a delirium of decadent sweetness.

• • •

Journal Entry: October 2

A turquoise light bathes the Louvre tonight as I sit in a nearby café, glazing my chafed, cramping hands with tiger balm. I've worked the tempered muscles and stretched out the needy ligaments of what seems like all of *gai Paris.* I've dutifully tended to the carnal desires and unnamable eccentricities of my paying clients for months now, so I'm happy for the opportunity to simply sit in a beautifully tufted green-velvet chaise at Café Marly. I am worn out but happy to be writing here in my journal and sipping raspberry cassis and champagne like the citizen king Louis Phillipe. My garçon is handsome and attentive (with a smile like *Mona Lisa*'s, with that reassuring knowledge of a secret joy), and, who knows—maybe he'll appreciate a free rub-down after he gets off work.

I watch the long line of impatient tourists standing at the glass pyramid entrance, stoop-shouldered and fidgeting, waiting to be transformed by world-famous art. I hold up my kir and notice that my hands are the hands of an artist too. *These hands can create masterpieces as good as any Van Gogh,* I assure myself, *treasured moments set apart from the ordinary world.*

The twisting line into the museum barely budges and, looking through my champagne flute, I see the crowd beginning to meld into one snarling snake, a long sheath of scaly skin good only for endless rubbing, endless shedding. I watch the cobra rise and move; I hold my sore hands up and tell myself that I am not afraid of its sudden death rattle, its oozing venom. I can put my fingers near the pointy fangs and he will not strike. I can stroke him and he will not, he dare not, pierce this tender hand, my warm flesh offered.

season of marriage

➳

MARY ANNE MOHANRAJ

SHE WAS DIZZY WITH THE SMOKE. The traditional wedding had lasted almost three hours, and the heat and oil fumes from the ever-present lamps had combined to make Raji feel queasy. Kids were running around all over the place, dressed in too-vibrant colors that hurt her eyes. And the chanting. It went on and on and on in incomprehensible Sanskrit. Raji knew no Sanskrit—she even spoke her little Tamil with a New England accent. She was suddenly homesick: for America, for Massachusetts, for forests and hills and snow and people around whom you could speak your mind without treading on some custom you didn't under-stand. For cold pizza for breakfast and frozen yogurt for lunch. For slumber parties and stolen dates and the friends who had covered for her. Despite the cold heart and the pain that had driven her to this wedding in the baking heat of Colombo, America was home. And it was much, much too late to go back.

She was married now. The wedding reception was ending, and it would soon be time to leave with this kind-seeming stranger, to go to the house of his mother (whom Raji already disliked), to go to his bed. And all her American casualness about sex, the casualness and experience she had counted on to see her through this ordeal, suddenly was meaningless. She was scared. Why, oh why, had she agreed to this?

The answer to that was easy: because she didn't care anymore. After she'd found out about Jim and that other girl, after all the broken promises and shattered dreams, it simply didn't seem to matter. The heat and incense combined to bring on a wave of brutally clear memory.

• • •

They'd just collapsed, Jim on top of her, as he always insisted. He was crushing her with his weight. Raji managed to roll to the side, and then turned to gaze into his eyes, still amazed that this gorgeous man would really want her.

"You were wonderful," Raji said.

"Uh-huh." He was still panting, but in a very sexy way, she thought.

"Jim?"

"Uh-huh."

"I love you."

There was a disconcerting pause. Before, he'd always responded, "I love you, too." Now, he said nothing for much too long.

"Ummm…" Jim said.

"Yes?" she asked, eagerly.

"I should probably tell you something. Now don't get too upset, OK?" And he proceeded to tell her about Sharmila. Indian. Raji remembered her from Biology last semester. Drop-dead gorgeous with unfairly huge breasts. Sharmila, whom he'd been sleeping with for three weeks. His conscience had finally kicked in. Or maybe he was just bored with Raji, and this was the easiest way to make her break up with him. Which, of course, she did.

...

Looking back, she realized how stupid she had been. Not in dating him, but in caring so much about somebody who had obviously cared so little. She had gotten so worked up about what she had seen as the ultimate betrayal that she had sunk into a black fit of depression during which she had let everyone else make decisions for her. She'd ignored the advice of her friends, both Asian and American, and decided that maybe her parents were right, after all. Maybe American men really *were* slime. Maybe she'd be happiest with someone like herself. So she'd agreed to meet some Tamil men, and the next thing she knew she was flying to Ceylon to meet this man Vivek. And he was gentle. And kind. Rich and generous; he'd given her a lovely ruby and pearl necklace the day after they met. And though she'd only known him for a few days, her parents thought he was very suitable and his parents liked her and it was suddenly all arranged and they were asking her and she said yes.

And now she was remembering all the sweet guys she'd grown up with and wondering where they'd gone. She was finally shaking off the depression that had lasted the four months since Jim, and suddenly knew that she'd have been happier with an American she understood rather than with this stranger from a strange land that she'd left when she was six. And it was still too late. She was married, and though she could probably get a divorce, Raji wasn't the sort to give up on anything that easily. A divorce would mean that she had failed...again. Not to mention that a divorce would break her mother's heart. Her dear, scheming, conniving, thoroughly manipulative mother. Sometimes Raji couldn't figure out whether she loved or hated her mother. Not that it really made much difference at this point.

Her silence was noted by Vivek, who asked her in his perfect, if heavily accented, English if she felt all right. Raji was touched that he had noticed—Jim would never have noticed if she were quiet; he would have been too busy talking. She nodded to Vivek that she was OK, then stood with him as the interminable reception finally came to a close. He gave her a tentative smile, a sort of "buck up" look that *was* heartening. Raji wondered what this shy and probably virginal man would think of an experienced American. She'd find out soon enough.

The women took her to the bedroom and helped her undress, giving her fragments of advice in broken English as they helped her into a flowing white nightgown, incredibly demure and perfectly opaque. Raji barely heard them, caught somewhere between tears and laughter. She waited patiently, allowing them to dress her as they chose and lead her toward the crimson-draped bed. One woman, who Raji thought was her new sister-in-law and recently married herself, touched Raji's shoulder before she left, kindly. Then they were gone.

Vivek appeared, ghost-like in the doorway, dressed in flowing white to match her attire. He walked toward her silently, carefully: a hunter afraid of startling some strange, wild creature. Raji was determined to try her best to make this marriage work, and so she smiled, slightly trembling. Vivek returned her smile with a tentative smile of his own, and reached up to touch her cheek. His hand was not damp and sweaty as she had somehow feared, but warm and dry, as if lit by some inner fire. He had not touched her before this, in all the days of wedding preparations during the short month since they had met. Even when placing the gold *thali* wedding necklace around her neck, he had taken care not to touch her. She was suddenly grateful for his gentleness and, stepping boldly toward him, stretched her slim brown arms to encircle his thick neck, surprised to find that he was shaking too.

Vivek was not very handsome, but was sturdily built, with hair thicker and richer than her own, and deep brown eyes. Raji had thought them dull and calf-like before, but suddenly she was not so sure. There was a hint of laughter in those eyes, and a sparkle of intelligence. Of course, he was a doctor (nothing else would have satisfied her mother) and so couldn't be entirely stupid. Now, with her hands locked behind his neck and her delicate body inches away from his, Raji found herself bemused, not sure what to do next, or how fast she should take this. He solved that problem for her.

He placed his arms around her waist, gently. Tilting his head, he kissed her. She was startled, not at being kissed, but at being kissed by him, and stiffened in his arms. He raised his head questioningly. "Is this not customary in America?"

"Yes, yes it is. I didn't think it was, here."

"We are not as ignorant as you Americans assume. We do watch movies, after all."

Now Raji was sure that he was laughing at her, as he leaned down to kiss her again. Despite his claims to knowledge, she was fairly sure that kissing was new to him, and so responded gently to the firm pressure on her lips. They kissed chastely for long minutes, until Raji, greatly daring, opened her mouth and touched her tongue to his lips. He broke away for a moment, plainly startled, but then returned to kissing her with enthusiasm, opening his own mouth and tasting her lips, her teeth, her tongue with his own. She tilted her head backward, hoping he would get the hint, and he did—kissing her cheek, her nose, her ear, tracing a delicate line along her cheekbone with his tongue. He went slowly, and Raji stood still, eyes closed, feeling him touch her so gently. This was new to her—this gentleness, this seeming reverence. She had enjoyed sex with Jim, but it had always been hard and fast, a summer storm: quickly started, quickly over. Vivek was twenty-five, years older than Jim had been, but he smiled with the wonder of a child. Raji felt an odd constriction in her chest.

Continuing to explore her coffee-colored skin, Vivek's tongue slid slowly down her neck. Shivers were racing through her now, and Raji tried to hold still, starting to wonder how long she could act the shy virgin, how long it would be before her impatience broke through. His kisses were abruptly stopped by the laces at the top of the gown, and he froze and locked her eyes with his. Raji slowly reached up and, almost teasingly, pulled free the tangled white ribbons and laces. Vivek undid them completely, sliding the white fabric off her creamy brown shoulders, continuing the slow kisses that had fallen as cool rain but now began to burn. Despite a ceiling fan, the room was stiflingly hot to a woman bred to New England winters, and Raji began to sway, dizzy with heat and unexpected passion. Vivek caught and held her, as the gown slid from her bare body to pool on the green-tiled floor. Cradling her against him with one arm, he pulled aside mosquito netting and drapes with the other. Picking her up, he gently deposited Raji on the bed and pulled the sheet over her. All this happened so quickly that Raji had no moment in which to become embarrassed in her nakedness before this almost-stranger, this husband. And then he was undressing too, undoing the wrap of white fabric and climbing in to sit beside her, pulling the mosquito netting closed so that they might be undisturbed.

"Are you all right?" Vivek asked.

"Yes, I think so. Are you?"

"Of course I am. I'm a man."

Laughter again, from both of them this time, which trailed away into silence. He looked suddenly vulnerable, Raji thought, as he sat there naked and cross-legged on the wide bed. The silence grew more and more awkward until Raji finally raised herself a little on her elbows, letting the sheet fall down to bare her curving breasts. Smiling, she puckered her lips for a kiss. He laughed again, and suddenly he was swooping down on her in mid-laugh, slipping his broad hands around her fragile frame. Raji began drowning in a hail of fierce kisses and caresses. In the lamplit dimness his hands explored what he could not see, curving to surround her small breasts, which fit neatly into the palms of his hands. He fumbled a little, sometimes touching her too softly, sometimes too fiercely, but always kissing as she arched into his touch.

Vivek slid his hands down her stomach, across her hips, gently pushing apart her trembling thighs. She stiffened, remembering what she had not told him, and opening her eyes wildly searched for his, until he, looking up, caught her trapped gaze.

"Don't be afraid," he reassured her, though his voice was trembling. "I'm a doctor, it's all right." He smiled again, inviting her to share the joke. Raji wished it could be that easy....

"I'm not afraid, it's just...there's something I need to tell you."

"Shhh…don't worry."

Vivek smiled at the confusion in her eyes, and leaned down to kiss her. At the moment he kissed her he entered her, and Raji was suddenly so hot, so wet and ready for him, that she thought she might scream. But, remembering his despised mother in the next bedroom, she buried the sound in her throat and only moaned, softly. She curved up to meet him as he began long, hesitant strokes that stretched through her long-neglected body, giving it the attention it so desperately wanted.

The world blurred for Raji to a haze of cloudy netting above her, lit by the lamp glow and measured by the rhythmic movement of this man, her husband, inside her. Sometime during that long eternity it began to rain outside their window, but the thunder and lightning couldn't begin to match the pleasure arcing through her. He began pounding faster and faster to match the storm, and came suddenly. Raji was caught in a moment of purest frustration underneath him. She opened her eyes a few seconds later to see his concerned face above her.

"That didn't work very well, did it? I'm sorry," Vivek said.

Raji remembered the numerous times Jim had left her frustrated without even noticing. She decided not to think of Jim again—he didn't deserve to intrude on this, her wedding night. This man, her husband, was thoughtful, considerate. She could have done much worse. Raji smiled up at him, feeling warmth unfold within her. "Shhh…it's fine. We have lots of time to practice. But there are a couple of things I don't understand."

"Ask," he said, smiling gently.

"Well, for one, why is it still raining? I thought storms in Ceylon were short."

"Usually they are, but this one will last a while. It's the beginning of monsoons, remember? It will be storming for the next three months."

"Oh. I knew that."

Raji *had* known that, but she had the distinct feeling that he was laughing at her again. Vivek smiled brightly at her, rolling her toward him to rest in the crook of his arm. The storm raged more fiercely outside, no doubt churning the dirt paths to mud, soaking the very air and making it hard to breathe.

"Want to ask one of the harder questions now?" he asked.

"There's just one more. Now you know that you didn't marry a virgin. Do you mind?"

She closed her eyes and clenched her fists against the answer, suddenly wanting desperately to make this gentle man happy, especially happy with her.

"I knew from the beginning. Your mother seemed to feel I had a right to know what I was bargaining for," he said, quietly.

"She told you? How could she? She didn't even know...." Raji was caught somewhere between anger and relief. Vivek chuckled.

"You would be surprised what mothers know. Mine really isn't so bad; she's just not looking forward to my leaving with you, so she's a little irritable."

"Leaving?" Raji was now completely confused.

"For America. Lots of work for doctors there. The problem here is that everyone who can become a doctor does so. There aren't enough jobs. I've been hoping to live in America for a long time, and I could hardly expect my beautiful American wife to be like the innocent girls of the villages here. Not that many of them are really that innocent." He grinned down at her then.

Raji didn't return his smile, suddenly troubled by a depressing possibility. Maybe he had married her only for her citizenship, so that he could get a visa and emigrate to America. She had certainly heard of plenty of arranged marriages where that was one of the prime requirements—a spouse with American citizenship. Raji tried to ignore the thought, though. If it were true, it was too late to do anything about it now, and he had certainly acted as if he wanted her and not just a ticket to America. She didn't want to believe that the man who had been so sweet to her could be so mercenary.

Vivek appeared troubled by her silence. "That is..." and he was suddenly hesitant, "if you want to go back to America."

"If I *want* to?!" and Raji started laughing, smothering her doubts. "Oh, yes. Yes, my husband. Soon, please."

"Soon," he agreed, smiling. "I already have a job offer there, actually. As soon as I get my work visa we can go. I just wanted to make sure that was what you wanted, too."

And now she knew that he could have gone on his own, that he had wanted her and not just any American. Now Raji was free to begin to care for this man beside her, and to acknowledge to herself just how much she longed for apple trees and miniskirts and roller-coasters. Ceylon had its own strange beauty, its passion and mystery, but she was an American at heart.

Vivek touched her cheek then and said, "Shall we try that again? My mother will be very upset with me if you continue to be so quiet. She will think that I have been too rough with you and that you are crying."

Raji held herself still for a moment, looking up at the face of her new husband. He was such a mass of surprises. Then suddenly she rolled over so that she was lying on top of him. Raji began kissing him wildly, ignoring his startled eyes. She stopped for a moment to tell him, "You're about to find out just how rough American women can be..." before she returned to teasing him unmercifully, rubbing her small breasts across his smooth chest. Vivek responded with renewed passion, pulling her close so that her pointed chin rested in his hands and her hair fell forward, veiling their faces. Raji finally left behind all thoughts of mothers and matchmaking, allowing herself to go spiraling downward with her husband, losing herself in the touch of sweat-slick skin on skin.

Any sounds they made were soon drowned out by the pounding of the monsoon storms.

fuera compás

⌖

NATASHA ROSTOVA

HE FOUGHT HER. FOUGHT HER AND WORSHIPPED HER.
He wasn't supposed to feel these things, these emotions that
scorched his blood. And because of her, because she cracked the
strength of his discipline, he would return to watch her night after
night. He saw this woman at the market with a basket dangling
from her tapered fingers. He saw her at church, her dark head
bent over a prayer book. And he watched her nightly transformation into a fierce, whirling dervish with sweat glistening on her
brow and fire in her eyes.

He sat at the back of the tavern with a hat pulled low over
his forehead, feeling his sex grow hard and thick in his trousers.
Smoke varnished the air. His nostrils filled with acrid smells
of liquor and sweat. Raucous shouts beat against the walls like
the violent, fluttering movements of a trapped bird. Mateo could
not help but think that the seven deadly sins blossomed in places
like this, as if they found such energy to be moist and plentiful
fertilizer.

"Devotion," the bishop told him repeatedly as they sat in the library. "You must cultivate devotion and compassion as if they were precious plants. Never allow them to die."

"Yes, Father." Mateo comforted himself with the thought that he cultivated such holy thoughts daily. Only when he watched Carmen did they disappear like evaporating ice.

He would enter the tavern through the front door, but always after the performances began, after all eyes were riveted on the flurry of red cotton and black lace that Carmen became when she danced. The skirts of her dress flew about her like water that rippled only at the provocation of guitar music and the hoarse modulations of Gabriel's voice. Carmen never used castanets, relying instead on the power of her own hands as she clapped them together in staccato *palmas* to accompany the tones of Fernando's guitar.

Her feet stamped on the ground, the sound of a thousand horses' hooves, a primitive rhythm that vibrated in Mateo's blood and bones. A rhythm that defied death itself. Her movements were determined, a beating and clapping that matched Fernando's tempo so adroitly that it was as if the two were making violent love. Yet they did not appear to be aware of each other, each one enveloped in the cocoon of the dance and the music. And the audience, the collective voyeur, was the entity that compelled the merging of the two.

• • •

Flamenco gave Carmen an intense awareness of her own body. Her heartbeat echoed inside her head, her chest hurt with the force of her breathing. The tightness of her calf muscles stretched to her lower back. Her feet developed calluses in defense of the nightly beating, the *zapateado,* she required of them. And yet she would dance on and on, for her whole being came alive when she did so.

Not that she was ignorant of her audience. Oh, no. She reveled in the stares burning through her skirts, the excitement caused by the glimpses of her shapely, muscular legs and the erotic twisting of her hips. Rough, male voices yelling *"Eso es!"* and *"Olé!"* penetrated her ears as she spun and stamped and clapped within the confines of the small stage until her body forced her to cease.

And then, still stimulated from the vehement exertion, she would meet Tomas in the back room and let him fuck her on the bare table, her skin still damp with sweat and her breathing harsh in his ear.

• • •

"You'll never leave here, will you?" Carmen slipped another olive into her mouth and wiped her greasy fingers on her skirt.

Fernando shrugged, strumming his fingers lazily over the guitar strings as he gazed at the hills and valleys of Andalucía. "Part of me wants to," he admitted. "Every flamenco guitarist has *pasión de viajar.*"

"Why is that?" Carmen bit into the salty flesh of another olive.

"I suspect it's in our nature," Fernando replied. "Nomadic music breeds nomadic people."

Carmen smiled. She understood what he meant. Unwilling to conform to the dictates of musical convention, flamenco resounded with the echoes of gypsies, Iberian folk music, and Arabian poetry and song. The guitarist's love for flamenco, even after so many years, bubbled from his every pore. He stroked the curves of his guitar as if he held a cherished woman in his hands, with a loving precision that spoke of bliss.

Fernando glanced at her through eyes wrinkled from burnished days and smoky, café nights. "Why do you ask me this now? Are you thinking of leaving?"

"I hope to leave someday." Carmen knew that the café *cantantes* were flourishing in Sevilla and that she might have to move there to continue dancing. Like a thin hemorrhage, people had begun abandoning the copper and iron mines of the Huelva province towns for larger cities. "I'm tired of the tavern."

Fernando nodded. "This is not the place for you. You are too good a *bailaora*. You are meant for more."

"I hope so," Carmen murmured.

She had once found charm in the province's *pueblos blancos,* which had been settled by ancient Romans and Phoenicians. She had once sensed a mysterious beauty in the medieval fortress walls, the churches built by the crusading Knights Templar, the natural caves, the Moorish castle that stood on a distant hillside like a nursemaid watching her charges.

Now, she thought of it as a stark, barren place where nothing thrived. Nothing except her lust for dance and for Tomas.

"I must go." Carmen stood, brushing off her skirt. "I'll see you tomorrow night."

She left Fernando sitting under a tree in the company of his beloved guitar. People strolled and sat in the town courtyard, some watching the energetic children and others gossiping. On Sundays, the shops shut down to allow everyone to socialize and worship. Carmen suspected that people sometimes confused the two ideas—herself included.

She entered the small, whitewashed church. Faded, smoke-smudged frescos seemed to break through the stucco walls, providing glimpses of color and artistry in the hallowed space.

"Bless me, Father, for I have sinned." Carmen's teeth bit into the flesh of her lower lip as her knees sank into the grooves of the confessional bench. "It has been one week since my last confession."

"What are your sins, my child?"

Carmen liked Father Navarro's voice. He spoke in low, even tones that held the same comfort as a loaf of warm bread. His words never sounded imperious or sharp, unlike those of the other priests, who seemed to revel in the sins of their confessors.

Carmen took a breath. "Three times I took the Lord's name in vain. Twice I lied to my father, and once I had impure thoughts. Once I experienced hatred of another woman."

"What woman?" Father Navarro asked gently.

"Maria Alegre."

"The painter's wife?"

"Yes."

"Why?"

"She's ignorant, Father. Ignorant and stupid."

A frown entered the priest's voice. "That is unkind."

"I can't help it." The air in the confessional closed in on Carmen. A bead of sweat trickled down her spine. "I dislike her."

"For no reason?"

"Yes."

"Concealing a sin is a sin in itself," Father Navarro reminded her.

"I know, Father."

"Very well. Say five Hail Marys as your penance. Go in peace."

Carmen quickly made the sign of the cross and left the booth. She liked the semi-anonymity of the confessional, but she didn't expect to see the priest later that afternoon at the fruit market.

"Good afternoon, Carmen." Father Navarro carried a basket filled with ripe figs and strawberries. He moved easily through the small crowd with the poise that came from knowing that one was respected.

"Father." Suddenly uneasy, Carmen's fingers clenched on her satchel.

"I've been meaning to speak to you about your thoughts on dance lessons for some of our young girls," Father Navarro said.

"Yes, well, I have a...an appointment in an hour," Carmen replied. She couldn't help staring at him, realizing that she had never seen him this close in such brilliant sunlight. He had strange eyes—flaxen brown swimming with flecks of gold. Jewels trapped in amber. "Perhaps some other time?"

Father Navarro nodded, reaching up to scratch his ear in a movement so utterly human that Carmen couldn't help but find it endearing.

"That would be fine," he said. "If you would contact the office this week, we can arrange a meeting."

"All right. Goodbye, Father."

Carmen hurried away, a bit unnerved at how the father could be so matter-of-fact after just hearing of her weaknesses. She turned once to glance at him. He was still watching her with those unusual eyes — eyes that made him seem more human than holy. A shiver raced down Carmen's spine as she realized he was looking at her the way other men did.

Pushing the unsettling thought aside, she continued on her way. While she honored the sanctity of Sundays by not dancing at the tavern, she always met Tomas in his studio. There, he stripped off her dress and fondled her breasts, leaving smears of black and red paint on her skin.

"I saw Father Navarro at the market this afternoon." Carmen watched Tomas as his mouth moved over her breasts.

"And...?"

She thought briefly of telling him of her confession, but then shook her head. "Nothing."

"You're beautiful." His voice was rough, his eyes glazed as he slid his palm down her belly to the thicket of hair between her legs. Warmth uncoiled in Carmen's body as he touched her, then clutched her hips to turn her around.

She bent over the back of an upholstered chair, letting Tomas push her legs apart with his knee and open her body to him. Her body jerked forward at his first thrust, his pelvis slamming against her with tender brutality. Carmen's heavily lidded gaze locked on a half-finished canvas of Don Quixote on horseback. Paintings of flamenco dancers and guitarists lined the walls, but none were of Carmen. Tomas wouldn't paint her, he said, for fear of revealing their secret.

She gasped, digging her fingernails into the arm of the chair as he pushed back and forth, driving her to the edge. "Promise me," she panted. "Promise me someday you'll paint me."

Tomas's fingers raked down her moist back, his penis plunged farther into her. "I...I can't."

A wave of frustration rose in Carmen. "Can't paint me or can't promise?"

"Both." He pulled away from her, turning her so that he could look into her face. His eyes burned like two black coals. "I want you. God, how I want you."

Carmen hugged her thighs around his hips and pressed

her breasts against his chest. His hands gripped her almost desperately, his breath scorching her skin as he pumped into her with increasing urgency. Carmen wrapped her arms around his shoulders, reveling in physical pleasure even as her gaze fixed on another painting, one of a famous Sevillian *bailaora*.

She failed to see how a painting of herself could reveal their adulterous affair, but she didn't really mind that Tomas wouldn't paint her. He was not a particularly good artist — at least, not in her opinion. His subjects appeared awkward and inept, thickened with too many layers of oil paint and harsh colors.

But, oh, could he fuck. The hot-wax sensation of his cock drove out thought and replaced it with pure carnality. Carmen was content not to allow Tomas to ungracefully render her likeness on canvas, as long as he repeatedly spread her thighs and filled her with hard plunges of his cock.

When the sky began to resemble the thick layers of a spongy, pink cake, Carmen took Tomas in her arms. He lowered himself onto her, and their sated bodies unfolded from voluptuous tension as slices of evening light splashed into the room.

"Someday," he gasped, "someday I'll marry you. Someday I'll paint you."

Carmen frowned slightly. "No, you won't."

Tomas lifted his head to look at her. "Why do you say that?"

"Because you love your wife."

"I love *you*." Tomas's dark eyes suddenly brimmed with tears.

"Oh, stop it." Impatient with her lover's excessive devotion, Carmen pushed him away and reached for her clothes.

• • •

"Toma que toma!" "Olé!" "Eso es!"

Voices rose like hundreds of black crows into the hot air of the café. From his table at the back, Mateo stared at the length of Carmen's leg as it appeared in intermittent flashes beneath the swirls of her skirt. She moved with the fluid rhythms of a raging current, slicing her hands through the air, slamming her energy into the earth, her body rippling.

Mateo's eyes gleamed hotly as he watched the sinuous movements of Carmen's body. His member throbbed ceaselessly against his thigh. He felt such a thick pain that he sometimes had to clutch himself through his trousers, hiding the evidence of his desire beneath the table.

He watched her until she could dance no more, despite the *jaleos* and encouragement spilling from the audience. After Carmen left the stage, the men grumbled good-naturedly and returned to their drinks and card-playing. Mateo stood and made his way to Carmen's dressing room. He stopped when he saw Tomas Alegre slip through the doorway before him.

Mateo knew. He didn't have to step forward silently to peer through the crack in the door. He didn't have to push the door open a few more inches to enhance his perspective. No, he didn't have to. But he did.

And he watched with a dry mouth and pounding heart as Tomas Alegre slid the black stockings off Carmen's legs, all the while gazing at her face. His hands, probably soft like those of the priest and the scholar, stroked over the curves of her thighs. He lifted and spread them to reveal the fleshy dew of her sex.

Mateo tried to swallow. His head throbbed, his thoughts gaining momentum as he watched Carmen's sex engulf Tomas's penis. And then the two bodies collapsed together in a mesh of animalistic grunts, accompanying the harsh beat of their thrusts. Drive, energy, total surrender to the appetites of the flesh.

And the priest stood on the edge of this circle and feared that it would never break open for him.

• • •

Say it. Say it. Say it.

"And twice I took the Lord's name in vain." Carmen stopped. Shadows flecked her face behind the lattice screen separating them.

Say it! Mateo forced himself to keep his voice even. "That is all?"

"Yes, Father."

"Nothing else?"

She hesitated for a breath and then said, "No, Father."

Mateo's heart filled with disappointment. He gave her penance, blessed her, and closed his eyes as she left the confessional.

· · ·

Carmen picked up a towel and wiped her damp forehead as she walked to her dressing room, ignoring the shouts of encouragement for her to return to the stage. She switched on the single light bulb and kicked off her shoes. Her blood hummed with lingering energy, even as her body pleaded exhaustion.

She sat down at her dressing table and looked at her reflection in the cracked mirror. Wide, dark eyes, reddened from smoke and smudged with cosmetics, stared back at her. Yes, she would leave this town someday. Café *cantantes* were blossoming all over Sevilla. That was where she wanted to be, not this stinking tavern filled with miners.

"You've forgotten something."

Carmen turned at the sound of the male voice. A man stood in the half-opened doorway, his shoulder leaning against the doorjamb.

Carmen frowned. "What are you doing here? No one is allowed here."

"Except the painter — is that right?"

A gasp nearly choked Carmen's throat as she recognized the temperate voice of her visitor. Fear came swiftly on the heels of shock, as if Father Navarro had the power to damn her for all eternity.

She stood, fumbling for the edge of the table to steady herself. "F-father, I…what on earth are you doing here?"

He entered the room, closing the door behind him. Carmen realized she had never seen him without his vestments. The priestly garments had always given him an air of holiness. Now, he wore creased trousers and a linen shirt. He looked as if he could be any one of the miners in town. Carmen suddenly remembered how he had watched her almost hotly the other day in the marketplace.

"I could tell you that I'm concerned about your soul," Father Navarro replied.

"And I would be concerned about yours if you tell me that you frequent this place," Carmen replied, then clamped a hand over her mouth in horror.

To her further shock, the father chuckled. He had a nice laugh, one as moderate as his voice. "I should tell you that my soul is in definite danger."

"And that's why you're here?" Seeing him now was so out of context that her dancer's body suddenly felt unbalanced.

Father Navarro paused in front of her. She stared at him with unabashed curiosity, realizing that the lack of vestments changed his face. The pointed collar on his shirt gave his features a harder edge, strengthened the soft line of his chin.

"Actually, I wanted to ask you why you continue to refuse to confess your adulterous affair with Tomas Alegre."

Carmen drew in a sharp breath, knowing the answer to her question even before she asked it. "How did you know about that?"

His shoulders lifted. "I saw you."

Carmen's hand jerked up to slap him firmly across the face, but the nagging reminder that he was a priest stopped the movement. She brought her hand to her throat instead, feeling her pulse thumping a rapid drumbeat underneath her skin.

"God," she whispered, her voice raw. "My God."

"Why didn't you ever confess?" Father Navarro asked, as if they were discussing the psalms of the Bible.

"I didn't...I couldn't...how dare you ask me this here?" Carmen finally spat. "I don't care if you're the priest! You can't come in here and force me to tell you anything. So go ahead and damn me if you want to!"

"Ah, I would never do such a thing." Still, he did not move away from her. In fact, he placed his fingers on the collarbone exposed by her scooped neckline. The warm pads of his fingertips traced the ridge as if it were the most fascinating thing he had ever touched.

A conflicting wave of shock and intrigue crested in Carmen. Her skin tingled where he touched it, and yet he did not move his fingers beyond a two-inch span.

"If you think," she said, struggling for breath, "that I sell my body or that I—"

"No," Father Navarro interrupted gently. "I don't think that. I never have."

When he lowered his head to place his lips against her collarbone, Carmen trembled. Part of her wanted to pull away from this blatant wickedness, but she could not, for the life of her, deny her fascination. Her fingers closed around the edge of the table so tightly that her knuckles hurt.

"You can't do this," she gasped. Her heartbeat echoed inside her head the way it did when she danced.

He didn't reply, instead sliding his tongue along the valley at the side of her neck. A tremor shuddered through Carmen, swift as a hummingbird. The warmth of his body created a fold of heat between them.

"I want this." Father Navarro's voice hoarsened with growing desire. "I want you. I've watched you dance, you know. Many, many times."

"And you think you can just walk in here and have me?" Carmen snapped.

Father Navarro lifted his head to look at her with those unusual eyes. Eyes that fairly melted with heat and a hint of desperation. "Just once. Once. Please."

His hands reached up to cup her breasts. Carmen couldn't move to stop him, although she became increasingly aware of her body's response to this man and the sheer illicitness of his request. She often found herself aroused after dancing, but this was wholly different. This was both captivating and utterly immoral.

Father Navarro stared at the bulge of her nipples as they pressed against her bodice. With hands that shook, he grasped her neckline and pulled it down to bare her breasts. The cool air brushed against her skin, evaporating droplets of perspiration.

She watched Father Navarro touch her breasts, tracing the tight peaks as if he were touching something cherished. Carmen realized that no man had ever touched her like this, not even Tomas.

His breath rasped against her skin as he pulled the dress over her hips, going down on his knees before her as he unclothed her body. A surge of excitement swelled inside Carmen as she stood naked before this priest, feeling his palms travel over the curves of her hips and the muscles of her thighs. Her legs trembled as Father Navarro's hands moved between them, parting them to allow him access to the folds of her sex. When his finger slid into her, Carmen's hips bucked involuntarily toward him. She knew how moist she was; she could feel the slickness of her sex and the ease with which the priest touched her.

"Put your finger in me." Carmen forced the words out of her throat, reaching down to grasp his wrist. "Touch me there."

A sheen of sweat broke out on his forehead. With a moan, his head sank against her belly as one, then two fingers slipped into her. Carmen shuddered. Her inner muscles clenched around him, but it wasn't enough.

"Once," she whispered. "You can do it once."

She urged him to stand, barely able to control her shaking fingers as she unbuttoned his trousers. She took the compact length of his penis in her hand and wondered suddenly if she should treat his cock differently, if it was somehow holy. Maybe her own ablutions were enough to absolve them both. The thought caused a bubble of laughter to rise inside her.

She eased onto the dressing table, parting her legs to allow him access. His penis glided into her, a delicious pressure collecting in her sex. She grasped the father's arms, her gaze on him as his expression tightened from the sheer pleasure of carnal union.

"God," he gasped. "How I've wanted this. You have no idea how many times I've watched you."

His fingers dug into her waist as he thrust into her, accelerating the pace of his movements until the friction sent waves of rapture through Carmen's blood. She closed her eyes, letting her head fall back against the cold mirror as Father Navarro fucked her. Her calves closed around his thighs as she shed any lingering reservations and abandoned herself to him. Whatever sin they were committing, she knew there had to be worse.

This lust was like flamenco, full of rhythm, movement, and sheer improvisation. Only when she danced or fucked did Carmen feel the same sense of pure dynamism moving from the depth of her being. The kiss of *el duende.*

With a careful movement in complete contrast to the urgency of his thrusts, the priest lowered his head and brushed his lips against Carmen's. Slowly, like the sweep of seagull wings, their breath danced and their lips grazed. Father Navarro continued his exploration of her sweat-polished body, curving his hands over every inch of her that he could reach. And then, with a force that surprised even her, he groaned against her skin, plunging into her until his body shook violently. Carmen clutched him to her and went over the edge with him, brilliant colors coursing across a black sky.

"You have no idea how much I've wanted this," Father Navarro gasped, his chest heaving as he pulled away from her and reached for his trousers. Sweat dampened his shirt. "I can't take my eyes from you when you dance. You're possessed, you possess others."

Carmen picked up a cotton wrap and pulled it around her body. Lingering sensations pulsed gently through her.

"*El duende,*" she said, reaching for a glass of water on the table. "That's what flamenco dancers call it. The demon, the spirit. When it arises from the innermost core of blood, it takes over and you lose yourself in dance."

Father Navarro's lips curled into a half-smile. "It is the same with the bullfighter," he said. "And, like the matador, you perform these violent rituals to battle the forces that would see you subdued."

"And the priest?"

"No. Not so for the priest. Your movement is a stark contrast to my life, my quiet obedience."

Carmen smiled. "I see little evidence of that, Father. I think you're wrong. Even priests can find themselves at the mercy of *el duende*. It simply requires that you be passionate."

• • •

Sunlight glistened on the ripe fruits and vegetables that sat piled in neat pyramids at the market stands. Textured oranges contrasted with the tight, red skin of tomatoes fairly glowing in the light. Juicy strawberries and purple figs basked in the warmth like rows of jewels.

Mateo bit into a fig, letting the sweetness burst over his tongue. He realized that he had never before seen just how beautiful fruits and vegetables could appear. He picked up a strawberry and held it up to the light. How perfect it was, each little seed embedded so delicately in the crimson flesh!

"Father."

Mateo turned at the sound of Carmen's voice. She stood a short distance away, her hand clutched around the handle of a valise. She wore a long, cotton skirt and white blouse with her dark hair swirling around her shoulders like raven's feathers.

"Carmen. You're leaving?"

She glanced away, her gaze skimming over the Huelva province hills. "Yes. For now."

"What about—" Mateo stopped.

Carmen shook her head. "I told him to go back to his wife."

A surge of satisfaction almost caught Mateo off guard. He knew that his own submission and Carmen's command were crucial elements of their souls. They would not exist without them.

"Will you be back?" he asked.

"Someday, perhaps. Goodbye, Father." She hesitated for a second and began walking away. Then she stopped and turned back to look at him. Sun sparked in her eyes, eyes as dark as the black grapes piled nearby.

"It's amazing, you know," Carmen remarked. "Flamenco."

Mateo nodded. "Yes. Yes, it is."

"You dance on such a small stage, a square really, some-times not much wider than the span of your arms."

"I know. I've seen you."

"And yet within that space," Carmen said, "you can do anything."

wanna Buy
a Bike?

࿔

ALISON TYLER

IN AMSTERDAM, YOU CAN PROVE the Rolling Stones wrong. Here, you actually *can* always get what you want. That is, if what you want are drugs—any drugs—or sex—any sex. Sex with men. With women. Orgies. S/M. B/D. Name the perversion and you can make it come true.

Sure, I understand the benefits of having such readily available pleasures. In the states, you have to search out the seedier sides if you've got a taste for trouble. So I realize how someone might enjoy being able to walk down an alley, point to a window, and buy the person behind it for an hour of frisky fun. Yet the type of free-wheeling environment found in Amsterdam poses a problem for girls like me. Girls who like the darker side of things.

The rush, I've always found, is in delving into that cloak-and-dagger ambiance and plunging down the steps into the unknown. What's illegal in Amsterdam? You can walk into a coffee shop and buy your marijuana, walk into a pharmacy and purchase magic mushrooms. No need to skulk through alleys after your personal yearning. For some, it's a fantasy come true. But I fucking hate it.

This is why I was sulking miserably through a rainy Amsterdam afternoon, a scowl on my face, my long black hair windswept, my eyes troubled. In each cozy café, college students sent fragrant plumes of smoke toward the lazily spiraling ceiling fans. Content and flush-cheeked, the smokers slipped deeper into their daydreams, looking as if they were right out of a painting—Norman Rockwell for the new millennium.

In the red light district, I knew I could find someone to take care of whatever I craved, which made me crave absolutely nothing. While others tightened their coats against the harsh autumn storm, I rebelled in the only way I could, pushing back the hood of my heavy black jacket, pulling open the buttons, letting the water hit my skin.

The one thing I do love about Amsterdam is the setup of the city: intricate circles and circuits of canals. Wet and pungent, filled with houseboats, fallen leaves from gold-flecked trees, ducks, and debris. I like the idea of the circles, one slipping inside the other as they get closer to the center. Rings around rings, like the spiraling efforts of a lover's tongue nearing the bull's-eye of a woman's clit.

With thoughts like that on my mind, it was no wonder that I was aroused. But I felt as if I were on the verge of coming without ever being able to reach the climax. Searching for something unknown in a city where you can get anything as long as it has a name and you have the price....

"Wanna buy a bike?" a voice asked as I rounded a corner, breaking through my unhappy haze. Turning, I saw the first evidence of the Amsterdam underground. A scruffy-looking youth with tousled, birch-colored hair and a dead-eyed green stare captured my attention. Handsome, but weathered about the edges, he had the look of someone who'd been up all night. It's a look that I find seductive.

"Excuse me?" I asked.

"Pretty girl," he beckoned, and I took a step further away from the crowds of tourists and into the mouth of the stone-cobbled alley where he stood. "Do you wanna buy a bike?"

And now I understood. Where, in any other city, this man would be offering me drugs or sex or something not easily found on the street, he was hawking bicycles instead. Good as gold in Amsterdam.

"Cheap," he added in perfect English. "With a seat and handlebars. Everything."

In Amsterdam, you have your choice of how to get around. You can walk—like I do—or use a trolley, a boat, a car (if you have balls of steel), or a bicycle. The problem, in my opinion, is that everyone is stoned on something, and they drive as if to prove that you can handle a vehicle while your mind is flying. Trolleys split pedestrians and make them scurry for safety. Bicycles cut off cars. I might trust myself on two wheels, but I wouldn't trust those around me. Still, the excitement of embarking on something illicit made me shift in my wet jeans. Danger is my all-time favorite aphrodisiac.

"Where is it?" I asked, looking around.

"Don't carry the product on me," he said tersely, and I thought I saw a sneer on his attractive face, as if he was thinking, *What can you expect from a foreigner?*

"How much?"

He leaned forward to quote the price, and I saw the way his eyes looked at me. As if he'd suddenly noticed that my jacket was open, my lipstick-red T-shirt wet and tight on my slim body, my jeans soaked through.

The price he quoted was high for a bike, but low to fulfill my need. I nodded, and he motioned for me to follow him, back down that alley to another. Quick-stepping as we made our way to some unknown destination, I heard the way my boots sounded on the walkway, that staccato beat, heard the echo of my beating heart in my ears. This was adventure, excitement, the reason I'd come to Amsterdam in the first place. And why was I getting all warm and aroused? Silly girl, silly girl. It was because I was about to buy a bike.

"This way," he urged, "just down that street."

I tried to keep up with him, but ended up walking behind, and that was OK. The rear view of this youthful dealer was something to be admired. Like me, he had no qualms about getting wet, and his Levi's were a dark ocean blue, tight on his fine ass, slicked down on his lean legs. He had on a black sweater, also drenched, and that unruly white-blonde hair that seemed bed-rumpled instead of just plain wet.

When we got to our destination, he wanted the money. But I've made deals with street salesmen before. It's important to see the merchandise before you put up the cash, regardless of the country you're in.

"Don't trust me?" he asked, grinning, and I shook my head. "This way, then," he said, and we continued on our route, around one of the comeliest canals of the city, where even the ducks were now hiding beneath the arched bridges to get out of the cold driving rain. What did they have to worry about? They lived in water.

"Just a bit further," he said, and I wondered as I spotted a familiar-looking kiosk whether we were going in circles. Didn't matter to me. I'd have followed as long as he led. But soon he stopped again, this time in front of one of the skinny, gingerbread-colored houses that tour-leaders love to point out as the "charm" of Amsterdam. Chained to a railing was a shiny blue bicycle, just as he'd described. Two wheels. Handlebars. A seat. Everything.

"You believe me now?" he asked, and he took a step closer as he held out his hand for the money. His fingertips could have brushed my breasts through the tight, damp shirt, could have stroked the line of my chin, tilted my head up for a kiss. I felt my breath speed up, but I didn't let on. I can play as streetwise as I need.

"The key?" I asked, pointing to the bike lock, and the corners of his eyes crinkled at me as he smiled again. He seemed to have more respect for me now, sensed that I was willing to play any game he named.

"A little further," he said softly, turning on his heel and continuing the walk. Such a smart-ass, I thought. He'd have taken my money at the first place, then told me to wait while he got the bike, disappearing forever. At the second stop, where I could actually see *a* bike, he would have made more excuses — "I need to get the key" — and then vanished. Now, we were testing each other. Him to see if he could get the money from me. And me to see if he might sense something else that I wanted.

Once again, we were walking down another alley. At the end stood a long metal rack, with at least fifty cycles attached. The dealer nodded toward the mess of metal. "You choose one," he said, "tell me the color, and I'll get it for you. *Then* you pay."

"I'll need a lock, too," I said.

"Locks are no good. Watch what I do to one."

I looked over the rack of bikes and found one that I liked. "The emerald green."

He smiled. "Five minutes. Meet me back there," and he pointed down the alley to a bridge. "On the other side."

This was fine with me. If he didn't show up, I wasn't out anything. If he did, well, we'd just see. For the first time, I felt happy to be in Amsterdam. The city *was* lovely, even rain-streaked, and the abundance of drugs and easy sex made the people around me seem at peace. Who *isn't* blissful when they've just gotten laid, or smoked a big fat one, or done both simultaneously?

At the meeting spot, I waited in the rain, shivering, and in less than five minutes he was there, wheeling the bike ahead of him. Now it was my turn to pull a fast one.

"I have to get the money," I said. His eyebrows went up and he frowned at me, but I shook my head quickly to reassure him. "I have it, but it's at my hotel," I told him, naming the location. My smile must have let him know what I was offering. More than payment for a bike. "Don't you trust me?"

"We'll ride there," he said. "It's quicker."

I found myself perched over the back wheel as we sped down the streets, cutting off taxis and trolleys, wreaking havoc with pedestrians, and then joining a sea of other cyclists until finally we were at my hotel. He carried the bike into the lobby for me, where the concierge promised to watch it. Then we headed up the stairs together, soaking wet, dripping little puddles on the carpet as we walked.

At my room, I paid him first, just in case that was really all he wanted. He took the money, folded it, and slid the bills into the side pocket of his jeans, just before he slid his jeans down his legs. Smiling, I stripped, as well, and soon we were naked together, pressed against the wall of my hotel room. Our bodies were wet and cold, at first, then wet and a little warmer as we created heat together.

I like sex. Especially unexpected sex. And this beautiful boy seemed perfectly ready to give me what I needed. He took his time. Starting with a kiss, he parted my lips with his, met my tongue, moving slowly, carefully. Then he grabbed both of my wrists in one hand and held my arms over my head, pinning me to the wall. With my wrists captured, he brought his mouth along the undercurve of my neck, then kissed in a silky line to my breasts. I arched my back, speaking to him with my body alone, making silent, urgent requests. He didn't fail me. First, he kissed my left nipple, then my right, then moved back and forth between them until I was all wet again. A different type of wetness from being soaked to the skin outdoors. Now, I was soaked within.

It was time for him to fuck me, and I wanted to say this, but I realized to my embarrassment that I didn't know his name. I felt a moment of panic, then decided it didn't matter. We had our agreement, our arrangement, and that bond of dealer to seller should have been all the information I needed. So I locked onto his clear green eyes and tilted my head toward the large bed in the center of the room. He grinned, lifted me in his arms, and carried me to it.

There was romance in the gesture that pulled at me deep inside, from the base of my stomach to the split between my legs.

Even though I was the same girl who had gotten off in the past by being taken in public, being tied down with leather thongs, bound with cuffs, spanked with paddles, fucked with dildos. Kink has always tended to make me come. But this time was different.

The thrill, I have always found, lies in the unknown. Plunging down those steps into darkness has always been my favorite way to play. Yet, usually, the need for danger takes me into extreme situations. This time, I found myself on a normal bed in an average hotel room, doing something extraordinary with a stranger.

"Trust me," he said, and I nodded.

The boy spread me out on the bed and continued with his kissing games, making his way to the intersection of my body, then tracing a map of Amsterdam's canals around and around my clit. His tongue slid deep inside me, then pulled out, went back in to draw invisible designs on the inner walls of my cunt, and then out again, leaving me breathless and yearning.

"Now," I murmured, and he nodded, understanding. But then he moved off the bed again, rummaging through his pile of wet clothes until he found the bicycle lock and chain that he'd removed from my new cycle. Back at my side, he used the heavy metal links to bind my arms together over my head. No lock needed, just the chain wrapped firmly around my slender wrists. That was perfect, divine—just the type of rush that I craved.

Then, sitting up on the bed, he used his hands to part the slicked-up lips of my pussy, and his fingers slipped into my wetness. I sensed it a second before his cock pressed into me, and I stared into his eyes as we were connected. And, oh Christ, that feeling was almost overpowering, the length of his rod as he thrust deep inside me, following the same route made by his tongue moments before. Only now, I basked in the fullness of it. Thick and long, his cock filled me up.

Before I could even think about what I might want next, his fingers came back into play. He kept my pussy lips spread apart, stretching me open, and then the tips of his fingers began to tap out a sweet and unexpected melody over my clit. I sighed and ground my hips against him, letting him know how much I liked what he was doing. Then I squeezed him, from deep within, and this time he was the one to sigh. Open-mouthed, eyes wide and staring into mine, he watched me for the whole ride. Held me with a gaze so intense that I couldn't look away.

This sent me over the edge. His fingers, his eyes, his cock, his tongue all combining to take me there, to lift me up. To send me. My body closed in on his, and then opened up, squeezing and releasing, bringing him right up there with me. Pushing him over.

"Beauty," he whispered, stroking my still-wet hair away from my face as I came.

• • •

When I went downstairs later in the afternoon, the bike was gone, of course.

"Your friend, he took it," the concierge told me with a smile. "But he left you this." The money was sealed in one of the cream-colored envelopes kindly provided by the hotel. Fair trade. He knew I didn't really have use for a bike in Amsterdam, and if he'd taken the cash, that would have made him a whore instead of simply a street dealer. It was a wholly complete transaction, and I knew that I should have been satisfied.

Still, the next day found me walking through the city with a mission, pausing at each darkened alleyway until I heard the words that made me wet.

"Hey, pretty girl," he whispered, his voice low and seductive, "wanna buy a bike?"

Bullshit

ॐ

Jim Provenzano

BELOW MY HOTEL ROOM WINDOW, the Botanical Gardens sat amid a small, snow-blanketed park like a sunken Congress. The central dome and outlying wings were glass and steel, but shaped the same, is what I'm trying to say.

The Gardens were on my list of "things to do if nothing better happens." While my president's hide was being whipped stateside, I'd decided to escape my country in Toronto, where a simple Web-content-crap contract job, plus a free roundtrip flight, beckoned.

Also, two guys from Toronto that I'd talked to in a chat room seemed nice and e-mailed jpegs as proof of handsomeness. I sent mine. Their return messages claimed attraction. Potential near-blind dates were arranged.

I'd heard about the gay club called Remington's, where you could sip a beer while watching guys strip all the way. Hmm… sip 'n' strip. That was still problematic at home. I love watching men dance naked, but the spaces where this pleasure is provided are increasingly limited and smelly. Remington's sounded reputable, with the added potential for solicitation—something I'd always wanted to try.

I'd befriended whores, considering them the last honest businessmen, even dated a few, but never paid. It wasn't until later that I realized some people thought I did, or had to.

When a former friend in New York pulled the prank of calling up a bunch of escorts and impersonating me, I was livid. He said it was a joke, but only after I'd caught him. One of the escorts had saved the message, and e-mailed it to me as a PureVoice MPEG. Despite my computorial hesitance, it worked.

I even got to watch the wavering voice signal wiggle up and down as the soon-to-be former (if I had my way) media director of a huge AIDS organization said:

"Of *course* I'll leave a message at the tone, George. I'm a polite kind of guy. I'm calling because I saw your, um, ad in the back pages of the *Bay Area Reporter*, and I wanted to know what your services included. It says, and I quote, 'rubdown.' I don't think it says anything else, just has your name and phone number. So, um, what do I, what more do I need to know? Please let me know. My name is Jim. I'm at...." He then gave my phone number twice and wished the escort a happy new year.

Months later, still stinging from this fraud, and hurt by what I can only imagine as his other numerous nonrecorded libels to members of our increasingly limited and carnivorous community, I figured paying for sex was about the last palatable and unfelonious kink I hadn't tried. Why not take the advice of my evil former pal, since everyone else is?

So when a bit of business came my way, and a paid trip to Toronto, I planned my minivacation and débauche over the border.

I forgot to plan ordinary tourist things. My purpose was to get laid, or at least inspect the places where men get laid in Toronto. Having written gay-ghetto travel articles, it was hard to break old habits.

The usual listings amounted to a mirror site for any other large city: the leather bar, the college guy bar, the mixed gender/New Wave club/restaurant, the posh place for older gents. It's like those variety packs of little cereal boxes my brother and I fought over as kids. "No, I want the Sugar Pops!"

Shuttle bus, plane, bla bla. No lucky penis sightings in airport men's rooms. I used to play that game. No longer. I'd had my little loo adventures when spotting dicks was a thrill. Nowadays I can pick gay guys in waiting lounges at fifty paces. Cute teens always duck into stalls. The only lookers are Uncle Fester doppelgängers.

Generic room, individually wrapped soap, etc. The hotel lobby was continually full of burly men standing around in packs, talking like rolling gravel. Friday featured a herd of lacrosse players. Saturday, a truckers' convention.

Sure, they seem sexy in the porno mags—the mythos of trade—but up close, they're less than charming. They also can't stop staring, since I am neither faggy-looking nor amenable to their lingo. These men don't modulate their voices. It's just ON or OFF. "How 'bout dem Rangers, eh?" Grunt, grunt.

Calling the two potential dates revealed a wrong number and another guy who, to sum up, invited me over immediately and turned out to be the gay male equivalent of Miss Havisham. His eccentricities shook my nerve so badly, I hightailed it back to the hotel for recon and a shower.

I perused the horrifyingly banal sightseeing options in the little lobby rack. I'd forgotten that Niagara Falls was nearby. Oh.

The Church Street strip: restaurants, with their tasty, nice waiters, bla bla. Bars: where I sat or leaned near posters of fascistically gorgeous men, proved unproductive. I can't drink two beers without getting sleepy while some diva screams that I'm "free to do what I want."

I switched to club soda when a cute guy gave me an appreciative glance. He would have served my goal of bedding a local of the classic Canadian mode: late twenties, Gallic features, prominent nose, milky skin, slightly witty, hopefully uncircumcised, and a bit superior-acting toward Americans.

But as I sidled up to the bar for a refill, prepared to utter a

dismissive joke about the projection screen's nude wrestlers—
"Yeah, but their technique is lousy"—thereby ingratiating myself
into his life, arms, anus, perhaps, he began chatting with a
woman to his left, deliberately turning away.

Buh-bye.

I should add that I also tried a few bathhouses, and got
exactly what I'd feared: murky, eerie caverns with angular, maze-
like halls worthy of De Chirico. Patrons consisted of the usual
suspects: pasty, potbellied men with concave chests; rail-thin
Asian wisps who swarmed into the showers to watch me bathe.
The only hunk would play polar opposites, always being at the
other end of a hall, before I gave up, worrying more about foot
fungus than any STD, my throat constricted from the unventi-
lated surplus of cigarette smoke.

Next cereal box: the leather bar.

Let me preface this scene with a bias—I still don't get it.
You want torture, don't give me theater. I'll give you a headlock
if you're into pain, but I'd prefer affection. Roughly? If that's to
your liking. Frankly, I have my own form of S/M: discovering
photos of ex-boyfriends gracing gift cards in shops thousands of
miles from home.

But the nut job I met topped all others. He was the least ruf-
fled-looking or hairy, and not adorned with cuir utensils, so I
thought he'd be less...specific in his needs.

(Blurt out loud as Pee Wee Herman:) Ha!

"Hi." Handshake.

He wore a black leather vest, no shirt, jeans and boots. He
was incredibly handsome from the neck down. His eyes read
Instant Spousal Abuse.

I wore jeans, brown hiking boots (*faux pas!*), and a wrestling
T-shirt from a school where I actually wrestled. Would authentic-
ity prove enticing?

"How's your ass?"

"Huh?" I sputtered.

"Your cock. Is it big?"

"Is this your idea of chit-chat?"

"I don't like the bullshit. I'm just into fucking."

I was about to recommend a petting zoo, but instead smiled, said, "How about I finish my beer…?" then did so. "And you can watch my ass—which is, quite honestly, the best, firmest, youngest, most fuckable ass here"—I glanced around—"which is not saying much, and walk out this door and out of your sad little world."

Which I did. I felt great, until it started to rain again. I walked in it, so my physical state could match my emotional state, wondering, What are we without the bullshit?

The Torontonian equivalent of Times Square? Yonge Street. Blinking lights, sneaker stores, Adult XXX. Irony: Youth Center next door to the strip club. At least there's employment nearby.

So I chose the strip club, where the smoke irritated, a speaker blew out, but the men danced—and took it all off. Some, aided by rubber bands, sported bouncy boners, while others went *au naturel*. Some danced like pros. Others merely strutted. I didn't care. I had a seat, a drink, and the best show on earth. All tease, all skin.

Watching the boys expose themselves with varying levels of assurance and self-degradation touched both my groin and my heart. I adjusted my pants, making room for an occasional boner of my own. The black light exposed spots on my jeans where detergent had over-cleansed the fabric, creating glow-in-the-dark faux-come stains.

In shorts, the dancers strolled about the club, feigning interest in customers, luring them to a back room for private dances. I partook of a few, I admit, shot a wad, monetarily, but declined those with bronzer, guys with long hair, or boys named Cory.

I put my cynicism aside when a dancer of utterly boyish proportions hopped up onstage, his cock already denting his shorts. He was porn star Dano Sulik if he'd been born in Ontario and not Eastern Europe. I would charm him with tips, then allow him to seduce me with commerce.

As I was about to move to a small table ringside, a gaggle of Asian drag queens entered in a cloud of cigarette smoke, taking the stage-side table. Pouting, with bags, coats in faux-something, and frouffed-up hair, they seemed concubines of Imelda Marcos delayed by traffic, completely distressed to be there, and determined that everyone else noticed.

One of them, not cross-dressed (a drag hag?), blew smoke directly onto the stage while neo-Dano arced his curved bottom toward them. Their turned-away heads and dismissive chattering shattered his performance. His cheerfully flirtatious smile cracked. His dick wilted.

What nasty creature would heckle a go-go dancer? Why did they sit so close and block several views of the most perfect young man as he shook his booty? How could they turn away when a musical anatomy lesson worthy of Gene Kelly was being so beautifully displayed? Was this some sort of gender civil disobedience? Isn't there any place left on earth where a dick can hang free?

As neo-Dano left the stage, all it took was a touch on his shoulder, and he offered to do a "private dance." His near-authentic smile sparked my interest. I would reward him for his endurance.

He wiggled about, let me fondle him, feel the curve of his back muscles, the folds of tight muscles, the indent of his navel. This was in one of the half-private booths where you sit and let a guy contort inches from you for ten dollars (Canadian). For twice that, you can touch him. For ten times that, you get take-out.

"You like me?" he cooed as he sat on my lap, writhing in a manner that reminded me of the *Metropolis* movie poster crumpled in my coat pocket. I'd peeled it off a construction wall as a souvenir. Hel, the whore of Babylon, could not outdo this boy in mechanized charm.

"I adore you." I licked the dimpled curve above his ass.

I had not expected to dole out so much cash, and when it came time to pay up, I only had a twenty and a few U.S. fives.

"Oh, those are fine," he said. I felt like an invader exploiting a small country. I wanted cosmopolitan, not desperation.

"You want me to come to your hotel?"

"Sure. What can I get?"

"Lemme put it this way. We'll both...arrive."

J'arrive. I'm coming. I'd be his last client *du jour,* get the money shot. Not only could I get a porn star stand-in, but one I could imagine as underage, plus a guarantee of body fluids.

"One-thirty?" The black light gave his eyes an eerie, metallic cast.

"OK. See you." I scribbled my hotel address and room number on a Remington's card. I imagined entrapment, burly vice cops bursting through the door. I almost panicked, but as I walked to the hotel, three truckers were luring a pair of busty black street-"hos" into the lobby.

No problem.

Bank machine, convenience store, hunger, elevator, gobbling down plastic-wrapped flavored pies.

If you're expecting a hot sex scene, you may notice there are few words left.

He did not show.

I had the cash in a Best Western envelope, with a tip prepared. I had a tape of soft music cued. I'd bathed. As my evil friend said, "I'm a polite sort of guy."

Did he even try to get in, I wondered, by pretending to be a pizza boy? I hoped for some elaborate catastrophe to have prevented his walking the five blocks to meet me—anything but mere disinterest.

He'd said I would sleep well, knowing I'd had a great time. I slept fitfully, hoping every straggling hotel guest passing my door was him. He would be cold pizza: late, chewy, but still pizza.

What did I get? At least the heart thuds of anticipation. A chance to memorize ceiling spackling. The next day, home, online, I would download neo-Dano's jpeg from the Remington's website. I think it was him.

Perhaps the dancer's absence had much less to do with me than his short attention span, or even a preference for older men with daintier hands and less stamina. I remembered the last time I'd edged this close to being a John, how the muscle-bound go-go pup had said, in excusing his passing me over for a man of 70, "But I gotta *do* stuff with you."

Is it my fault I can't even get laid by a whore? That I don't know how to respond to wolf whistles and silent gawking with anything but shyness? That I can't strike up a "bullshit" conversation while hackneyed porno glares from a screen on high? That paying for incredible beauty seems like more fun than forcing attraction to a nice guy who's free, but who will reduce my body's interesting features to brunch chat-fodder only hours after sending me on my way?

• • •

Before the airport bus ride, during which I comforted myself into worldly delusion, since I could tell what the elderly French couple behind me were saying, before I sat comfortably in the Air Canada plane, before the captain announced in two languages that we were presently flying over Casper, Wyoming, I remembered that this is why I must have a window seat — to hide my face, because flying over the crinkled terrain where that boy was killed forced up a snot-filled choke of overwhelming grief.

Before I enjoyed watching *Ronin* dubbed into French while still enjoying the plot, I realized that I, too, am a terrorist, but of sex: a suspect, a criminal, but also one within the gay realm. To the sexual performers, I'm pathetic for desiring the emotional trappings surrounding sex — cuddling, intimacy. As the trappings of our commercialized community continue to fail us, the "bullshit" remains while we pass through it, transients burrowing through the cereal boxes.

But before I did all that, I visited the Botanical Gardens, because I had three hours until my shuttle bus and nothing better to do.

• • •

After dropping my bags off with an indolent concierge, I traipsed through the park's lawn, avoiding the shoveled sidewalk. Memory patches of childhood forts and snowmen rose to greet me. The snow approached liquid death, but the crunching under my boots revived and tortured me. "Once I was a little boy," the Smashing Pumpkins song rolled by in my head.

Entering the Gardens, I felt the moisture transform me, felt the verdancy, the arranged beauty, manicured yet wild. Exoticism in a great glass box. I almost felt the bits of pollen, or whatever these plants exuded, entering my lungs. I felt better, being a citizen among the clusters of other people: straight couples, a family, a few stray gay men, a homeless guy, two black squirrels.

And then, the small sign identified it.

Aralaceae
Hedera
Helix
(descended from the English Ivy)

One of the doorways, draped by an almost hairy ivy, forced passersby to be grazed about the head and neck by the hanging vines. I shivered, startled by the contact, and retreated to a private, moist area. Intoxicated by the plants' aroma, perhaps, a flood of tears, an emotional slow-motion sneeze, erupted on my face just as a tourist snapped a picture of the goldfish pond.

Aralaceae. Hedera. Helix. It would become an incantation, a spell. Without presumption or performance, without insult, an admission fee, or the sacrifice of humiliation, finally a living thing had touched me.

Bottomless
on Bourbon

⁊

MAXIM JAKUBOWSKI

HE HAD OFTEN PROMISED to take Kathryn to New Orleans.

But it had never happened. They had spectacularly fallen apart long before the opportunity arose. In fact, the travel they had managed to do in between feverish fucks had proven rather prosaic. So much for promises. They hadn't even visited Paris, Amsterdam, or New York either.

So, whenever he could, he now took other women to the Crescent City.

For sex.

And fantasized about Kathryn's face, and eyes, and pale breasts, and cunt and more.

New Orleans was for him a city with two faces. Almost two different places—the aristocratic and slightly disheveled languor of the Garden District on one hand and the hustle and bustle of the French Quarter on the other, contrasting like night and day.

The touristic charms concealing darker, ever-so-venomous charms. The heavy, placid flow of the Mississippi River zigzagging in serpentine manner through the opposing twin shores of Jackson Square and Algiers. The gently alcoholic haze of New Orleans days and the enticing, dangerous attraction of fragrant New Orleans nights. Nights that smelled and tasted of sex.

He loved to see the women sweat as he made love to them, enjoyed the feel of bodies sliding against each other, in moist, clammy embraces as sheets tangled around them. He took unerring, voyeuristic pleasure in watching them shower afterward, washing his seed away from their openings, cleaning away his bites, the saliva that still coated their nipples, neck, or earlobes that he had assaulted with military-like, amorous precision.

Those were all memories he treasured. Stored away for all eternity in his mental bank vaults. The curve of a back, the soft blonde down slowly being submerged in a small pool of perspiration just inches away from her rump, highlighted by a solitary light bulb, as she kneeled on all fours on the bed and he breached the final defenses of her sphincter and impaled himself in her bowels. The sound of a moan, of pleasure, of joy. Ohhh…. AAAAHHH…. Chriiiiiist…. The tremor that coursed through the girl's taut body as he discharged inside her or she rode the ocean waves of her oncoming orgasm.

Yes, New Orleans, his city of sex.

Endless walks through the small streets between hotel room episodes. Invigorating breakfasts of beignets and coffee and ice-cold orange juice at the Café du Monde; oysters and thick, syrupy gumbo at The Pearl off Canal Street; loitering hand in hand in the markets full of the smell of spices and seafood, chewing on garlic-flavored pistachio nuts; obscene mounds of boiled crawfish at Lemoyne's Landing; hunting for vintage paperbacks through the dusty shelves at Beckham's; po'boys at the Napoleon House; zydeco rhythms at the House of Blues — a routine he could live on for days on end. Until he would tire of the woman, because she bored him, once past the mechanics of fornication: never said the right thing or talked too much or simply because she wasn't the woman he really wanted to be with in New Orleans.

There had been Lisa, the software executive; Clare, a lawyer who looked like Anne Frank had she ever grown up and liked to be handled roughly; Pamela Jane, the investment banker he had met at the hotel bar who wanted to be a writer; Helene, the biology teacher from Montreal. He didn't feel he was being promiscuous—four women in six years since Kathryn. Some he had found here, others he had brought.

But somehow none had fitted in with this strange city and, even though the sex had been loose and fun, and the company never less than pleasant, something had been lacking. Even at midnight, his women buckling under his thrusts on bed or floor or sucking him off under the water streams of the shower, he knew they were creatures of the day, anonymous, predictable; they had no touch of night, no share of darkness. And the darkness was what he sought. In women. In New Orleans. What he knew he had once detected under Kathryn's lush exterior.

He had high hopes for Susi, though.

• • •

She was Austrian, in her late twenties, and worked in a managerial capacity for a travel agency in Vienna, which made it easier (and cheaper) for her to jump on a plane for purposes of pleasure.

They had met in New York some months earlier. It was spring and the weather was appalling for the season. The rain poured down in buckets, and all Manhattan was gridlocked like only that island can manage. He'd been in town promoting a book and negotiating the next contract with his publishers there (he never used an agent) and was booked on an evening flight back to London. He'd been staying, as usual, in a hotel down by the Village, off Washington Square. He had booked a car to JFK and it was already half an hour late. They had checked at reception and found out that the driver was still blocked in traffic near Columbus Circle. He had promptly cancelled the car and rushed with his suitcase to the hotel's front steps to hail a yellow cab.

They were few and far between, and he wasn't the only hotel guest heading for the airport. Both he and the tall, slim, red-headed woman went for the same cab, which declined the airport ride, on the pretext of the conditions. They agreed to share the next cab to come along. She was even later than he, as her flight preceded his by twenty minutes.

"My name is Susanne, but my friends call me Susi, with an *i*," she said, introducing herself as the driver made his slow way toward the Midtown Tunnel.

Despite clever shortcuts through Queens, the journey took well over an hour and a quarter, so they had much opportunity to talk as they inched nearer their planes. She had been in town for a week, visiting her parents, who both worked as diplomats for one of the big international organizations.

She did miss her flight, while he caught his with a few minutes to spare. But they had exchanged e-mail addresses and had remained in touch since.

They had quickly become intimate. He'd sent her one of his books, and she had remarked on the sexual nature of many of his stories and confessed to some of her own sexual quirks. She was an exhibitionist. Would sometimes take the subway back in Vienna dressed in a particularly short skirt and without underwear and allow men to spy on her genitals. She was shaven, so they had a full view of her naked mound. She was also in the habit of masturbating in parks, where she could be seen by passersby, actually encouraged voyeurs to do so, and knew that, sometimes, men were jerking off watching her just a few meters away.

She would pretend her name was Lolita. He asked her why.

Because, she answered, she had little in the way of breasts, and her bare pubis evoked a child or a doll. She was submissive by nature, she told him.

She e-mailed him a series of photographs taken by an ex-boyfriend she had broken up with shortly before the New York trip. He found them wonderfully provocative, in a tender sort of way. In the first, her long, skinny frame stood in contrast to the sluttish, traditional black lingerie of embroidered knickers, suspender belt, and stockings almost a size too big for her. Yes, she had no breasts, barely a hillock worth of elevation, and no cleavage, and, he imagined (the photographs were all black and white) pale pink nipples like a gentle stain in the landscape of her flesh. Her hair was a bit longer than when she had been in New York, her eyes dead to the world. In the second photograph—he could guess the sequence they had been taken in, pruriently imagined what the boyfriend in question had made her do, perform, submit to, after the camera had been set aside— she was now squatting clad only in suspender belt and stockings, her cunt in sharp focus, lips ever so ready to open, her head thrown back so that you could barely recognize her features. Photograph number three saw her spread-eagled over a Persian carpet and parquet floor, one arm in the air, both legs straight, holding herself up by one arm, like a gymnast, her face in profile, a most elegant and beautiful vision of nudity with no hint of obscenity at all, her body like a fine-tuned machine, a sculpture. In the fourth, she was standing and the photographer had shot away from crotch level and her body was deformed as in a hall of mirrors by the skewed perspective, the focus on her enlarged midriff. The one thing that struck him as he kept on examining the photos on his laptop screen was how her sex lips didn't part and how he wished to see inside her. The final photograph she had sent him (were there more? more explicit or extreme? She answered that others were just out of focus, though his imagination as ever played wildly on) was both the sexiest and the most vulgar. She was on all fours, her arse raised toward the camera in a fuck-me pose, long legs bent, rear a bit bony, the line of her cunt lips straight as a ruler and continued by her arse crack and darker hole. Every time he looked at this one, he couldn't help getting hard. And he knew that she enjoyed knowing that.

He told her about the delights of New Orleans and invited her to join him there one day.

To explore possibilities, he said.

Initially, she only said maybe.

But he persisted, courting her with a modicum of elegance, and she finally agreed. It took a couple of months to find a week when both could free themselves from previous commitments (ah, the sheer logistics of lust!) and arrangements were made. Flights to New York were coordinated — her job came in useful — and they both arrived in Newark an hour or so apart. Neither flight was delayed.

Curiously enough, there are no direct flights between New York and New Orleans, and their connection went via Raleigh-Durham.

As they emerged from the airport luggage area, Susi smelled the heat that now surrounded them like a blanket and turned toward him, kissed him gently on the cheek, and said: "I just know I'm going to like it here. Thanks ever so much for bringing me."

By the time the taxi dropped them off at the small hotel he had booked on Burgundy Street, it was already dark.

It was summer. Moist, no wind from the Gulf, the air heavy with the powers of the night, the remains of the day lingering in patchy clouds. They were both sweating, their bodies not yet acclimatized.

They dropped their bags and he switched the air-conditioning a notch higher and suggested a shower.

He undressed her. Now she was no longer black and white. The nipples were a darker pink, closer to red than he expected and darkened a shade further when he kissed them. Her pale body was like porcelain. Long, thin, exquisitely supple. Since Kathryn, none of the other women, here or elsewhere, had been nearly as tall.

He escorted Susi to the shower cubicle and switched the water on. She looked at his cock, growing slowly at the sheer sight of her nudity. He soaped her with infinite delicacy and tenderness and explored her body under the guise of washing, refreshing her from the transatlantic journey with its grime and tiredness. He fell to his knees and wiped the suds away from her crotch. Her gash was red against the mottled pinkness of her pubic mound. She hadn't shaved there for a week or so; they had agreed she would let him shave her clean, a delight he had long fantasized about. He parted her thin lips, as if opening a rare flower, and darted his tongue inside to taste her. Susi shuddered.

The first time was good.

They were shy, affectionate, slow, tentative, testing pleasure points and limits with great delicacy.

She was extremely self-conscious of her lack of opulence breast-wise, so he lavished particular care on her there, sucking, licking, nibbling, fingering her with casual precision until he caught the precise pulse of her pleasure behind the gentle swell of her darkening nipples.

They came closely together. Silently.

. . .

The later days filled quickly between wet embraces and ever-more feverish fucks as they grew used to each other's quirks and secret desires. She had always wanted to take a riverboat down the Mississippi, and they spent a day doing so, passing the Civil War mansions and great lawns and observing the rare crocodiles still lingering in the musty bayous. Just like tourists. Which they were. Sexual tourists with, so far, no taste for the local fare. Breezing down Magazine Street in midafternoon as the antique shops reopened for business. Taking a tram to the Garden District. Lingering, with verbose guides, in the atmospheric cemeteries, with their ornate crypts and walls of bones. Visiting the voodoo museum, trying to repress their unceremonious gig-gles. He covertly fingering signed first editions at the Faulkner House.

Susi never wore a bra—she had no need for one—and neither did she slip knickers on when they would go out walk-ing. Long, flowing, thin skirts revealing the shape of her legs when she faced the sun, only he knowing how unfettered her cunt lips were beneath the fabric, sometimes even imagining he could smell her inner fragrance as they walked along hand in hand and conjuring up the thoughts of other, lubricious men passing by, had they known of her naked vulnerability. It turned him on, this constant availability of hers, this exhibitionistic desire to provoke. Walking along Decatur, passing one of the horse-drawn carriages waiting there for tourists, they saw a dog held in leash by a small black child wag its tail frenetically and brush against Susi's leg. He smiled. She asked him why.

"He could smell your cunt," he said.

"Do you think so?" she remarked, her eyes all wide.

"Yes," he told her. "You smell of sex. Strongly."

Her face went all red, approximating the shade of her short bob, and he watched her flush spread to her chest and beneath the thin silk blouse.

"It turned him on," he said.

"Oh…."

"And me, knowing how naked you are under those thin, light clothes," he added.

She smiled.

Later, back in their hotel room, she insisted they keep the curtains open when they made love, knowing any passing maid or room-service staff might see them in the throes of sex as they walked past on the steps outside the window, and as he moved frantically inside her, he saw that she kept her eyes open, was actually hoping they would be seen. The idea excited her.

The same night, a few blocks before Bourbon, she suddenly said:

"I have to pee."

They'd only left the hotel a hundred yards or so ago, so she must have known the need would arise. He offered to go back to the room.

"No," she said. "The side street there. That will do."

It was dark, no one around, although the risk of passersby emerging off Toulouse was great.

Susi pulled her long skirt upward and bunched it around her waist, her thin, unending legs bursting into pale view, the plumpness of her cunt in full display under the light from the illuminated wrought iron balcony above them, and squatted down. He watched, hypnotized, as the hot stream of urine burst through her labia and splashed onto the New Orleans pavement. Her eyes darted toward the main street, begging for someone to come by. None did. Her bladder empty, she rose to her feet, the skirt still held above her waist in insolent provocation.

"It's a bit wet," she said to him. "Would you dry me?"

He got down on his knees, wiped her cunt lips clean with the back of his hand, then impulsively licked her briefly. Her clit was hard, swollen. Susi was in heat.

"Fuck me here," she asked him. "I don't mind if people see us."

"I can't," he said. "We've only just got out of bed. I don't think I could get hard enough again so quickly."

Susi glanced at him with disapproval.

She dropped the folds of her dress.

They began talking.

"Does it turn you on?" he asked.

"Yes."

"What is it? A feeling of control over men, that they can see you but not touch?"

"I don't know," Susi remarked. "My body is nothing special, but I love to show myself. Gives me meaning. It's a bit confusing."

"Your body's great. You shouldn't underestimate yourself," he answered. "But you must be careful. On the nude beach outside Vienna, with your girlfriend along, there's an element of safety, but elsewhere it could be risky, you know."

"Yes."

"Some people could read other things in your need to exhibit yourself. You could get yourself raped."

"I know," Susi answered, with a slight sigh in her voice. "Sometimes, I even imagine what it would be like. Several men."

"Really?"

"Yes. Five of them. First they fuck my every hole, then I am made to kneel, still naked, at their feet, and they all jerk off and come in my face and hair."

"A bit extreme…."

"I know…."

He tried to lighten the mood. Already anxious as the darkness neared.

"The ultimate facial treatment. Better than soap!"

Susi laughed and led the way back toward Bourbon Street.

. . .

He described how Bourbon Street would be when Mardi Gras came. The noise, the colored beads, the floats, the beer, the wonderfully hedonistic atmosphere that gripped the whole French Quarter, the fever that rose insidiously as the alcohol loosened inhibitions and the music from the bars on either side of the street grew louder, competing rhythms crisscrossing on every corner, clouding minds and bodies.

How the revelers on the balconies would bait the walkers below, sprinkling them with drink, offering beads for the flash of a nipple or a quickly bared backside, to massive roars of approval from the wild crowds.

He could see Susi's eyes light up. Yes, she would enjoy Mardi Gras here. No longer require an excuse to bare her parts to one and all, and the more the merrier.

"And what happens behind closed doors?" she asked him.

He shuddered to think. He'd only stayed in New Orleans for the first night of Mardi Gras. Had heard mad rumors of uncontrollable excess, of sex in the streets. He'd once come across a range of videocassettes in a Seventh Avenue porn joint in New York documenting the sexual side of Mardi Gras here year after year. But as with wine, he was unaware which were the good years or the bad years and had never sampled any of the cassettes in question.

His mind raced forward. To a clandestine video in a white box with a Polaroid cover shot of Susi's porcelain-white body, face covered with come, labeled "SUSANNE 'LOLITA' WIEN, MARDI GRAS 1999." A vintage performance, no doubt.

Bourbon Street night deepened as the beer flowed ever more freely, spilling into the gutters from plastic cups being carried up and down the street by the Saturday night revelers.

The music surging from all around grew louder, the lights more aggressive, and the crowds swayed uncertainly. Young kids tapped away for a few cents or break-danced outside the bars, the neon signs of the strip clubs entered battle, pitting male strippers against female ones, topless joints against bottomless ones. A row of mechanical legs danced a cancan from the top of a bar window, advertising further displays of flesh inside.

Susi was curious.

"I've never been to a striptease place before. Can we?"

"Why not?" he said, acquiescing.

They entered the dark bar. A woman who had stripped down to a shining, lamé bikini was dancing around a metal pole at its center. A few men sat by the stage desultorily sipping from half-empty glasses. They ordered their drinks from a sultry waitress and watched the stripper shed her bra with a brief flourish. The performance was uninspiring, and the most exciting thing about the dancer for him was her gold navel ring, which shimmied in the fluctuating light. His mind went walkabout as he tried to recognize the rock 'n' roll tune she was (badly) dancing to.

Several shimmies and swirls later, with a liberal shake of her silicon-enhanced mammaries, the song (some country and western standard given an electric and gloomy Americana twist) came to an end and the stripper quickly bowed, picking up a few stray dollar bills thrown onto the stage by the isolated punters on her way off.

"Is that all?" Susi turned to him, asking.

"I think so," he said.

"But it's not even bottomless. She didn't even show her cunt!"

"Maybe because it's a bar. I don't know," he said, "there must be some local bylaws or something. Don't know much about the rules in American strip clubs," he continued, surprised by Susi's interest.

Another stripper, black, stocky, took to the stage and a soul number burst out of the speakers. The previous performer worked the other side of the dance area, soliciting tips from some of the men. One whispered in her ear as she accosted him. She nodded. The man rose and he followed the woman, who now wore a dressing gown, to a darker corner at the far end of the bar. Susi nudged him and they both peered in that direction.

They could just about see the stripper throw back her gown and squat over the lap of the man, who had now seated himself.

"A private dance," he said to Susi.

"Wow! Cool!" she said, one of the more irritating mannerisms he had picked up on when they chatted online back in Europe.

There wasn't much to see. The stripper moved in silence. The man appeared to keep his hands to himself, but the darkness engulfed the couple.

"I'm turned on," Susi said in his ear.

"Really?" he said, finding the atmosphere in the bar quite unerotic, the black stripper now strutting her square rump a few feet away from his face.

"Yes," Susi added. "I don't think I'd make a good stripper. No tits, as you well know. But I sure could lap or table dance. I'd like to do that for you…."

He grinned.

"Sure. Later in our hotel room, I'll look forward to your demonstration."

"No. Here," Susi said, a deep tone of excitement in her voice.

"Here?" he queried.

"Yes." He could see that her right hand was buried in the folds of her dress, that she was fingering herself through the material. "Can you arrange it? Please. See the guy at the bar? He appears to be in charge. Get him to agree. Please, pretty please?"

He shrugged.

It cost him fifty bucks and some haggling.

He walked back toward the stage where Susi was downing the rest of her Jack Daniels.

He nodded.

"It's yes," he said.

She rose, a mischievous glint in her eye. She took him by the hand and led him to a chair, nowhere near the darkness that offered shelter further down the bar but in full view of all. She pointed a finger, indicating he should sit down, which he did. Sensing what was to happen now, the bar attendant stationed himself at the door to Bourbon Street to prevent further spectators and a possible loss of his license. Susi camped herself facing the chair he now sat on and pulled her dress above her head. You could hear a pin drop as the barman and the few spectators dotted around the stage witnessed her naked form emerge from the cocoon of the fabric, whiter than white, shaven mound plump, and so bare, like a magnet for their disbelieving eyes. A couple of the attendant strippers peered out from the dressing room on the side of the bar counter.

The music began and he had no clue what it was, his mind was in such turmoil.

Susi began writhing a few inches away from him, knowing all too well how much she was the center of attraction.

She danced, wriggled, swerved, bent, squatted, obscenely, indecently, her hands moving across her bare flesh in a snake-like manner, her fingers grazing her by-now-erect nipples, descending across the flatness of her pale stomach and even (although he hoped he was, because of his close proximity to her dance, the only one to notice) lingering in the region of her cunt and actually holding her lips open for a second or so.

He felt hot. Even though he had come to know every square inch of her skin, this was a new Susi, a creature he had only guessed at.

It was quickly over.

He held his breath.

A few people clapped in the background.

Susi's face was impassive but flushed.

She picked up her discarded dress and slipped into it.

"That was good," she said. "Can we go now?"

On their way to the door and the muted sounds of Bourbon Street, the barman handed Susi a card.

"You're quite a gal," he said, as she brushed past him. "My name is Louis. If you're seeking more serious fun, just call me."

Susi slipped the card into her side pocket without even acknowledging him and emerged into the twilight.

"I'm hungry," she said.

One of the nearby hotels had an oyster bar. They shared a plateful each of oysters and clams. She smothered each with a generous helping of tomato-flavored horseradish as she gulped them down.

"One of your fantasies realized?" he asked her.

"You might say that," Susi answered. "But there are others."

"I have no doubt," he smirked, still uncertain of the path they had embarked on.

"Don't look so glum," she smiled. "You did say we would come to New Orleans and explore possibilities, didn't you?"

"I suppose I did."

The rawness of their sex that night was compelling and savage. She sucked him with hungry determination and wouldn't allow him to withdraw from her mouth when he felt his excitement rise. Usually, he would hold back and penetrate her, which prolonged the pleasure. He came in her mouth. She let him go and he watched her tasting his come before she finally swallowed it.

"You taste sweet and sour," Susi said.

The following day, she insisted they visit a place called The Orgy Room. On Bourbon, of course. As pornographic films were projected on the walls, a group of people, pressed together like sardines in a can, were force fed into an exiguous room and allowed to jostle and play on pneumatic fun-fair carpets, or were they waterbeds? Most were drunk. The constant contact was, he felt, somewhat unpleasant, and far from arousing. Soon, he was separated from Susi in the swaying crowd but could still see her at the other end of the room. She deliberately exaggerated her movements and rubbed herself against others, often pulling her short, black-leather miniskirt up her thighs so that her genitals were fully visible to those closer to her. He observed, as various men took note of her and soon congregated around her. He could see her face flush amongst the laughs, and the human wave of bodies soon directed her against the back wall where she stood motionless, her skirt now bunched at her midriff and a couple of men frantically fingering her as she pretended to ignore them. He watched from afar, not quite knowing what he now felt. Eventually, the siren rang and the crowds thinned and made for the exit. As Susi reached him, trailed by the puzzled men she had snared in her net, she took his hand in hers. The men observed this and interrupted their progress toward her. Sweat poured down her forehead, her thin red hair was plastered down against her scalp. They walked out. He looked up at the sky. A storm was brewing.

"I came," she remarked. "Jesus...."

"Susi...."

"Take me back to the hotel," she ordered. "Tonight, I want you to fuck my arse."

• • •

The next morning, she expressed a desire for breakfast in bed. They had woken up too late for the hotel room service. He volunteered to fetch food from a nearby 24-hour deli. The night rain had swept away the heat momentarily and the cool air came as a welcome relief as he walked the few hundred meters to the shop and back.

When he returned to the room, Susi was speaking on the phone. She put the receiver down as he walked in.

Maybe he shouldn't have asked, but he did. Force of habit. He'd left the hotel number with a few friends back in London, in case of sudden business, magazine commissions.

"Was that for me?" he asked Susi.

"No," she replied. "It was Louis, from the bar."

"I see."

"I wanted to find out about the...secret places, the real New Orleans, so to speak." She looked down as she spoke, the white sheet lowered down to the whirl of her navel. There were dark patches under her green eyes, from lack of sleep and the intensity of the sex. He'd never found her as attractive as now, he knew.

He set the bread, snacks, and fruit juice bottles down on the bedside table.

"And?"

"And he's given me a few addresses. Said it's his night off, offered to show us around."

"We barely know him. Do you think it would be safe?"

"You always told me that New Orleans was a city of sex. Not of vampires or voodoo. That it was constantly in the air, you used to say, remember."

"I did."

"Well, it would be silly not to find out more, wouldn't it?"

"I suppose."

"He's picking us up from the hotel lobby around nine tonight. He'll show us beyond Bourbon."

They walked through the market at midday. Beyond the food area full of Cajun spice mixtures, chicory blends, pralines, nuts, and colorful fruit and fish, a flea market of sorts contained stalls that sold souvenirs, bric-a-brac, clothing, counterfeit tapes of zydeco music, hand-made bracelets, and all the flotsam that brings people to a tourist town. On a previous visit on their second day here, Susi had spotted a black felt table where a long-haired, superannuated hippy was selling fake body jewelry, which could be worn without the need for piercings. Now she selected several pieces.

Late in the afternoon, back in the room, she retreated to the bathroom for a shower. She emerged half an hour later, splendidly naked and scrubbed clean, her dark red hair still wet.

"Do you like it?" she asked him.

He looked up from his magazine.

She took his breath away. How could her body be so damned pale and so heartbreakingly beautiful? She had rouged her nipples a darker shade of scarlet and accentuated the bloody gash of her sex lips with the same lipstick. A courtesan adorned for sexual use.

She had also strategically placed the small rings and clips she had purchased in the market across her body. A ring hung from her lower lip, stainless steel clamps swung from her hardened nipples, and a stud appeared to have been pierced into her clitoris from which a thin golden chain hung, which she had until now worn around her wrist.

"Like a creature from a dream," he said. "From a very dirty dream, may I add. You look great." He could already feel his cock swell inside his boxer shorts.

"Come here," he suggested.

"No," she said. "I have to dry my hair. Anyway, I also want you to conserve your energy. Your seed..." she concluded with a smile.

"As you wish," he said, unable to keep his eyes away from her jeweled cunt.

"This is my fantasy night," she said.

It felt like a stab to his chest.

He already knew what she had arranged with Louis.

· · ·

It was a very private club on Ramparts, at the other end of the Quarter. From outside, it looked like any other house, slightly run down and seedy. But the moment you passed the door, you could almost smell the familiar fragrance of money and sin.

"You sure you still want to?" Louis asked her as they walked into the lobby.

"Yes," Susi said.

Louis guided them into a large room full of framed Audubon prints and a fake fireplace and asked them to make themselves comfortable. And left through another door after showing them the drinks cabinet.

Alone with her, he said nothing at first. Then, seeing his unease, Susi said:

"It's not quite the fantasy I told you about. Just the second part, really...."

"Oh...."

"And I want you to be one of the men...."

"I'm not sure I...."

"I'd feel more comfortable with you there," she said, interrupting him. "You'll enjoy it, you'll see. Anyway, you knew what I am, what I like, when you suggested we come here. You'll get a kick out of it. You like watching. I see it in you. Even when we fuck, your brain is like a machine, recording it all, storing away every feeling, every tremor, every moan. Memories that will last forever."

Before he could answer her, the door opened and Louis came through it with three other men. Two of them were black, tall, built like football players; the other white man was middle-aged, stocky, silver-haired.

"Here we are, Susanne," he said, without introducing the others. "You're in charge now...."

The thought occurred to him that he had called her Susanne. "Friends call me Susi," she had told him all those months ago as they caught that New York cab. So Louis was not considered a friend!

Susi indicated the center of the heavily carpeted room.

"Make a circle around here," she said, with something more Germanic than usual in her voice as she ordered them to clear the heavy chairs away from the room's epicenter.

The circle soon emerged, as the furniture was set aside.

Susi stationed herself there and undressed.

"You all stay dressed," she said to the five men. "Just cocks out, OK?"

She positioned herself and as the men's eyes followed her every movement she opened her legs and stuck a finger inside herself. She was visibly already very wet, and there was a squishing sound as the finger penetrated her. Louis unzipped his jeans and pulled his cock out. The others followed his example. One of the black guys, he noticed, was enormous, at least ten inches and thick as hell. He discreetly examined the other cocks, and was reassured that his was still reasonably sized in comparison. Joint the second biggest, he reckoned, not without a wry thought.

Susi introduced a second finger into her cunt, secretions now flooding out and dripping down the gold chain.

There was both a sense of the ceremonial and a sense of the absurd about them all. Six human beings masturbating frantically. Five men with their cocks out, fingers clenching their shafts, rubbing their coronas, teasing their glans, heavy balls shuddering below as the woman in white at their center teased her cunt in a parody of lovemaking.

"Not yet," she warned. Had one of them intimated he was close to come?

It felt as if time had come to a standstill, swallowing all their halting sounds of lust.

She adjusted her stance, now kneeling, her hand buried deep inside her crotch, almost as if praying, and indicated she was finally ready for her baptism of come.

The men came, one by one, spurting their thick, white seed into her face, as she leaned forward to receive them. He was the third to orgasm and noticed the arc of his ejaculate strain in the air, separating him from her body and the final drips landing in the thin valley between her muted breasts. Soon, she was covered with the men's seed, like syrup dribbling across her thin eyebrows and down her cheeks. He didn't think she herself had actually come, although all five men had.

There was a long silence as they all stood there, the men with their cocks shriveling already, the drenched woman in quiet repose.

Finally, Louis spoke.

"Well, Susanne, just the way you wanted it?"

She nodded as the men began zipping up.

"Care to move on to your next fantasy?"

What next fantasy? he wondered. What else was she after?

"Yes," she said, rising to her feet and picking up the green towel Louis had previously left on a nearby chair and wiping her face clean.

"Good," Louis said. "There's quite a crowd out there waiting."

Still not bothering to put her clothes on again, Susi asked him: "Can you give us a few minutes alone, before, please?"

"Sure, Susanne," he said, and the four men trooped out of the room.

"So," he asked her the moment after they had closed the door. "What else have you planned for the menu, Susi? It must be a fantasy I am unaware of. You're full of surprises."

"I know," she answered. "I should have told you before. I'm sorry. It'll only happen once and then I shall return to my boring life, you know. Maybe the time will even come for me to settle down, marry some decent guy, and even have kids. A nice *hausfrau*."

"What are you talking about, Susi?"

"I want to be fucked in public…."

"What?"

"Just one man, that's all. But I have to know what it feels like with people watching, you see. You said this was a city of sex, I'll never have the opportunity again. Just this once. We're miles away from home, no one knows us, we'll likely never come here again. Only you and I will know…."

"You mean with me?" he asked.

"Yes. If you wish to be the one."

"I…." He was at a loss for words.

"It's all arranged with Louis. We'll even get paid five hundred dollars."

"It's not the money…."

"I know…I understand if you don't want to. Arrangements have also been made for another man, if you decline. But I *do* want you to watch…really…."

His thoughts were in turmoil. This had all gone too far. He had played with fire and the flames were now reaching all the way through to his gut. As they always did. He never learned the lessons, did he? Long before Kathryn, he'd been going out with a woman who was avowedly bisexual, and it had planted a bad seed in his mind. Not for him the common fantasy of watching two women together, no. The idea of bisexuality had preyed on his mind for months and one day, curious to know what it must feel like to suck a man's cock, from the woman's point of view (after all, they never minded sucking his, did they?), he had agreed to an encounter with another man. He distressingly discovered he enjoyed sucking cock and had been irregularly doing so for years now, in secret, whenever a woman was not available and the tides of lust submerged him. He had never told any woman about this. Feared they would misunderstand. Blamed his insatiable sexual curiosity. Even Susi wouldn't understand, he knew. Not that this was the time to tell her. He always went that step too far. And paid for it. Emotionally.

"I just can't, Susi. I can't."

"But will you...."

"Yes, I will watch."

• • •

There was a crowd in the other room of the house on Ramparts. They had been drinking liberally for an hour or so, it appeared. There was a heavy air of expectation about them.

Louis led Susi in, as in a ritual, him holding the thin gold chain secured to her clitoris, her eyes covered by a dark blue piece of cloth. This is how she had wanted it to happen. She didn't wish to see the audience. Just feel it and hear it around her as she was fucked.

They had cleared a low table in a corner of the room and Susi was taken to it, carefully installed across so that all the light was focused on her already gaping and wet red gash and positioned on all fours. Her fake jewelry was taken from her body and she was helped to arch her back and raise her rump to the right level. The man who had won the quickly organized auction came forward. He looked quite ordinary — late twenties, an athlete's build, not very hairy. He had kept his shirt on but his cock already jutted forward as he approached Susi's receptive body. He was uncut and his foreskin bunched heavily below the mushroom cone of his glans. He was very big.

The man found his position at Susi's entrance and buckled forward and speared her. A few spectators applauded, but most remained quite silent. From where he sat, he couldn't see Susi's face, only her white arse and the hypnotizing sight of the dark purple cock moving in and out of her, faster and faster, every thrust echoed by a wave of movement on the periphery of her flesh, like a gentle wind caressing the surface of a sand dune.

It was lasting an eternity—longer, he knew, than he would ever have managed. The guy was getting his money's worth. And the audience was rapt at the sight, many of them blatantly playing with themselves in response to the spectacle unfolding before them. She would be very sore at the end of this. Sweat coated Susi's body like a thin shroud as the man dug deeper and deeper into her, and he watched her opening enlarge obscenely under the pressure of that monstrous cock.

Shamefully, he couldn't keep his eyes away from the immediate perimeter of penetration, noting every anatomical feature with minute precision: the vein bulging on the side of the invading cock as it moved in and out of sight in and out of her, the very shade of crimson of her bruised labia as they were shoved aside by the thrusts, the thin stream of inner secretions pearling down her inner thigh. Neither could he help himself getting hard again, watching the woman he knew he had fallen in love with getting fucked in public by a total stranger.

That night, she curled up against him in bed in the hotel room, drawing his warmth…and tearing him apart.

• • •

They had packed and were waiting in the hotel's lobby for the airport shuttle they had booked earlier that morning. One suitcase each, a Samsonite and a Pierre Cardin. They hadn't discussed yesterday night, acted as if nothing had happened. They had the same flight to Chicago, where they would part—he going on to London, she to Vienna. Now he knew: he would want to see her again, in Europe. It would be easier. They had come through this crazy experience, and he realized how much she had touched his heart.

The blue minicoach finally arrived, ten minutes late, and he picked up the suitcases and carried them to the pavement. As he was about to give her case to the shuttle's driver, Susi put her hand on his arm.

"Yes?"

He had never realized how green her eyes were.

"I'm not coming," she calmly said. "There's nothing for me back home. I'm staying in New Orleans."

"But...."

She silenced him with a tender kiss to his cheek. When he tried to talk again, she just quietly put a finger to his lip, indicating he should remain silent.

"No," she said. "No explanations. It's better like this."

The driver urged him to get on board.

As the shuttle moved down Burgundy, he looked out of the window and saw Susi walking to a parked car with her suitcase. Louis stood next to it. The shuttle turned the corner and he lost them from sight.

The short drive to Moisan was the loneliest and the longest he had taken in his life.

He would, in the following years, continue to write many stories. That was his job, after all. In many of them, women had red hair, green eyes, and bodies of porcelain white. And terrible things happened to them: rape, multiple sex, prostitution, drug addiction, even unnatural forced sexual relationships with domestic animals. But they all accepted their fate with a quiet detachment.

He would continue to occasionally meet up with strange men and take uncommon pleasure in sucking them off. This he did with serene indifference, because in his mind it didn't count. It was just sex, meat—it was devoid of feelings.

He never visited New Orleans or saw or heard of Susi again.

the sun rises

~

Michael Gouda

"HOLY ONE," WHISPERS THE VOICE, low and deferential, from out of the darkness.

Dreaming. The Goddess Nut, gigantic face, features spread over the sky, eyes the size of galaxies, expressionless, open mouth, waiting patiently, teeth monoliths apart, tongue blood-red, covering viscous oceans, endlessly in motion, waiting, waiting as the orb of the sun sets, grows bigger in the evening mists, disappears into that vast waiting mouth and is swallowed. Lips clamp shut.

"Holy One," repeats the voice.

Lips clamp shut. The world is in darkness. The sun makes its journey through that darkness, through the giant body, down the esophagus, stomach, guts, and foulness. Death and corruption. Stink and contamination. Then the womb, to nestle there, comforted by placental juices and moist warmth before being expelled into the day again. But before then, the terror of darkness.

"Holy One," a third time, accompanied by a gentle, reverential touch on the shoulder.

It is still dark. Menkheperre stirs. He sits up in his wooden truckle bed, struts groaning at his movement. The sweat of his nightmare runs down the center of his shaved chest and cools in the darkness. A guttering flame from a clay oil lamp reveals the youthful face of the merciful despoiler of his dream, anxious yet determined, the alabaster pots of purified water and oils, the folded linen garments. It is the boy, Ahotep.

"My Lord," he says, now that he sees Menkheperre is awake, "it is time to prepare."

Menkheperre swings his legs out and stands up. He is naked. The other looks at him, at the tall figure, from the shaven crown, over the young face serious with the solemnity of the moment, the body still angular with youth and the rigors of training, to the long legs—but he spends the most time on that which clusters in the fork.

"May I wash the Holy One?" Ahotep asks, using the prescribed formula.

"Purify my body," says Menkheperre, "so that it may be worthy to carry out the actions of the Most High God."

Ahotep dips his sponge in the water and washes away the sleep from his eyes and the sweat of the dream. Rivulets of water run down his body and reflect the flickering oil flame with points of light. Menkheperre gasps at the coldness of it. Then Ahotep washes the clefts and fissures of his body, cleaning out any dirt or uncleanness. As he passes his sponge over the genitals, the scrotum contracts, forcing the testicles under, while the cock diminishes from its former distinction. Ahotep regrets this but knows that later actions will remedy the imperfection.

He dries the body with a linen towel.

"Who is the Receiver?" asks Menkheperre.

"The God has chosen me, Lord," says Ahotep, "unworthy though I am," yet Menkheperre looks pleased.

Ahotep pours some perfumed oil into the palms of his hands and commences to rub it onto the skin, over the shoulders and down the chest, across his narrow hips and over the limbs, until his skin shines luminously. The air is full of the scent of jasmine, heady and intoxicating. As Ahotep reaches his genitals, he gently massages the scrotum until it hangs down, the balls heavy with their weight of sperm, then rubs the penis with long, supple strokes until it grows, proud and tall under his ministrations, worthy indeed of the God himself.

Ahotep finds himself hardening in sympathy. He would like to continue the massage, but time will not permit.

"May I dress the Holy One?" he asks.

"Cover my body," says Menkheperre, "with the finest of linen, so that it may be arrayed in order to"—he hesitates for a second, and Ahotep holds his breath: not a mistake, he prays, not this first time!— "to pay tribute to the Most High God."

All is well. Ahotep breathes again.

He puts the pleated loincloth on Menkheperre, tying around his slender waist. It hides the erection and again Ahotep is sad. Then comes the *kalasiris*, fastened high up under the arms and falling almost to the ground. It is made from material so fine as to be almost transparent. Ahotep can see the olive brown of his legs through it and the broad sweep of his chest, the nipples peeking through like two brown halos. He covers the priest's shaven head with a black wig—and Menkheperre is ready.

He stands in a hieratic pose, the new High Priest of the God Amun Re, Lord of the Thrones of the Two Lands.

• • •

It was still dark, but the professor hadn't been able to sleep. And the little sleep that he had been able to catch had been troubled by strange dreams, dreams of darkness in which the sun sets and never rises again. Now he was fully awake. He rinsed the crust from his eyes with the water from the ewer that stood in the corner and wiped clean his armpits and groin with soap and a cloth. It was almost a ritual with him. He was a fastidious man and, though he knew he would soon be sweaty and grimy again in the heat of day, he preferred to start the day with as clean a body as possible, however primitive the conditions.

And some of the conditions Professor Maximilian Pontifex had endured had been primitive indeed. Although only twenty-four years of age and the youngest professor of Middle Eastern archaeology ever, he had already been on a number of digs that would have satisfied many an archaeologist twice his age.

But this one, the excavation of the temple of Amun Re at Thebes—the Southern City, as the Ancient Egyptians called it—would be his greatest triumph. He was certain that he was on the brink of discovering the Sanctum Sanctorum, the Holy of Holies of the God itself. No longer would he have to wear a pair of (plain glass) pince-nez and struggle to cultivate a moustache to make himself appear older than he was. (He gave a wry smile as he thought of his jejune attempts at obfuscation.) His peers would now have to respect him for his achievements. The year of grace A.D. 1883 in the reign of Her Majesty Queen Victoria would go down in archaeological history as an *annus mirabilis*.

The previous evening they had worked right up to the very doorway of what he truly believed was the inner sanctuary. Only the waning light and the reluctance of his native workers to continue had stopped him from excavating the whole night through. He put on his fine linen shirt and knotted his tie around the starched collar. It was hardly the sort of clothing that helped excavation in this land of scratchy sand and burning sun, but a certain standard of decorum was expected of British scholarship. He put on his frock coat and took up an arc light from the pile of equipment. He hesitated with his pince-nez but finally decided to leave them behind. Without them he looked young and vulnerable.

Outside the tent flap and wrapped in his *djellaba* was Achmet, his young Egyptian assistant. The professor tried to step over him without disturbance—he could do with his sleep, certainly, for he had never known a more willing and cooperative worker—but Achmet was up and ready, his eyes shining in the starlight and lips smiling to expose regular white teeth, an almost fluorescent gash in his olive brown skin.

"Early start today, *effendi,*" said Achmet, and touched the professor companionably on the arm.

Together they set out across the sand to the dig.

. . .

Menkheperre and Ahotep set out together, though once outside Menkheperre's room they are joined by the prescribed number of junior priests and acolytes who will accompany them along the way.

In daytime this will be a sunny courtyard fronted by two mighty, towering pylons, the wooden doors plated with gold and silver alloys and electrum and flanked by pillars shaped and colored into the likeness of lotus flowers. The walls will be bright with painted images of the God in his glory, inlaid with lustrous stones and finished by glistening glazes. Now, though, it is full of dark shadows and the sound of bare feet slapping on the stone. Above them the stars flare.

As they go further down the straight processional way, the lesser priests and their attendants drop away, their part in the ritual over. Only the ritually pure can proceed to the Holy of Holies; and eventually, at the door, there remain only the High Priest, Menkheperre; the Receiver, Ahotep; and four Watchers (or Witnesses).

The Sanctuary is a small chamber with no windows and only a narrow doorway, at the moment closed. This part of the immense temple complex is not meant to be impressive, but its holiness means it will never be violated. At the doorway the little procession of six halt while Menkheperre reads from the painted inscription on the wall:

"Hail to you, Amun Re, Lord of the Thrones of the Two Lands, foremost in the Southern City and the Northern City, you of the massive thighs and member, wide of stride that encompasses the earth, foremost in Nubia, Ruler of Punt, most ancient in Heaven and eldest in all the world, whose mighty orgasm creates all things and makes the sun to rise."

The door is opened and they enter.

• • •

"Well, Achmet, what do you think of the work of your mighty ancestors?" asked Professor Pontifex. He gestured at the ruined remains of the pylons and rows of half columns that lined the processional way down the center. They made a curious couple, the English professor in his correct coat and trousers and the Egyptian in his loose-hooded cloak that touched the ground. The cloak was probably the more practical of the two and certainly, at this time of day, the warmer. Despite their differences, however, in color, education, and religion, there was a certain similarity between the two, a compatibility that transcended all else.

"It is impressive, *effendi*," said Achmet, "but at the same time a little sad."

"Sad that they should expend so much effort on a mistaken idea, or sad that the magnificence has come to this ruin?"

"Perhaps a little of both, *effendi*."

The professor took a breath. "You could call me Max," he said. "It is what my friends call me."

Achmet appeared to be trying the strange-sounding name over to himself. Eventually he said, "Max," and laughed.

"How many years — er — Max, has this been here?" he asked.

"Well, this part, according to the wall inscriptions, was erected in the XXIst Dynasty, the reign of King Psusennes I (1041–993 B.C.). The High Priest was a man called Menkheperre. It is after the great period of Egyptian history, the time of the Rameses, but to rule for forty-eight years shows a time of stability and strength."

They reached the small, square building that they had been digging out from the sand over the past few days. Professor Pontifex lit the arc lamp and by its flaring light they could see the inscriptions and the doorway, now blocked by some pieces of stone that had fallen from the architrave.

"See," he said, "here is the Royal cartouche of King Psusennes, and here" — he pointed lower down — "is the name of the High Priest."

"Can we open the doorway by ourselves?" asked Achmet.

"Though we are only two, we have the strength of a hundred."
Achmet looked puzzled.

"It says so here," said Pontifex, pointing to yet another inscription.

They struggled with a large piece of limestone and eventually got it free. The professor was sweating by this time and, casting convention to the winds, he took off his coat and his detachable collar and tie. He opened the buttons of his shirt. Achmet looked at him. "You have a good physique…Max," he said. Pontifex felt a little embarrassed — one doesn't make remarks like that to another man — but pleased, all the same.

After the removal of the large piece, the rest of the stones came away easily, and soon they could peer, or indeed crawl, into the building. He shone the light through. The walls bore illustrations in colors as bright as the day they had been painted, the glazes clear, the outlines sharp.

• • •

The Witnesses carry oil lamps. The sole lights, they barely illumine the wall paintings, yet their bright colors stand out. Here is the Great God in all his sexual prowess and glory, the phallus erect and far beyond the dimensions of mortal man.

Ithyphallic Amun Re frots, sucks, and ruts, and his seed spurts — forming the world, creating the everlasting verities of Egyptian life, the daily passage of the sun, the annual flooding and irrigation of the fields by the Nile, and, of course, the mysteries of the Afterlife.

Menkheperre bows low to the images and prays that he may be allowed to undertake the duties of the God. Every day of every year for millennium after millennium, in the shadowed chamber of a perfect elegance, at the temple's core, the priest administers the offices of the cult. Now it is Menkheperre's turn.

Ahotep kneels before him and opens the *kalasiris*, then unties the fastenings of his loincloth. It drops to the ground, never to be used again, for the God has worn it and it is holy. He takes the penis of the God reverentially into his hands and, in their warmth and movement, it enlarges and stiffens. He pulls back the foreskin so that the glans appears, a drop of crystal fluid at its head.

"I take the member of the God in my hands," Ahotep says. "And it is good."

He gently rubs the ball sac and reaches under it to massage the perineum. The God's member twitches, and Ahotep knows it is time. He puts more scented oil on the cock, now engorged to its fullest extent, and then lies on his back on the altar stone. He raises his knees so that the access to his body can be seen and entered.

Now the God moves to him and presses his penis to the offered hole.

"I take the member of the God into my body," says Ahotep, and Menkheperre pushes himself, oiled and willing, the full length.

Ahotep tries to restrain a cry of pain. He manages to turn it into the ordained response. "And—it—is—*good*." The words are choked out.

Now Menkheperre withdraws and then plunges in again. Speared beneath him, Ahotep looks into his eyes, but they are glazed and unseeing. He has become the God, and it is Amun Re who pushes the prick of heaven into the earthly anus. The tempo quickens, and the God's head suddenly jerks upward. Now Ahotep must remove himself from the God's thrusting and ejaculating member, for the Watchers must witness the Holy Emission.

Forcing backward with his legs, he groans as he feels the twitching cock leave him and then the warm semen spatter onto his stomach and chest. It is a goodly discharge, and the Watchers take note and murmur their approval.

Menkheperre grasps his own cock and holds himself while the spasms jerk and the last drops are caught by the chosen Receiver.

In the eastern sky the sun rises.

• • •

They clambered through into the room and stared round at the glorious riot of sexual extravaganza.

It took Pontifex a few seconds for their import to register and, when it did, he gasped. In scene after scene, a godlike form, wearing the headdress that identified him as Amun Re, sporting an erection that defied belief, fucked, frotted, rogered, and sucked with an assortment of slender, ephebic partners. Embarrassed, the professor tried to look elsewhere, but the sexual marathon continued all around him and, despite himself, as he made out the pictures, he felt a pleasurable stirring in his loins.

Achmet showed no such inhibitions. He danced from one scene to the next, alternately crowing with delight or gasping with happy amazement.

"Look, *effendi* Max. Look what they are doing. Is that possible?" He laughed with the irrepressible humor of the young. Max envied him. He himself was scarcely a year or two older than the boy, but his own strict education and upbringing had loaded him with inhibitions so strong as to make him feel generations older.

"They are"—he searched for the word—"incredible!"

"And the two there...." Achmet was at his shoulder, his breath warm on the side of Max's face, laughter and—was it excitement?—in his whispered words. "I think they are...enjoying themselves."

His body leaned lightly against Max's, an arm around him, the hand resting on his shoulder. Through the *djellaba* and his own cotton shirt, Max could feel the youthful litheness of the torso, touching him from chest to hip. He felt he should step away but wanted the contact to remain—forever? What was happening to him?

"I wonder what it would feel like to do that," said Achmet softly, his breath a tender caress.

"It would be very, very—wrong." The statement started firmly but faded into indecision.

"But perhaps pleasurable."

Max's erection grew. It would be obvious, he knew, within the confines of his tight trousers. Achmet's *djellaba* hid all.

Max turned inward to break the contact of the arm around him but found his face was just inches away from Achmet's, the eyes bright and shining, his lips full and inviting. He could not help himself. He kissed the lips — and was lost.

Their bodies were pressed together, and Max knew what the Arab cloak had hidden: that Achmet sported an erection as great as his. The spear of hard flesh pushed into his groin. Achmet's arms and hands were holding him, stroking his back through the thin material of his shirt, and then going down to cup his buttocks and pull him into even closer contact.

Achmet's kiss was strange. His mouth blocked the air, and then he suddenly sucked so that the breath was out of Max's mouth, out of his lungs. He experienced slight pain but immense eroticism, and had to pull away to breathe.

Then Achmet slid down his body, covering with light, feathery kisses the exposed flesh of his chest and abdomen, the flat surface of his stomach. His fingers felt for, found, and swiftly undid the buttons on his trousers, releasing his stiffness. Then his lips were on his penis, taking it into that warm, moist place with the fibrillating tongue. The pleasure was almost intolerable. Max groped for Achmet's groin, wanting to feel him, to do the same for him. He staggered and fell, and the two of them were struggling together on the sandy floor. Achmet's *djellaba* was raised to waist level, Max's shirt torn off and his trousers kicked away.

Then they found the position, mouth to groin, groin to mouth — and it was good. A scent of jasmine arose from the boy's body, and the cock in his mouth was both rigid and silky soft, the ball sac in his hand full and virile.

The mouth on his cock lunged up and down, and he knew he would come. He could not control himself — nor had he any wish to. Achmet was making strange whimpering noises, and he heard other sounds that he knew must come from himself.

Suddenly his mouth was filled. Knowing it was Achmet's semen drove him over the top. He came, again and again, the pleasure pulsing from his loins, his legs, arms, his whole body, until he thought he must be drained dry, a desiccated husk. Then he swallowed what had been given to replace the loss — and at last he knew fulfillment.

The rays of the morning sun touched the entrance to the Sanctuary.

Gloriously in the eastern sky, the sun rose.

The Mermaid's sacrifice

۶

CHRISTOPHER HART

WE WERE IN THE GARDEN BEHIND THE VILLA when he came to call.

Kit was hunched up on a sun lounger in the shade, reading a book. He wore a distant frown. I was wandering around on my own, in my usual daydream, skimming my palms ticklishly over the heads of the bougainvillea flowers, the oleander and hibiscus and the green tracery of the jasmine. It was very hot. There was a light wind but it was humid, the *libeccio*, blowing in from the southwest across the Mediterranean from North Africa and picking up all the summer mist of the sea as it came. It muffled everything, made everything, even the lizards on the crumbling villa walls, dreamy and slow. My thin cotton dress clung to me with light perspiration. I thought of nothing. Except maybe Kit.

A man was standing just the other side of the gate when I looked up and saw him, gasped, almost swallowed my tongue.

I held my hand up to my mouth, schoolgirlish, infuriated by my own timid reaction. He smiled. He had a wolfish smile.

In fact, all his features had the properties of beasts of prey: the wolfish smile, the aquiline nose, the leonine mane (albeit graying at the temples), the deep-set eyes of some other unnamable hunter species glaring out of the dark night. "Signorina?" he said. His voice was a low growl, of course.

"Signora," I corrected him, lowering my eyes briefly to check for the shirt unbuttoned to the navel, the extravagantly hairy chest, the gold medallion. But he wasn't like that: navy blue shirt, only top button undone. No jewelry that I could see except a fine gold wedding ring. I opened the gate to him.

He was lean and rangy, with a high sunburned forehead and a wide sensuous mouth that looked good when he smiled, which was rarely. His hands were large, with strong, prominent veins; his stare piercing but not hostile—well, not quite. I guessed his age to be about mid-fifties, maybe older.

He held his hand out to me. "Leopoldo," he said, in a cultivated Italian accent. "My wife and I live next door."

I shook his hand. "Nancy," I said. "My husband and I...." I paused, bent my head, smiled self-consciously. I was beginning to sound like the Queen. I looked up again. "Kit—my husband— we're just staying here for a couple of weeks. It's lovely here."

He nodded gravely, said nothing. He stared at me for fractionally too long for comfort, and then said, "We would like to invite you over to dinner tonight. Just a simple dinner—the four of us."

I babbled that it was very kind of them to invite us, and what time should we be over, and we'd be delighted. He told me, nodded again, and turned and strode away. When he was gone I felt my shoulders relax.

. . .

Kit, of course, doesn't want to go.

He lays his book down on his chest and looks up at me and holds his hand up to his forehead to shield his eyes from the setting sun. A hank of hair flops over his hand. So young. I love him so much. "Do we have to?" he says.

"I've already accepted."

"You could have consulted with me first."

"I thought you'd...."

"I came here to get away from all that, and now you've gone and fixed up some tedious dinner party with a couple of old farts who'll have nothing to talk about and expect us to entertain them all evening. Thanks a lot."

"He didn't *look* like an old fart."

"Who didn't?"

"Leopoldo."

Kit mouths *Leopoldo* back at me in a sarcastic fashion, and then slams his book down and struts off into the villa to get ready for dinner.

I love him even when he's petulant.

• • •

Kit wears his ivory linen suit that he knows I like him in. So that's OK. I'm not so sure about the tie — too hot, surely? But I don't say anything.

I wear my long emerald-green dress with the narrow shoulder straps, and some bright red lipstick. Really bright. Kit looks quite startled when he sees me, and then smiles. "Hi, beautiful," he says, kissing me delicately on the forehead.

We walk next door arm in arm.

• • •

Leopoldo's wife is called Teresa, and she is extremely beautiful. She is perhaps ten years younger than he, very elegant and self-possessed, with eyebrows permanently arched high over her big eyes. Not plucked, just arched: skeptical, amused, worldly, permanently set for flirtation. Her skin appears finely stretched over high cheekbones — but not, please God, face-lifted — and her lips are quite thin. She compliments me immediately on my dress *and* on my lipstick, and she kisses me warmly on both cheeks. She herself is wearing a long black evening dress, and a gorgeous hematite choker, and, would you believe, long black gloves up and over her elbows. Like some 'fifties film star: subtler than Sophia Loren, more voluptuous than Audrey Hepburn…a darker, more Mediterranean Grace Kelly?

Teresa obviously likes dressing up for even the smallest occasions. She must notice me eyeing her gloves because she looks down and caresses them lightly, each one, and gives me her most charming smile, and says, "Oh, any excuse to dress up these days, my darling!" in her charmingly accented English. Leopoldo takes my right hand and kisses it, his eyes fixed on my face from under his heavy brows as he does so.

• • •

Dinner is taken out in the garden. And what a garden.

We couldn't see it from our side because of the dense row of cypresses that they have growing around their private patch. Leopoldo leads us immediately round the side of the villa—I can tell it is large, and in rather better condition than the one we're renting—but other than that we don't get to see inside it. Behind, a wonderfully elegant, classical-style lawn stretches down to a grove of almond trees at the end, and down the center of the lawn runs a very ancient-looking, stone-clad, long and narrow pool. Walking beside it I see that the pool is lined randomly with colored tiles that reflect through the water and give it a strange metallic sheen. Leopoldo to my right, taking my elbow in his large hand, says, "Perhaps a swim later on, if we have not eaten and drunk too much?"

I nearly blurt out that I haven't brought a swimsuit, but I stop myself just in time, realizing that it would only justify his making some lecherous remark about skinny-dipping. I bite my tongue. Something lurches, deep inside me. I feel a slick of sweat over my upper lip.

• • •

It is all impossibly beautiful. The night is warm, and we dine outside, among the grove of almond trees that thickens into an orchard beyond. To either side are citrus orchards too, their tangy fumes filling the night air. The *libeccio* has dropped off, leaving the air still and sultry. An oval pine table and four chairs stand in the grass, surrounded by flambeaux on chains and poles dug into the ground. When we sit down, the orange light from the naked flames leaps and dances over our faces, emphasizing the brightness of our skin and our eyes, and (I imagine with a thrill) the sluttish scarlet of my lips.

Teresa and Leopoldo — "Call me Leo, *please*" — have a cook, of course: Tancredi. (No one could afford so palatial a villa along this bit of coastline and not afford a cook as well.) Tancredi mixes us our drinks — Kir Royales all round to start with — and then brings us our meal: *zuppe di cozze,* mussels in a hot-pepper sauce. Leopoldo tells me they were fresh this morning, relishing their taste, his wide lips glistening in the torchlight. Kit by my side starts to relax, I can feel it, and with the second glass of wine — some unidentifiable but perfect floral white — he begins to talk. And when Kit actually chooses to talk, he is wonderful. Soon he is deep in passionate argument about the real significance of the bull-run in Pamplona, and then the bull-leapers of Knossos, and then he even engages Teresa in conversation about the sad decline of haute couture. Teresa used to be a model — naturally. She often stays with Yves St. Laurent in his pad in Morocco, it appears, and she tells an amusing story about Yves and the time he unwittingly ate a raw potato.

Leopoldo doesn't laugh, I notice. He watches her from the other end of the table, taking a steaming mouthful of sea bass — our main course — his dark eyes fixed on her, weirdly adoring. Teresa, it seems, rather ignores Leo. Clearly she knows him well. I feel I do too, already: and his name may be Leo, but if he's not a Scorpio — I'll swim naked in that pool, indigestion or not.

There's cheese, and fresh grapes and almonds, and peaches baked and drizzled with sweet almond wine, and we are all a little drunk, I think, but not so drunk that we will feel ill tomorrow morning. Drunk only on conversation and good food and fine wine and flirtation and the strange and unexpected beauty of this hidden garden and these two enigmatic people—as old as our parents but, I have to admit it, far, far cooler.

. . .

I need the loo. Teresa gives me directions—"Go in through the sitting-room doors and turn left and then right down the corridor and…." Something like that. But by the time I've got there I've completely forgotten, so I stumble around the darkened villa, giggling softly to myself, wondering at how huge it is, and badly needing a pee.

Somewhere down one of the hallways I find myself in a smaller room, with bare terra-cotta walls and a small, circular fountain in the middle, of gray-green stone, maybe marble, and looking very ancient. The fountain is running softly, trickling down over the stone into the basin, and above it is the figure of a naked girl. But not the kind you'd see in a civic fountain—not doing what she's doing. Not with that brazen abandon, her eyes stone-blank and closed, entirely absorbed in her own erotic oblivion.

And then I am abruptly aware of Leo beside me. He doesn't look at me, only at the naked figure there over the fountain. "Isn't she beautiful?" he says.

"I…yes, I suppose…" I stammer, wishing I could think of something wittier to say.

Then, only then, he turns to me and says, "I will tell you all about her. But later. First you need a bathroom, I think?"

At last! He shows some sign of chivalry!

But it doesn't last. The "bathroom" he leads me to doesn't have a lock on it. In fact, it doesn't even have a door. It is a beautiful little room at the back of the villa, tiled in sand and terra-cotta with marine motifs in the walls and floor—but no door. Quite open. Leo sees me hesitate and shrugs. "Go ahead," he says. "I won't watch."

I could have been offended. But suddenly I think, *Fuck it,* and do as he says. And what does he do?

He lights a cigarette. And watches.

Afterward we walk back to dinner arm in arm as if it is all quite normal.

Maybe it is, round here.

• • •

Kit by now is gently, sweetly drunk. He gets drunk quite easily, and becomes even more boyish than ever.

Teresa looks up and smiles at me. "Your husband is a university *professor*," she says to me. "So clever—and so young!"

"You wouldn't think it to look at him, would you?" I say dryly. Kit grins at me.

"Ah, poor darling," says Teresa, reaching out and squeezing his thigh. "I think he is—*delicious*."

Delicious, but drunk. Which is, no doubt, why he has completely forgotten, by the following morning, about their second invitation: to the island.

• • •

Instead, after final *grappe e caffè corretto*, and kisses and *arrivederla*'s and *domani*'s all round, we stumble back to our villa and fall into bed. And I want to make love to him then, across our bed, or rather for him to make love to me, pulling my dress up, not even taking it off. I so want him to make love to me. But he is too drunk. And even if he wasn't, I know too well that he would probably just turn away from me and murmur that he was tired, another night, and then fall asleep.

I do not sleep. I feel the blood coursing through my body and it is full of wine and a certain anticipation or even fear, as if I know something is going to happen, something beautiful and terrible, before this holiday is over. And my blood is awake, wide awake. Some time later, lying there, ears straining to hear the waves breaking on the shore below, I hear louder sounds: splashing, and screams. They are coming from next door. I get up and go to the window but I can see nothing beyond the cypress trees. As if in a dream I go down into our garden and across the cool

137

grass barefoot to the trees, and the cypress branches brush against my skin and I press in close and look through.

Leopoldo and Teresa are making love. Still clothed, or at least half-clothed, they are wrestling with each other, standing waist deep in the shallow end of the pool, Leo grimly silent, Teresa bucking away from him, screaming and laughing as he holds her tight. Then they fall silent, first as he closes her mouth with a long and ardent kiss, then as he flings her back across the side of the pool and falls on top of her. She is wearing only stockings now, and her black choker, and the long black gloves. She wears them for him, I realize. She still knows how to make herself desirable to him. Hungrily he trails kisses down her belly and between her thighs. I see her move her thighs wider apart, raise a hand to her mouth. They make love then in silence.

I return to bed and lie on my back and my hand creeps between my thighs and I come, weeping, eyes closed, mouth clamped shut in silence.

· · ·

The sky is still gray with the very earliest dawn light when I hear through my sleep the front doorbell ringing. It rings a second and a third time before I get to it, eyes half-shut, in a tatty white bathrobe that I know is far too short for decency.

When I open the door, Leo and Teresa are standing there, Teresa with a slightly enquiring smile, her eyebrows arched.

"Ah," she says. "You're not quite ready yet."

"Ready for what?"

"The trip to the island."

"Hmm?"

· · ·

It seems that last night when I was indoors, Teresa asked Kit if he and I would like to join them for a boat-trip out to the island in the bay tomorrow morning, and maybe a picnic. They would pick us up early. Kit had accepted with alacrity—and then forgot all about it.

I wake him up with a vigorous thump on the head with a pillow. He's grumpy at first, and then hungover, and then gradually, as he showers and shaves and rehydrates with tea, he begins to whistle and hum and I know that he is suddenly rather looking forward to the idea of a day on the island.

He wears jeans and deck shoes and a T-shirt and his linen jacket, and, just to cap the Italian playboy image, his shades. I'll wear deck shoes too, and my short white cotton dress, and will sling my red jumper over my shoulders. Carry my straw hat.

"Swimming trunks, do you think?" he asks me.

"Shouldn't bother," I say, feeling mischievous. "We can always skinny-dip."

He reaches out and pinches my bum. "I'll see you downstairs when you've showered."

• • •

Head back, eyes closed, face and breasts and belly and thighs streaming with hot water, when I hear the bathroom door open and then the shower curtain part, I'm thrilled. It's been ages, too long, since Kit and I showered together. His gentle hands start to soap my back, massage my shoulders, plant tiny kisses in the dips and hollows, and I arch my back as his hand reaches down between my thighs and I twist my head to see him.

It's Teresa. She has undressed, I can see her clothes on the bed in the room beyond, and her hand is between my thighs, caressing softly, her eyes steady on mine, knowing I am transfixed, helpless. I cannot move. She puts her other hand around the back of my neck as if to hold me still. But she needn't bother. I am helpless and still, a willing victim, burning, immobile. I even slide my feet a little further apart over the slick tiles to encourage her to touch me. I want to feel her fingers inside me. I have never done this before, with a woman, and never thought I would. It cannot be real. She moves her head slowly and sensuously under the falling water, as if feeling it thrumming on the top of her head like a hundred tiny fingertips, then she raises her face up to it, her mouth a little open, catching the warm water and letting it trickle out again over her face and throat. Then she presses herself hard against me, our naked flanks slippery against each other, and turns my head and devours my lips with hers. The water pours down over us, plastering our hair to our cheeks, mingled maybe with my tears, and I cannot move or speak and I do not stir. The kissing is slow and deep. I pull back a little so as to trail my tongue over her lips more lightly, but she does not let me, pulls me closer in again, our breasts sliding against each other, our nipples hard and tingling. She turns me half-sideways so that she can skim her flattened palm over my nipples, murmurs endearments in my ear, punctuated with flickers of her tongue against my earlobe, in the shell of my ear, gently probing—endearments in a language I do not understand, but that I understand perfectly. Then her hand moves down over my arched belly and between my legs again, and she reaches her other arm around my waist and holds me tight against her, curved into each other like spoons, and I stretch my legs apart even wider and feel weak and I have to turn and hold myself steady against her and bury my face against her, my mouth closing on her breasts and sucking them in deep, greedily. She rests her head on top of mine now, almost motherly, whispering what a beautiful girl I am, what a beautiful young girl, what a greedy girl, how hungry! Her fingers slick between my swollen lips and ease back and forth over the head of my clitoris, too slowly. I want to beg her to press harder, to reach down and press her hand harder into me with my own hand, but she will not let me, I know. I rest against her, utterly passive and obedient, knowing she knows best, and as I come, richly and shudderingly against her warm, moving hand ticklish with foam, I raise my face up to her again and want her, need her to kiss me again. She kisses me and then murmurs what a good, sweet, beautiful young girl I am, she kisses me on the top of my head, she nuzzles her mouth into my wet hair, she covers my face and neck with quick little kisses, she croons softly like a mother to her baby. I fall against her then as I might have done against my mother years ago, and she raises my face gently with a forefinger nestling under my chin and kisses me on the lips and parts my lips with the tip of her tongue and we stay like that for hours, it seems, just kissing, and the water cascades down around us and over us and through us, melting us, it seems. Melting the very heart of us.

. . .

And none of it matters. Afterward we kiss and laugh and dress and return to normal. As if it is all normal.

Leo and Teresa are highly organized. I knew they would be, somehow. It's bliss.

The car is a huge silver Merc. When Leo opens the boot for me to put my bag in, I see there's this vast, old-fashioned hamper filled with bottles of wine and bread and cheese and olives and oil and...the Full Mediterranean Diet Plan.

Kit and I sit in the back and keep smiling conspiratorially at each other on that long drive down to the coast. The black leather of the seat is warm under me and I feel wet again already. I cannot stop thinking about it, and more of it, please, more. Down and down we go, round the hairpin bends, down from the hills to the sun-scorched coast, through olive orchards and lemon orchards, among cork oaks and sweet chestnuts, and toward the sea, ancient plane trees and stone pines with the heat shimmering on their evergreen-gray canopies, and the odor of pine in the air so rich and intoxicating that I feel almost like bursting into tears, like a little girl. I squeeze Kit's hand.

The harborside is chaos, as usual, especially as the local fishermen are landing a huge catch of pilchards that they have just ring-netted out in the bay. It's a cliché, I know, but these young Italian fishermen, these gods—glossy black hair, lean-muscled shoulders tanned dark and slick with sweat, their tight, white sleeveless T-shirts stretched across their chests, flecked brilliant red with fish blood, shouting and laughing and swaggering at each other—Teresa knows I'm admiring them because she is too, and a knowing girls' grin flickers between us. I can't believe it, but that brief exchange of looks makes me feel breathless, wetter still between my legs. What on earth is going to happen? I wonder. *Everything,* murmurs an inner voice. *Everything is going to happen.*

Leo gets a local boatman to motor us out to the island: hard-faced, bearded, scarily competent, navigating out past the rocks in the bay with one casual, strong hand on the wheel. Cigarette dangling from his grim mouth.

On the way out, I ask Teresa if anyone actually lives on the island.

"Not without our permission," she says mildly.

I gawp at her. "You don't mean…?"

She smiles, lays her hand on my arm, a tiny caress. "I'm sorry, I thought you realized. It is *our* island. Leo's, officially." She looks away toward her husband and back to me again, her eyebrows arched even more ironically than ever. "My *marito* is, *officially,* you know, the Count of the Island of San Michele."

I swallow. OK: I'm impressed.

"There will only be the four of us on the island," says Teresa, raising her arms above her head and turning her face into the sun and stretching languidly. "Free as birds."

• • •

The journey out to the island takes almost an hour, and the middle passage gets pretty bumpy, but as we draw near to the island both Kit's and my nerves are calmed by the awesome view, and the thought that it is the private property of one man. On the south side, intimidating sandstone cliffs rise sheer from the sea, deeply ribbed and eroded like the sculpted relief of an ancient forest or the bones of a whale. Inland I can see further sheer cliffs of brilliant white — marble, surely. And directly ahead, where the boat is taking us, a deep gully between high cliffs, with a small jetty at the back, in cold shade.

• • •

We disembark, Leo extending a chivalrous hand to me, and then ordering the boatman to carry our hamper up the treacherous stone steps to the cliff top. We follow him up.

. . .

The island is a dream. It cannot be real. I know Kit is thinking the same, because we have both fallen silent in wonder.

We walk for ten minutes along the cliff top, and then strike inland a little way, down a slope to a kind of sunken plateau. And there, in the middle, surrounded by more trees, is an immaculate, tiny marble temple.

Leo gives one of his rare smiles. "Not an original, of course," he says. "Built by one of my more eccentric ancestors, in the eighteenth century. You would call it a folly, I believe."

The temple has a narrow, shady portico, and two cedarwood doors that swing open on massive hinges. Inside is just one small, stone-floored room, with a couch on either side, a small, low table in the middle, which looks incongruously Indian if anything, and a heavy oak dresser along the back. Leo orders the boatman to deposit the hamper on the dresser, and tips him generously for his pains. The boatman nods curtly and leaves.

Immediately Leo starts pulling the couches out onto the portico — Kit helps him — and then the low table, and finds plates and glasses in the dresser and brings them out too. Then he unloads the hamper and soon the table is covered in food and the glasses are filled with wine. In no time at all we are reclining on the couches twirling glasses of iced champagne between our fingers while Leo, more relaxed than I have seen him so far, extols the beauty of his island, and its ancientness.

He tells us that holidays were invented here, in this great bay sweeping south of Rome, overlooking the sparkling Tyrrhenian Sea. He says that Rome was the first city in history that people felt a need to escape from, on occasion. "We all need a break from the usual, the habitual," he says. "From custom. Something different, to reawaken us."

"*Otium cum dignitate*," he murmurs, conjuring brilliantly with faulty but vivid English, the poet Horace on his farm in his peaceful Sabine valley, and other wealthy Romans here, Emperors even, in their great villas, enjoying their rest and recreation.

"And what recreations!" he says, eyes half-closed. "You know about the Emperor Tiberius, I suppose? The notorious passage in Suetonius, where he describes how the aged emperor built an entire palace to lustful pleasures hereabouts, with grottoes where groups of two or three young people would perform sexual acts for him. And where little boys were trained to swim underneath him when he was swimming and nibble at him. He called them his little minnows." Both Leo and Teresa are smiling at this. "Do I shock you?"

Kit says nothing. I say, too firmly, "No." My mind is filled and distracted by weirdly vivid images of those groups of two or three young people, acrobatically entwined, murmurous and ecstatic, in grottoes and shady groves, on an island just such as this....

"Oh, and he kept a pet mullet, encrusted with jewels," he added. "Or was that Claudius? I forget now."

• • •

Later, we go for a walk. Just Kit and I, hand in hand, still dreaming, saying little, dozy with wine but excited too. It is all too marvelous.

We walk up a narrow valley thick with grasses and scrub: scrub oak, yellow broom and purple sage, thyme, lavender, all headily aromatic, broken here and there by the red bark of arbutus. And such wildflowers: cyclamen, and tall asphodel, and white star of Bethlehem, and higher up between the granite outcrops, brilliant purple and yellow rock-roses. There is terebinth and carob, and down below in yet another secluded valley we can see tamarisk and oleander growing and swaying gently in the breeze beside a trickling streambed. We see swallowtail butterflies, and a hoopoe, and way overhead a big bird of prey: a buzzard, probably.

"Can't we live here?" I say suddenly to Kit. I always say this when we go somewhere beautiful. "Rent the temple off them. I'm sure they wouldn't mind."

Kit smiles and says nothing. He knows it's all a dream.

. . .

That long summer day passed so slowly — that last day, as I think of it now, that last day of the old life. We returned to the folly and dozed along with Leo and Teresa, they in each other's arms on one couch, Kit and I on the other. Stirring and waking at one point, I saw that Leo's hand was between Teresa's thighs, and they saw me watching them and smiled back at me. I smiled, and closed my eyes, and tried to sleep again.

. . .

And when I awoke, much later, it was with a shock that I realized that the sun was setting over the mountains to the west and coming down over the bay to drown in the water before us, and it was rapidly getting dark. I asked when we were heading back, at which Leo stood abruptly.

"Soon," he said. "But first, I promised to show you something, to explain the statue that you saw at the villa — the girl in ecstasy, yes?" And he held out his hand to me.

I stood, and he led me away from the folly and down into the valley and we walked for a long time and it grew dark. I was afraid, but *more* than afraid — my palms damp with sweat, unable to speak. And then we came down from the valley to another cove, shut in on one side by fierce rocks that ran straight down into the sea. And from here we could see the sunset perfectly. Oh no, I thought — this is just too clumsy a seduction attempt. I'm going to giggle.

But rather than lay me down in the sand and tell me he needed me, he desired me, he had to have me, Leo retained a firm grip on my hand and led me instead into the shadows under the cliffs, to a small crevice in the black rock. He told me to go in ahead of him. And inside, everything changed.

. . .

Inside was a vast domed cavern with mineral walls that glittered as if studded with gems, traced with mica and quartz, encrusted like the skin of the emperor's pet mullet. Torches burned all around, set into the walls in iron bands; and illuminated most brightly, preternaturally illuminated, in the center of the cavern, on a stone dais, stood a white marble altar, elaborately carved with figures, sea-creatures, mermaids, tritons, and nymphs entwined in foam. The torches also made the cavern hot, much hotter than one would have expected, like some primeval sauna, so that the air shimmered in the heat, and after the evening chill of the cove, I felt my body warming again and my skin suddenly breaking out in a slick of perspiration.

I could hear Leo talking to me now, explaining, but my head was humming so, I could barely take in his words. And the sea breeze was blowing in now from the mainland of Italy, soughing in the crevices of the rocks and sounding like a soft and far-off bugle call in the entrance to the cavern. Leo was talking about how water was the stuff of life, how some worshipped fire but really water was the heart of life, most passive and most powerful, seemingly shaped by everything and yet irresistibly shaping everything by its own primal force over all the aeons. The most ancient feminine principle, out of which everything is born. And any place dedicated to San Michele, he said, Saint Michael the Warrior-Archangel, was originally an ancient site of pagan worship, which is nature worship—such as this whole island, an island of unnumbered underground streams, and springs, and fountains, where people worshipped the principle of water centuries before Christ walked the dry and dusty roads of Palestine.

"And the mermaid, too," he was saying. "What is she? Half-woman, half-fish: fertility? Sexuality? The personification of our eternal mother, the sea?"

From a darkened corner of the cavern Leo turned and I saw he was holding a white robe. He told me to undress and lay my clothes away and put this on. Even while my mind still hesitated, I did as he said. Round the waist I knotted the belt of golden cord. And then he took my hand and led me out of the cavern and we waited there on the beach hand in hand, my bare feet in the still-warm sand, saying nothing, thinking nothing. I was utterly passive and yet I knew I was nothing like his slave-girl. Leo had led me here, and told me what to do, and yet I was not under his command. I was — how can I put this? — I was only the servant to *myself*, and to something greater than myself. Leo held my hand no longer like some domineering father figure, but as my servant, honoring me. And I remembered the look of adoration I had seen him give to Teresa, so many times.

• • •

And then I could hear a distant drumming, hypnotic, antique, an inexorable, almost militaristic rhythm, getting closer all the time. I glanced at Leo, and he looked curiously serene, uncharacteristically dreamy, rapt. Content.

Then round the corner of the far rocks came those who were beating the drums. Some were naked, some were half-clad in white; some were walking slow and stately, holding torches aloft, others were dancing and cavorting around them, dressed in grotesque satyr masks and goatskin cloaks. Those who were walking slowly were all by contrast beautiful, male and female alike. The torchlight burned on their faces and their bare shoulders, and their skins were golden in the glow. As they came nearer their faces shone with sweat and their otherworldly rapt attention to the delirium of the music. They banged drums and cymbals and moved along the beach toward us as if themselves spellbound and bewitched.

"Who are these, coming to the sacrifice?" murmured Leo, and turned and smiled at me, reverential, a little sad.

Then he took my hand and led me back into the cave. There he took a black strip of silk and turned me round so that I faced away from him, and he tied it around my head and over my eyes and secured it firmly behind so that I was in utter darkness. Blinded. And immediately all my other senses came to life.

I heard a noise like someone shaking out a heavy tablecloth and I knew that he was spreading something over the altar, and then he laid me down on it and I felt it was a thick velvet and I pictured it as a deep golden color, almost inlaid, cloth-of-gold, and I could smell incense and woodsmoke and also human sweat and sex. And then I felt the presence of many more people as they filed into that cavern, and the air was warm and thick with the smell of pinewood and smoke rising up to the opening in the roof of the cavern, and they drummed softly now and hummed or chanted a low song that was in no language I recognized.

I felt human bodies pressing all around me, and hands running over me, lips and tongues running over my lips and over my neck and throat, and one who kissed me I knew was Teresa from her perfume and I turned my head a little toward her and smiled at her though blindfolded and she touched a fingertip to my lips and I sucked it softly. Unseen hands loosened my white robe from around my shoulders and drew it down to my waist. Other hands loosened the knot of my belt and pulled it free—I raised my hips slightly to help them do so—and more hands raised the hem of the robe and pushed it up so that it formed a crested white wave around my waist and the rest of me lay naked.

Then there was a pause, and I heard a noise I couldn't identify, and then the sound of hands being rubbed together, and when they returned to me I knew that they had been rubbing their hands to warm the oil they held cupped. Now they spread what smelled like olive oil over my skin, from my toes upward, trickling it even between my toes, applying it with both fingers and tongues, warming it on my skin as they went. They held my hands outstretched and poured oil into my palms and massaged my fingers. They spread the grass-sweet olive oil up my legs and over my thighs, and I couldn't hold back a sigh and a gasp as they slicked it between my thighs, so gently, lingeringly, and I parted my thighs and wished those unseen fingers would stay there longer. Then strong hands lifted my legs behind my knees and bent them right up, and they poured more oil over me so that it trickled down between my rear cheeks, and further hands held my cheeks apart, and then a slim, delicate hand reached down and a small, subtle finger—a woman's finger, her little finger, surely—insinuated itself between my cheeks and inserted itself, just the tip, inside me, and caressed me there in a circling of oil and I begged silently for more, never to stop, oh more and forever.

They oiled my breasts and my neck and they covered me with kisses as they did so, so that I was exposed and caressed and fed on by countless mouths, tongues circling in dance-like movements over my breasts and around my nipples and then down over me until I bucked and writhed and wanted to hold my arms out to touch their hair and to embrace these unknown lovers, these worshippers. At last I could remain the passive body no longer, and I reached my hands out and caressed the naked flanks of those who stood around me, and a low murmur of delight went up from the throng and I guessed from the voices that the cavern held a hundred people or more and that every eye was on me. I felt two boys, young and firmly muscled, quite naked, standing to left and to right of me, and I ran my hand down over their lean bellies, my mind lascivious, whore-like, and found them rigid, standing out, and my fingers curled around them, each boy my slave in each oiled palm, and began to squeeze and caress them, and I heard their little gasps and felt their whole bodies tauten at my touch.

More mouths tried to kiss me, and I turned sideways to each in turn and felt tongue after tongue — some gentle, some feminine, some hard and probing, some hesitant, some greedy — entwining with my tongue, and then one brought a mouthful of wine and we drank it between us from each other's ruby, wine-stained lips. Then one of the naked boys beside me pulled free from my hand and turned my head toward him and slid into my mouth and I closed my mouth tight about him and he tasted beautiful. I felt another naked form brush against me, and cool soft hands took my free hand and placed it between smooth thighs and it was a girl now and she pressed my hand flat into her curls and then, using my middle finger almost as she pleased, she used it to caress her lips and clitoris. Soon I was flicking my finger rapidly over her swollen bud, and she leaned forward and her mouth closed on my breasts and she moaned softly and lay half across me while I brought her into raptures.

Between my legs, I felt tongues taking turns, and even competing to squeeze into me together, one on my clitoris, long feminine hair tickling over my belly, while another, perhaps a man, buried his face between my cheeks and ran his tensed tongue back and forth, slipping a rigid forefinger in and out of me.

My mouth filled with hot sperm, and then wine again, and then more tongues and another man pushed into me, and a woman must have straddled me and I felt her lower her salty lips onto my mouth. Then I felt a blind, probing head between my thighs, rubbing up and down and over the head of my clitoris and then back, teasing me cruelly, entering me just a half-inch and then easing back, and I arched toward him. I longed to reach down and grab the naked buttocks of that unknown lover and pull him deep into me, but my hands were filled with greedy men who would not let me go. Finally the stranger eased into me, strong and wide, stretching me, and beginning to pump faster and faster, fingers buried in the flesh of my buttocks. Others slipped their arms beneath the small of my back and lifted me up, exposing me more, so that a tongue, a woman's again I guessed, could skim over my clitoris, circle it, her hair draped over my belly, while the man fucked me so hard. I forgot how many times I came, it was impossible to count. It was continuous, without respite, I knew no tiredness. I filled with sperm, the man still throbbing pulled out of me, sperm flowed free and mingled with oil. They turned me on my side and raised one leg and another man quickly slipped into me, while yet another nuzzled between my buttocks and, very gently, oiled and slow, eased into me behind. The unseen, naked orgiasts around me must have watched in delight, and held my cheeks apart for the men to ease in better, and I felt them stroke my skin and heard them murmur soft endearments in my ears as I took them in, took both men in, and lapped greedily on fresh, lemon lips that she, another lover, another worshipper, touched softly to my mouth.

And I thought how they say that the taste of a woman is supposed to be like the saltwater taste of the sea, and then I understood everything, not with my mind but with my body, and my understanding deepened, wordlessly, all that enchanted night as I lay there and was worshipped and adored and made love to by my lovers as numberless as the stars in the sky or the grains of sand by the sea.

· · ·

When I awoke I was lying under a soft woolen blanket on the sand, and Kit lay beside me. He was awake, propped up on one elbow, looking over me as I slept. Normally he was always asleep until long after me. But he was awake, and his face was alight. We looked at each other for a long time, and I didn't have a word to say. I knew everything was real. But where had Kit been? Did he know?

Then he leaned over and kissed me. "You were beautiful," he said, "last night." He smiled. "The Goddess."

Then I remembered. "The last one, my last lover—that was you?"

He kissed me in answer.

As the sun came up—and exhausted though I was, though we both were, so tired that we laughed out of tiredness like unruly children—we made love in the surf where the sea broke on the beach of the Island of San Michele. There was no boat, nor another soul around. We might be stranded on the island forever, and we laughed, and didn't care, and all we could think of doing was making love in the foam, fucking, laughing, he harder, harder, always harder, like a rock, a stone statue like that little smiling ithyphallic god that they worship in some places, and I melting before him and flowing around him like water like a mermaid like the spirit of the water that they worship here....

New York, N.Y., by way of Taos, N.M.

M. CHRISTIAN

VI CALLED IT "SPAGHETTI WESTERN WEATHER"—
a cinematic weather pattern highlighted by periods of near-clichés: dust-devils spinning against a too-blue sky, a too-red desert bed; tumbleweeds chasing each other down cracked streets; a solitary mesquite bush, looking harsh and sharp in its hunger for survival. Screen doors knocked open–shut, open–shut in a lazy rhythm—pushed by a sternly hot breeze, followed by gusts laced with eye-stinging dust, dirt, and crisped leaves.

"All it needs," Vi would say, part of a ritual worked up in the year they lived in the tiny trailer, "is a dog looking for somewhere to die."

For a couple together for only three years, they had a lot of rituals. In more thoughtful moods, Clarette would expound in a tired voice about how the desert was perfect for such things—beads on a wire of routine that made the heat, the dust, the boredom tolerable for just one more day. When she was in a less thoughtful mood, she didn't say anything; she'd just sprawl on their stained mattress in a once-white T-shirt and old, comfortable panties and try to think of anything except heat, dust, and the boredom.

The electric clock over the dirty stove made a gentle hum, clear if you tuned your ear to it—as Clarette did, a gentle reminder to herself that Vi would be home in just a few minutes. The hum was another of those Indian beads on a wire, a little ritual she did without thinking.

Sometimes, when she did think about it—the hum of the clock, the sun so close to the horizon, the obnoxious newscaster on their cheap little B&W teevee who always said, "We'll be right back," all these things that happened just before the truck pulled up, the door opened, the jingle of Vi's keys in her denim pockets—she called it her "ticket."

Because when Vi came home, it was a chance to leave the dry outskirts of Taos, New Mexico—at least for a little while.

• • •

The sun was gone, the movie over. A curtain of deep night, as only the desert can make it, over everything. The moon was gone, new, so the sky was only lit by hard points of starlight. It was a warm night, and for that Clarette was grateful—she didn't like the desert cold, the way it seemed to cut through her.

Next to her, in their big bed, Vi was radiant heat: her big breasts soft against her back, her strong legs casually draped over hers. If she wanted to, Clarette knew she could wriggle her toes and feel the scratchy calluses on the tops of Vi's feet, from the too-hard work boots she had to wear.

Behind her ear, the big woman's breath was sweet, with just a tiny hint of the beer she'd had with supper. They stayed that way, curled around each other, for quite a while, a nebulous component of a typical night. Finally, her breath growing even warmer as she spoke, Vi said, "Where do you want to go tonight?"

Clarette was quiet for a time, letting the earth spin through her mind. The day, the Sergio Leone weather, made her think of the movies, of totems and icons, and one thing, and one thing only, came to mind when she thought of classics, of places that seemed to exist only on their cheap teevee.

"New York," she whispered, taking Vi's hand and pulling it around herself tightly.

• • •

"On the subway, late at night," Vi said, her voice low and theatrical. "The city that never sleeps is dozing, so it's just us — just you and me — sitting on the hard plastic seats, watching stations flash by through the graffiti-painted windows. Sometimes we emerge from the tunnels and travel through the nighttime city, past buildings that mix bright windows with dim stars, blocking out the clouds even high overhead. Brilliant signs as big as…as big as anything you've ever seen: all the colors of the rainbow, spelling out big corporation names. There's an aliveness to the air, like electricity is running through it. There's so much to see, so much that your eyes can't take it all in — they even hurt, there's so much.

"But we're on a subway train, traveling through it together, holding each other, so nothing hurts. We're feeling the rumble of the rails, the sway as the car bends through the steel and concrete canyons."

Vi's hand moved, softly, gently, till she cupped Clarette's small breast. "We're alone, traveling through the greatest city on earth. You're wrapped around me, your head resting on my shoulder, my hair tickling your cheek. My breasts, full and warm, are heavy on your arms.

"We're rolling through the city, between the high buildings, down into the cool tunnels. You look up, and see the names you've always heard of on the transit maps: Broadway, Lexington, Manhattan, the Bronx, Queens, Greenwich Village, Wall Street. The stations roll past the dirty windows, they flash by as we clack and click down the tracks."

Vi's voice grew deeper, huskier, as she gently squeezed Clarette's breast, cupping the tiny conical shape with her rough hands. "I kiss you on the subway, breaths mixing as we roll. As I do, you feel my nipples harden, even through my sweater...did I mention I'm wearing a sweater? Well, anyway, you feel me get nice and hard—you know how I do...."

Clarette giggled, a little-girl sound, pulling the bigger woman closer, feeling her own nipples respond.

"I unwrap you and push you back into the hard seat, kissing you rough and mean, nasty. You feel my breath coming into your mouth, my breathing matching for a moment the sway, the rumble of the subway car. My tongue touches, then pushes hard against your own—and everything, all of you, gets that much warmer, hotter.

"My hands are on your tits"—and they were, warm and rough, cupping her, squeezing her hard nipples between long fingers—"kneading them, working them. You moan, in that delightful way you do, and arch your back into the hard plastic. I get down off my own seat and kneel between your legs, push them apart. You're wearing jeans, tight jeans, and you can feel your cunt get all warm and wet at just the thought of being there."

Vi's hand slowly smoothed her hip, a slow caress that started at the gentle rises of her ribs and ended at the fullness of her hips.

"Take me," Clarette said softly, pushing herself back against Vi, mixing their warmth.

Vi kissed her shoulder, pulled her till she was lying on her back. "I will," she said, kissing around the tiny rosebud of her right nipple. "I promise."

A light suck, a gentle draw of nipple into mouth. Clarette sighed, a heavy, wind-gust sound.

Vi looked up, for no reason, saw the alarm clock's harsh red glow, one of Clarette's medicine bottles, and the statue. "We're outside, and it's cold. The sky looks busy, filled with more than just stars—the dancing illuminations of the city, the mad glow from the famous streets. The wind gusts around us, pushing our coats this way, that. At our feet are stones; firm and stable...."

Clarette spread her legs, a loving, practiced motion, and Vi cupped her, being careful not to reach too far down. She rested there, feeling Clarette's furnace, the gentle heat from her cunt.

"Behind us, waves lap heavily on rocks, kicked up from great liners, huge vessels coming home after months at sea. Like I said, it's cold, but we're not cold. We're hot, baby—we're very hot."

She rested there for a moment, a heavy heartbeat, then kissed Clarette on the tummy, on her gently rising/falling belly, and turned to the chest of drawers, selected a glove and a small bottle of lube.

"Where are we?" Clarette giggled, spreading her legs wide and snaking a thin hand down to flick casually at a momentary tangle of long pubic hairs.

Vi smiled, nodded to the little statue next to the glowering alarm clock, the bottle of medications. "She's there, huge and powerful, above us. Lit by brilliant—so brilliant!—lights. She's *vast*, 'big' doesn't come close. She's a Goddess, Clare, as green as new grass. Her face is almost invisible, lost against the dark sky, but we can see her, Clare—we can see her smiling out to sea, looking out across the world."

A little squeeze of lube on two gloved fingers, a gentle caress with same, from majora to a crease hiding a warming clit. A few strokes to open her up, to make her ready: downward, from the little forest of curly hairs to the opening lips below. Clarette hissed, a primal sound of love and welcoming, and spread her legs ever so much wider.

"We're looking at her face, on her island, in the middle of the bay. It's cold, but we're hot, baby, so damned fucking hot. You're wearing this beautiful leather coat, like smooth darkness, and it feels so good wrapped around you. I'm there, too, baby, because you know I'm always there."

Another sweet hiss as Vi's fingers dipped in, pushing gently till plump outer lips met second joints. Moved there, slow in-and-outs that made Clarette's hips gently rock and clench around them.

"We're there, baby" — another nod at the cheap little Liberty trinket by the clock — "we've made it that far and even farther. We're standing at her feet, looking up at her.

"I put my arms around you, pull you close against me. You feel me, feel my tits pressing into your back, feel me there with you. I kiss the back of your neck, a butterfly graze that makes your skin dance with goose bumps, and your nipples get ever-so-hard. One of my hands drops down and takes hold of one of your tits, squeezes it through the coat. It feels like someone else, like a great leather hand grabbing you, pulling hard at you. You breathe heavily and you feel your cunt get real wet."

The strokes became more familiar, a simple little dance between the two of them. Clarette's breaths, too, became a tune that Vi knew too well, could have played in her sleep. Up and down, small circles around her clit, back down past warm, wet lips, and in, to tease the tight ring of muscles, then back up again. Repeat. Familiar, but still magic — a charming routine, a loving ritual. Part of home, part of them, together.

Vi bent, took a hard nipple into her mouth, and nibbled, adding a new tone to Clarette's sounds. Between gentle sucks — just the way she liked it — she whispered, adding to the scene.

"My hands rise to your face, stroking your cheek. You kiss my fingers, suck them in, tasting my cunt on them. Holding you, I have my fingers down between my legs, feeling my own lips, my own hard clit, getting myself all wet and hot, for you.

"You taste me, and know that I'm wet for you, baby.

"But there are other things to taste than just my fingers. I slowly drop my fingers down and slowly — almost too slowly — start to unbutton your coat. One, two, three: with each button your body tingles, your nipples get even harder, your cunt gets even hotter, wetter. Four, five, six — and then that's all. The coat parts and the cold slaps on your...yes, it slaps on your smooth belly, that spot, right there, between your tits, your thighs. You're naked, baby, hot and burning naked out there on that cold island. The coat hits the ground, and you're before her and me, glowing with fire, cunt juice painting your thighs. I turn you, look at my own goddess, my own Lady Liberty. I kiss you, hard and mean, tongues stroking each other, lips hot and slick. I kiss you, and my hand snaps up between your legs...."

Between her legs, Vi's hand had moved a new way, though still familiar—throbbing bead of a clit, a tiny hot bead, down to enter, full and deep into her, past the tight muscles, all the way till the rough spot. With each cycle, each tap at the down and deep down, Clarette's voice changed, becoming bass and fundamental. She was lost, somewhere else, floating on Vi's hand, her fingers and her words. She might not have been at the foot of the Statue of Liberty, but she certainly wasn't in a tiny trailer in Taos, New Mexico.

"Feeling your clit, so hard on that cold night. You push down, trying to get all of me onto you, and into you. I do it, there—under the shadow of Liberty—put my fingers in you, so deep and hard. I start to fuck you, quick and firm, with my fingers, ending each stroke with a strong press on your magic spot, your G. You moan, making sweet music too deep and primal to escape on the cold wind. You buck down, too excited to be patient and passive. In the distance, you hear a lone foghorn, and you realize that anyone floating by, anyone with a good telescope, could see us, could see you, standing there, pale and naked, excitement painting your thighs. You're on display, Clare; you're out there on the island for the whole of New York to see."

The motions of Vi's hand in Clarette's cunt became less formal, less simple, as her own excitement started to pull at her. Too close to ignore, Vi moved a bit, feeling the silken skin of Clarette's breast slide across her lips...until the hard tip of her nipple was there, and then in Vi's mouth. She sucked with a shocking intensity, making Clarette arch her narrow back and put a thin hand on the back of her head. Sucking as she stroked, and stroking as she sucked, Vi felt as if she was a great woman—a chain going from mouth to tit, from cunt to hand.

Breaking the pleasant suction with a soft wet *smack!* and another punctured moan from Vi, she breathed deep (one, two, three, four), then: "You're so hot, baby, so wet. There, standing on the cold flagstones in front of the statue, you push down, trying to swallow my fingers with your cunt, trying to get even more of my thumb on your clit.

"But I'm nasty—right, lover? You know that. Three fingers for your tight cunt, your wet cunt, thumb for your clit, and one finger, my teeny tiny little finger, that reaches back between the cheeks of your tight"—a kiss on her sweat-slick belly—"ass, and taps (one, two, three, four) on your asshole.

"Oh, yes, your sweet ass. A few gentle taps, then away to take just the smallest amount of cunt juice, and then back—no taps this time. Not this time....

"Look up at her, Clare—look at her. Great and green. You look up at the statue—recognizing her from photographs, movies, your little toy there, on the dresser, but seeing her might and majesty for the first time. Maybe you wonder, slut that you are, what her great copper snatch must look like. But whatever you think, you look up at her as I work at your own great cunt, and then at your asshole as my little finger *slips* so neat and nice right up into you.

"Oh, yes, baby—nice and full and hot, bare and shining in the hard lights around Liberty, staring up at her distant smile and the faint lights of the city beyond. You're there, you're right there and you're with me, and I'm with you...."

The come boiled inside Clarette, a rumbling body-come that opened her eyes, opened her mouth and shut it, clenched her legs around Vi's hand. The moans changed into a heavy avalanche of sounds, a growling bass escalation.

Within her, Vi felt her cunt grip her, matching for a long time the fluttering beat of her heart. Looking, smiling, happy that she was happy, Vi held her, stirring the last of her quakes with a few kind oscillations of her fingers. "Sweet, sweet baby," she crooned, putting her heavy arms around the smaller girl, the so-much-more-fragile girl.

Sleep floated down on both of them, much more so for Clarette, but quite heavily for Vi after a hard day of work, and they crawled into a comfortable spoon: Clarette as usual facing the side, the dark window sprinkled with very bright desert stars, and Vi a warm comfort curled against her back. Before the weight pressed her down into a dreamscape, Clarette turned her head to receive a gentle, sweet kiss from Vi. "Thank you for taking me." Vi waited till she had uncurled briefly to drop, carefully, the rubber glove into the trash, to curl back and say, "One day, I promise, I really will...."

To that, Clarette snuggled firmer into her lover's arms and was soon breathing slow and steady. Vi followed, a few minutes later, hoping—not for the first time, nor the last—that she'd really have enough time with Clarette to show her the real subway, the real statue, the real lights of that distant city.

ɛɾuption

ֆ

JILL NAGLE

SOMETIMES, ATTRACTION GROWS SLOWLY, ripening like a fine wine or cheese. One day you catch a whiff of someone you've known for ages, and notice that an odor, perhaps a taste, has shifted and you swear you feel your blood suddenly racing through your veins, though it has flown there all along. From the deep roots of long friendship one day blooms an exotic, unknown fruit. This often happens after a heavy rain. I like growing lovers that way. Then, there's attraction that rears up with no warning, like hot molten rock, sending villagers screaming. My meeting with Andre was like that.

I was on vacation in Hawaii, enjoying the remote lushness of the big island. Kalani Honua, an "eco-resort" with a significant gay clientele, had many of the tropical flora and fauna of my balmy Miami childhood: coconuts, papayas, tall pines with tiny cones that stuck to your feet, and needles composed of detachable sections. Walking across the grounds was eerily familiar, especially each time I ran across another forgotten living thing.

Like crab spiders whose webs caught the morning dew, and sometimes your legs, arms, and face. Oh yeah, those crab spiders. Only these were orange, and ours were black and white and red. Then there were those fat blades of soft, dull green grass that stood up to so many feet. Plants with drooping buds the color of green grapes with air inside that we kids used to pop. Hibiscuses, identical save for their orange instead of pink hue. Periwinkles peach, white, and lavender. Palm trees and ferns; mangoes and little fat bananas whose texture was slightly more dense and slick than their larger cousins, with hints of strawberry, apricot, and Fuji apple in their bouquet. When our banana tree at home bore fruit, the bunches grew thirty or forty little guys at a time, which Dad would haul inside and leave on the counter, where they took up half the space. They would ripen in a wave, from one side of the bunch to the other, and no sooner had another column turned from green to yellow than they were gone, leaving the lonely stems to harden and furl against the air. We couldn't get enough of them.

• • •

Oh yes, and passion fruit.

• • •

My second day there, I decided it was time to explore the island. On the way out, I stopped in the office at the end of the long driveway to pick up a copy of the local map, having left mine in the room. I noticed a notebook of massage therapists and other services. One of the pages had an ad reading "Weight Training: I'll show you when to train, how to train, and how much to train." Just then, a tall, chocolate-skinned, generously built man with dreadlocks walked in.

"Hi, Andre," the woman behind the counter said.

"Hey," the man returned. "I'm wondering if there are any appointments scheduled for this afternoon." She told him there was one at three o'clock.

"You do massage?" I asked him.

"No, just weight training."

I paused, reflecting. "Any special twist to it?" I queried.

"I'll make you work hard, if that's what you want." He grinned gently. Hard body, soft eyes, full sweet lips. One hand casually over his crotch the whole time. I fantasized he was covering a pulsing erection. I felt slightly off balance. We stood gazing at one another for a moment. I nodded nervously, thanked everyone, and backed out of the office, forgetting my map. Once I started the car, I remembered and ran back in. Andre, already in conversation with others outside, followed me for a moment with his eyes. A friendly, same-gender-loving brother intrigued by my pointy glasses? Not according to my gut and my cunt.

That night, I woke up about 5 A.M. with Andre firmly lodged in my psyche, my pores, my crevices. I wailed silently inside, whining and moaning, like a baby without her bottle, whose mouth doesn't feel the same for the throbbing lack, whose stomach can only cry with emptiness. I doubled over in my bed, grabbing my pillow half crazed, trembly with restlessness. There's attraction, there's interest, there's admiration of beauty, and then there's *have to have.* The last time I felt "have to have" was with Wynn, my current lover. Wynn and I ate of dripping-ripe summer fruit after tending a winter of warm, dry friendship. This time, I was shopping not for a permanent lover, but a teaming tidepool, ocean water mixing with heated spring from the earth's core, like those about a half mile down the road from the resort. A sweet bath, but one you can't stay in too long. You don't live in hot springs; you enjoy them briefly, and say goodbye.

I rehearsed the many ways I might approach Andre, and dismissed them all. Ah, Andre? I don't think I could hire you for a training session; I'd be too distracted. Too oblique. Hey. I know of something that wants to erupt around here. Oh God, too corny. What if I were completely honest? I would have to say, *I want to devour you.* What if he were offended? Maybe I should preface it. But I hate silly qualifiers. Ugh! But that had to be it. For when I thought of him, my jaws unhinged and wanted *him and only him* between them; my fingers curled and clawed to pierce his skin, rip his muscle. From my gut came *I want to devour you;* the desire, and then the words, over and over and over.

Five-thirty A.M. A half hour till the generator came on, so I had no light. Needed to pee. It was dark out, which made me scared. Then I remembered where I was. Here on a remote corner of the big island, I needn't fear theft of my possessions, mugging, rape; instead, I thought about whether I might witness a *tsunami,* one of those giant waves created by a volcano beneath the ocean floor. The last one, they said, hit ten or twenty years ago. When the *tsunami* warning goes off, you get in your car and drive to the highest point on the land, and pray you beat the tidal wave. For a couple of days, I carefully watched the crashing ocean. I also wondered if the local steaming volcano would blow during my stay, as some believed it might, heaving up a two-thousand-foot spray of liquid rock visible for miles. If you're nearby, said my new friend Dave, it's not neat, it's not cool: you *get the fuck out.* You won't be burned, oh no; you'll just be *crushed* to death. Rock is rock, liquid or solid.

I envisioned my body immortalized in cooled lava, caught forever in the earth's heat. A romantic death, I thought. I've never been terribly afraid of death. Pain and suffering, yes; death no. I think that's partly because I believe death will be yet another interesting experience. I have reason to believe my consciousness will live on in some form, so I look forward to seeing what life will be like without this body. Yet I fear for its vulnerability to harm and disaster. Realizing that stepping outside onto this land to use the bathroom put me at no great risk, I took my flashlight and braved the stairway.

Emptied of urine, and thus of some of the pressure on my G spot, I drifted more easily toward sleep. I like this body in some ways, I thought, and I also feel its limitations. This day, however, I would be grateful for some of my particularly female attributes and make excellent use of them. I would groom and perfume the bait of my body for the food I wished to devour. Who eats whom is debatable in these waters.

In the early lavender morning, I took a cool run up the coast, stopping on the walk back to greet the absurdly blue ocean as it dashed white and creamy against the dark, chunky lava rocks. Again and again the waves, furious, dangerous. Futile, I could say, from the vantage point of up on the cliff. I leaned into a palm tree that dipped precariously into the valley of the beach of rocks, hoping to get my hot body sprayed. I thought of Scotty, dear sweet water creature, and how this is something he would do. Place himself in the right environs and…hope to get sprayed. He's a magnet rather than an arrow, drawing in rather than seeking and piercing the target of his desire. And he loves the water. So I invoked Scotty's spirit, water nymph, show-off bottom, dessert tease. Oh, spray me, mother ocean, or I'll leave you and wander off in search of something that will! She answered my pleas with a few cool puffs that tingled my body. I sent a prayer to Scotty, back to the ocean, to *Pele*, Hawaii's volcano goddess, and kept moving, walking off the run.

I came back onto the land red and sweating. A dip in the pool, I thought, as soon as possible. Trudging back to my room, I passed Andre fifty yards or so from me, busy gathering pond debris (for mulch, I would later learn) from a small body of water next to the pool house. I felt his eyes in my back and kept walking toward my building while my heart thumped, then ascended the stairs, entered my room, and shut the door. I stood there only breathing, not moving, for a good long minute or two. Cards still covered the floor by the bed. That morning, I had asked the round Motherpeace Tarot deck what would become of Andre and me that day, which was today. I drew the Lovers card, completely upright.

I have owned this deck about three years and probably drawn the Lovers card a total of three times. I thought perhaps it was too good to be true—that the cards were reflecting my wishes and desires rather than the actual course of events. Then I remembered that the two were not necessarily independent of one another.

Stripping away my sweaty clothes, I surveyed my body in the mirror, shifting from instrument to object, from vehicle to magnet, from runner to centerfold. I plucked my favorite thong from the soft tangle of undergarments, the one that splices my ass cheeks and wraps around my tummy *just so*. I took off my pointy glasses. I combed my hair and wiped down my face with a wet washcloth. Back to the mirror. I wasn't half bad-looking, after all, once I ditched the nerd disguise. Instead of the immediacy of the thick black frames, I saw blue-green eyes, flushed peachy skin, and…cheekbones! Why had I never bothered with contacts? Then I remembered all the unwanted attention from men. Now was the time to take out those dangerous tools.

I took a shimmery sarong off its hanger and tied it over my breasts. I was aware of its sheerness, and that the slit in the front opened and closed when I walked, revealing the neat *V* of my thong, and my long, strong thighs. I silently planned my route. I would walk back to the pool, this time passing by the pond, and stop to say hello to Andre on my way. No glasses. Since I was walking toward the pool, I could easily end the conversation if (when) I became tongue-tied. I gathered my belongings, adjusted my breasts, and opened the door to my room onto the large common area just outside.

I took a few steps forward and stopped. An impossibly round ass scooped the air on a mat in the center of the room. Andre turned over when he heard my footsteps, to rest flat on his back with his knees bent.

"Hi," I said, moving toward him automatically, not thinking.

"Hey," he said. I couldn't tell if he had followed me here or not. I decided he had. Our eyes didn't leave each other.

"Is it OK if I join you for a moment?" I asked.

"Sure," he replied. I sat on the couch in front of him. He continued what looked like a yoga routine, and my breath shortened as I noticed his nipples stuck out a most improbable distance from the mounds of his pectorals. His chest was smooth, shiny and chunky like *challah*, but more the color of a light pumpernickel. His ass was like two new loaves of sourdough bread. I wanted to knead him, to toast him, to butter him up, down, and inside out.

I know we must have made some conversation, but I can't for the life of me recall what was said, except that we agreed to meet back here—at my building—after lunch, to "talk" some more. I do recall that the sarong had slid slowly down my breasts during those few minutes. I remember his eyes traveling partially down my neck to my chest, then back to my face. As I turned toward the light to exit, I felt the fabric fly out around my body. With my back toward him, I removed the wrap completely and retied it, then slipped through the door, forgetting my flip-flops.

After a few minutes in the sauna, I jumped into the pool, which was just the slightest bit cool, a pleasant shock that quickly became the perfect bath. Andre passed by the area a couple of times, and I was aware of my nearly naked body in the water, bare breasts peeking freely about. Men's nipples have always inspired lasciviousness in me, so I silently laugh at the cavalier way they get ignored, desexualized, as if those nubs of brown flesh meant nothing at all, as if I hadn't taken nipples like that between my teeth and made men scream and clutch. As if! Andre, bare-chested with a sarong covering the lower half of his body, seemed to grow new nipple flesh each time he passed me. I wondered if vigorous sucking over time hadn't distended his mammaries.

Twelve o'clock came and went. At about a quarter after, I headed toward the feeding corral. I lingered over lunch with two sweet gay boys from Oregon, dishing and such, and then headed back to the lodge. On my way, I mentally took stock of my body's state of cleanliness. The sauna and pool had washed away anything potentially offensive, I reasoned. Since I was on vacation, I wasn't about to perform any cosmetic rituals like shaving or makeup. My raw self had won me this much attention; it would take me the rest of the way. Andre was at his workstation by the pond. He looked up and saw me at the foot of the lodge stairs, and I waved to let him know I was "at home" and ready to receive...visitors.

The balcony was airy and moist, with just a hint of coolness. I plunged into the one soft chair and put my feet up, closed my eyes, and breathed. I ran a fingernail over the grooves in my teeth where I know food is most likely to collect, and removed the schmutz. Eventually, I heard footsteps on the stairs to my left. "I'm gonna take a shower first..." he called up. First?

When I opened my eyes again, Andre was dragging a chair next to mine, drying himself with a towel, his sarong still clinging to his loins. For the first time, I really smelled that body. Oh, that body! A clean and musky sweat wafted toward my nostrils, caressed my face. For the third time in twenty-four hours, our eyes made relaxed, relentless contact. The air thickened and warmed between us, and Pele bucked beneath the ocean with impatience. A voice inside my throat whispered silently, *Hold on and pray.* We both breathed. This time, when his lips moved, they said in a husky voice, "Can we go someplace more private?" I looked out over the vegetation. It had begun to rain very gently.

"In a few minutes. It's so beautiful here right now." Delight reared in my chest at tethering the ballooning tension. We both gazed outward at the stretches of green grass, the coconut palms and bursting red flowers, the light spray misting it all. With every breath, I smelled him again. His sarong was hiked up to his waist on one side like a loincloth, revealing a beautiful hollow just before thigh became ass cheek. The mist began to cling to his shiny skin. My eyes lingered, then fastened. A slight trail of fuzz began just below his belly button, a small knot of interruption over a hardened, ropy lava flow, and disappeared into the shadow that the fabric created as it loosely enveloped his torso. I couldn't believe I was this close. Yes, I could. No, I couldn't. My hand reached over and rested in the hollow of his thigh, finding the place of suction with my palm. Yes, I could! I let my fingers press into his hip as I met his eyes again.

"You are very beautiful," I said slowly. He raised an eyebrow.

"So are you," he replied. His lips. His thigh. His nipples. His chest. His stomach. Lips, thigh, nipples, chest, stomach, lipsthighnipplecheststomach, eyes starting to lose focus.

"Shall we?" I whispered.

We stood into the mist and swam toward the door. I don't remember the short walk to my room, only suddenly facing him, moist, tender, hard and raw, with a cool clean bed next to us.

Hands, then. Everywhere. Then mouths. Neck. Ah, neck. And here came Pele. With a cry from my gut, I forced him down on the bed, took his whole pectoral in my mouth, and teethed it right down to the absurdly erect nipple.

"Bite it," he begged, though he need not have. My weight on his hard, thick, silky body pressed him into the mattress and I began with his chest as a first course.

I felt a slight resistance and also a curiosity in him. More than to resist, he longed to know where I would take him. Or so went the fiction of my desire. I felt arrows, probes, and heat-seeking missiles grow from my groin, the tips of my fingers, my tongue.

When something comes forth, a baby, a spill of liquid rock from a passionate fissure in the planet, people draw near to witness. These moments abound in nature, ripe for holy reclamation. The tiny, pale green points of each spring. Newness opens our mouths in wonder. *Shehekiyanu,* we sing in Hebrew, to mark and honor the first time ever, or the first time that year.

"Have you ever been penetrated?" I asked him. He shook his head. I slid his right leg over my shoulder, kneading his ass cheek, tracing the groove.

"What about now," I purred, grasping the back of his neck, grazing his full, tender lips with my teeth. He looked at me with eyes I read as no more than five: open, wondering, sweet.

"I...think I'd like that." Without breaking our gaze, I stroked the outside of his rosebud, greeting the opening from many angles as I kept his massive body pinned. Was I ever more alive than this? Though he could easily have flipped me on a whim, we both knew that the will of my gaze restrained him firmly. The fingers of my left hand found the warm opening between his lips and he began to suck like a baby.

The human body is like a hollow tube, and our "insides" a second outside surface. A long donut. Toward the center of his body, throat to ass, in a perfect circle through miles of intestine, past heart, liver, lungs, adrenals, kidneys, through the deep, vacuous cavity of uncharted body, the tips of my left and right fingers sought one another. His cock throbbed, rigid as I have ever felt one. My soft cheek found the tender underside just below his glans and stroked softly again and again. Lips, so hungry, could not help but sample his textures. Eyes vanished in favor of these greatly exaggerated cheek, fingers, lips, all in rhythm, nested in and among his surfaces, hot crannies. Small noises escaped his mouth, following his breath. Tongue eventually granted his shaft small, lingering flicks, here and there, pushing his voice to the highest register, finally swallowing him whole. Delight!

I imagined all of me traveling through him, along the path between my fingertips, fucking the inside of him as I sucked the outside of him, as he fucked me inside and outside, images of his dick down my throat superimposed on his dick fucking my cunt deeper than I ever imagined. Dizzy, unwound.

This need to be inside something, to force one's way into unconquered, protected solid mass: Perhaps this is Pele's obverse. Her heat, contained and trapped within the planet, wants so badly to come out and cool against the air. Maybe it is this heat we absorb and drive back into hot, molten places, seeking each other's burning cores.

As I reached toward myself, through him, again and again, dick and cunt became fingers and mouth; inside became out, outsider became internal organs. Tears of gratitude remembered my eyes open and showed a stranger becoming lover becoming new lava flow, becoming a white river on a coffee landscape burning new earth with each crashing spill.

Outside, the ocean was quiet. Crab spiders shifted in their webs, sated. Bunches of strawberry-flavored bananas grew a shade yellower, a millimeter fatter. Pele the sacred witness, for the first time in weeks, breathed in peace, the circle complete.

Body of Sand

⁂

Debra Hyde

THIS FIXATION OF MINE, THIS TRIAL AND TRIBULATION of the libido, is rooted in my earliest days. I was born into sand, into the gleaming dirt of the desert, and my earliest memories are of its feel. Innocently, I sifted it through my fingers. Barefooted, I ran through it. Doggedly, I dug into it, believing with a child's faith that a spoon and some elbow grease would get you all the way to China.

Dig deep enough, especially in the shade and away from the hot desert sun, and you'll find brown, cool dirt, packed down tight as if it clings with all its might to what little moisture it holds within its grains.

Maybe it started there, with the feel of dirt. Or maybe it started with the sandstorms, those howling wind events that made my mother rush to put towels down at the back door, at the kitchen windowsill. Our house, our little stucco dwelling set purple against the beige landscape, never leaked water. It only leaked sand.

Maybe I stood out in the backyard as the winds ripped past me. Maybe I felt the sting of sand against my skin. All I remember are the thorns of tumbleweeds and the swarms of ants that littered our backyard afterward. Both could bite, each in its own way.

But the sand can bite, too, and at some point in my life I became enamored of its sting. I came to crave its touch.

That's why I stand here, now, in the Great Sandy Desert, far from the usual Australian sites. Far from the sparkling water of the Great Barrier Reef, from the rugged rise of Ayers Rock, from the sight of ancient petroglyphs. It isn't the sense of the primitive, the sound of the aboriginal, that drew me here. It was the sand and my lust for it.

On the edge of vastness, I stand with arms oiled and out-stretched. I wait to feel the fine, red dirt of the land rip against my flesh, here, where Aeolian sand dunes can stretch for a hundred miles. Where lakes are ephemeral, present one day only to vanish the next. Where cities are such faraway creations that they might as well be of another world.

The sound of the wind picks up. I close my eyes and purse my lips, even though I'm wearing only safety goggles and a surgical facemask. I steel myself and wait for fury to strike.

As I wait, I think of you, lover and adventurer. I remember how you eyed me as you oiled my skin, as you made me slick. Are you thinking of me now, as you sit within the van and wait out both the storm and my weird desire for it? Are you imagining how gritty I'll be, in all places but one, that deep cleft between my legs? Does the thought of that one place, the oasis that I'll make wet, get you hard?

The wind arrives and the first sting of sand strikes my skin. It burns, little granules of pain. But it clings and accumulates, and so does my arousal.

Every sting pierces me, just like you do when you spread my legs and find your way into me. Often, you hold me down, refusing my help. You like it when you have to fight your way into me. I like it when you don't just slip into me, when the grit has nothing to do with sand and everything to do with ferocity.

Like the ferocity that strikes me now. The pain is like hail, but without the cold. The roar of the wind isolates me, makes me feel alone in the universe—like when I masturbate and in the instant I come, I know only my own existence and nothing more. Now, my existence is the roar of the wind, the petite pounding pebbles of the desert. Woman against nature, struggling, then merging with nature, at once singular and universal.

The sting of the sand is like your fingers when they pinch my nipples, like the drag of your nails over my skin as they trail from the curve of my breast downward, to the nub of my clit. And, yes, the sand gathers there too, encouraging my wellspring.

But as the sand gathers on my oiled skin and clings to me in layers, its sting lessens and fades. Breathing becomes harder as the storm intensifies and I begin to feel taxed.

That's when I feel your grip on my upper arm.

"That's enough." I hear your voice within the wind. "Time to come in."

I open my eyes and dimly spy you as the desert swirls around us. You're bundled up in a parka and look like Han Solo, rescuing Luke from the ice world of Hoth. You guide me to the van and, as I walk in dull, stumbling steps, I realize that endorphins course through my blood, altering my perception, readying me for your every touch.

You urge me into the back of the van and, as I kneel, you close its back doors. You pull the goggles and the mask from my face. My sight clears and I see the look in your eyes, in your smile. You gleam with a sense of adventure that the rigors of our travels have nothing to do with. My naked body, now as roughened as a sprayed ceiling, has everything to do with it.

As you undress, I wonder what your kiss will feel like. I imagine your hand against my gritty breast, your finger, caked with sand, inside me. I imagine the feel of grit rubbing inside me and as I do, you lean forward and kiss me. Your tongue seeks me out. It's insistent, urgent, but it is, as yet, untouched by sand. I know your taste, but I crave to taste the desert in your kiss.

I crave the taste of sand and saliva. I want the desert to join you when you invade my body.

You don't pull me close as we kiss. You keep me at a distance. You know the detached approach makes me long for you; it arouses me because I must be patient and when I want to fuck, I'm anything but patient.

The anticipation builds within me as we kiss, our mouths touching, our tongues dancing, but our bodies rigidly apart. Finally, you reach out to me and brush your hand lightly over my left breast.

My entire body shudders at your touch. The wind and sand has sensitized my skin. Every little sensation roars through me.

Now, you bring your hands to my breasts. You grip them, capturing them within each palm. You knead them, small things that they are, and the clinging sand grates against them. My nipples go hard as the friction heats my skin.

Your head dips down to a nipple and your mouth grasps it, drawing it to your hard palate. The sensation of your mouth deliciously stretching me is more than I can stand. I feel a heat flame between my legs. I feel a throbbing. My cunt comes alive.

Lay me down my mind begs. *Lay me down and fuck me.* But I don't voice my desire. You'll take me in good time, and asking otherwise is useless.

Your tongue invades my mouth again. This time, there's sand on your kiss. The invasion begins. I stiffen, then shudder, at the raw taste of it, the taste of the earth between my lips. We are Adam and Eve, called forth from the dirt of the earth, now honoring that hallowed ground in our lovemaking.

Australia tastes pure, its sand untouched by loam or topsoil. It tastes wind-worn, ageless. It beckons with opal mines, with beauty buried inside desolation. I feel like beauty wrapped in a veil of the desert. Forget Melbourne and Sydney, with their cosmopolitan trappings and casual ways; give me the barren earth, void of civilization, any day.

You pull me close now, finally, and wrap your arms around me. Our bodies come together in a full body friction, skin and sand and skin. The friction sets us on fire, makes us frantic. We grapple to touch, to caress, to possess.

I pull away from you and look at your body. Sand dapples your chest, clumps on the head of your dick, mingling with your seeping pre-cum. I bring my mouth to your neck and lick my way to a nipple, cleaning you of sand as I go, taking it for myself.

You stiffen when my mouth clasps your nipple and I hear the breath seize in your throat. In swift little circles, I sweep clean your nipple. I suck and nibble; I stress you with a stream of little pleasures, each bite as hard and tiny as a grain of sand.

I trail my way down to your groin. Your cock, hard and expectant, waits for me there, bobbing in apparent throbs of anticipation. But before I take it in my mouth, I nuzzle into your pubic hair and inhale. It smells of sweat and sand.

I hope our fucking, when we finally get to it, will smell like that.

But for now I suck. I draw the tip of your cock, that little bit muddied by sand and pre-cum, into my mouth. I use the same little circles to wipe it clean, to take and taste the magical mixture of man and earth. I revel in sticky sand that globs in my mouth; I revel in the taste of it, salted by your moisture.

But you deserve to revel as well, so I go to work on you, traipsing my tongue up and down your shaft. I drive myself down, as far as I can go, on your hard length, gagging once as I do. Then I bring myself back to the head of your cock, sucking hard, plying my tongue to that sweet spot that is your weakness.

Will you just let me work you over like this, or will you get into it and fuck my face? I feel your dick throb, then bulge in my mouth, unmistakable cues that you love what I'm doing. But you have the same goal as I do, and you pull yourself from me. A small pop sounds as you break the suction I've created.

Finally—oh, finally!—you lay me down. I'm near to rapture as your body meets mine, flesh to flesh, accentuated by the dirt we share.

Your dick throbs against my belly. "Make it dirty," I beg you. "Please."

I realize how silly I sound, but we've grown so urgent that it hardly matters. Gracefully, our arms entwine while our bodies rush to connect. I spread my legs and, as you insinuate yourself between them, you seek entrance. It's the ballet of seasoned lovers, a *pas d'action* that plays itself out time and time again.

It takes you several tries before you part me enough to enter me — I am, I realize, as dry as desert winds. But I spring an oasis as you persist, as the feel of sand grates between our bodies, as I feel rough grit enter me, piggybacking its way into me on your cock.

You are like a knife wrapped in sandpaper. You stab and abrade me as you pump me with firm, steady strokes. I squirm, impatient and wanting more. You laugh and grab my wrists with one hand. You put your other hand on one of my thighs and push against it, pinning me to the floor of the van, rendering me immobile. You and your cock rule me in this moment.

The friction is delicious — the friction of captor versus captive, of two bodies grinding, of sand within and sand between, your body against mine, driving the dirt into my skin. My nipples blaze, aching for the touch of your lips — no, for your teeth, clamping down and hurting! But you're only interested in straight-up fucking. No acrobatics. No fine twists of tantric subtleties. You pound away in a rhythm as persistent as the winds that howl around us.

Still, you grant me one small moment: You let go of my thigh and slide your hand between us, snaking your way to my clit. Your finger, caked with countless grains of sand, rubs me and urges me to come. Insistence batters my clit and drills my cunt, cock and finger working in unison to drive me onward.

And ever between us lies what I came for: the smell and feel of desert sand.

Now the friction burns. My skin feels torn in a thousand little places, inside and out. You grate against me with every thrust as you work me. I am helpless against this heated assault, against your finger and your cock. I feel a familiar tightness form within me; I sense it rising from beneath your finger. It comes to you and explodes around you, showering you with its own breathless panting.

I cry out. I come. It's so primal that it's simple.

My satisfaction barely subsides when you pull yourself from me and let go of my wrists. Your move startles me; you never stop before coming, and you always come inside me.

But you smile as you rise up and kneel over me. You stroke your cock and your smile widens. It becomes lewd. I realize you're stroking yourself just like they do in porn videos, and I know what you're after. In mere moments, your breath grows ragged, hurried, and a quick gasp tells me you're there.

You come, grunting, but your spunk doesn't shoot across me in a mad shower of force. Instead, it spills over your hand and runs onto my belly, like water bubbling from a nearly dry fountain. It pools atop the dirt and clumps there, oasis and desert, way more apropos than a standard "money shot."

You reach down and rub the come into the dirt until they blend. "A little memento for you," you claim.

We lie there, then, wrapped in a peaceful embrace. We kiss, often and lightly. I run my hand through your thinning hair, thankful that you understand my perverted wanderlust. Tears well in my eyes. Gratitude knows no bounds in the afterglow.

Soon, though, as I listen to you sleep, my mind drifts. I come to the aboriginal tale of creation where it is said that when the ancients traversed this land and gave it life, they left a trail of music as they passed. I wonder if the song they sang in this place now whispers in the wind. But as I listen to the diminishing storm, my eyes grow heavy and I hear the faint tinkling of bells, bells that sound at each plodding step of…what? Visions of Bedouins and camels rise in my drowsy mind and, as I drift off to sleep, I sense that I won't be sated for long. Soon, I will wander toward sand again.

Neti, Neti

ॐ

S. F. MAYFAIR

THE DREAM BEGAN A WEEK AFTER ELLEN LANDED IN
Bombay. It pursued her throughout India. Each morning she rose
early and joined the other college students on the tour, ate a breakfast of hard toast and sweet milky tea, and embarked on the day's
itinerary. She looked for the dream during the harsh daylight; she
fell into it in the soft night. Sometimes she heard peacocks call.

He came to her during the night. Ellen called this a dream,
but as the weeks passed she began to think it real. His scent, a
mixture of sandalwood and smoking fires, lingered on her skin.
When He withdrew from her, the loss left an ache between her
legs she could not distract. It was then that she began to notice
the vultures hovering in the trees.

Sometimes He'd enter her from above, His matted hair
trailing fires across her skin. Sometimes she'd mount Him, and
her head would touch the sky as she moved to take His hard and
unyielding flesh within her. He never spoke—there was no need.
She gave Him a lotus. Devouring it, He savored each petal, and

left bites on her skin. Their flesh mingled and ashes fell around them. He came to her naked and begging, and she did not know His name.

Ellen caught glimpses of Him during the day. Once she saw Him coming out of a temple doorway in a crowded street in Varanasi. She tried to follow Him through the narrow streets and alleyways. She pushed past the women in their bright saris, and was deaf to the begging children who followed in her wake. She ignored the stares of men lounging in the open shops who called for her to stop. The smell of temple incense mingled with frying street food and rotting garbage. A cow wearing a garland of yellow flowers around its neck blocked Ellen until she gently prodded it out of her way.

She followed His scent down to the *ghats*. At the edge of the river people were washing clothes or bathing. An older man, naked except for his *dhoti*, tried to give her flowers and mark her forehead with the colors of his god. She paused at the top of the *ghats* and looked out over the Ganges. She saw Him disappear across the river amid the smoke of the funeral pyres on the opposite bank. That night He came to her, reeking of death.

Ellen no longer talked and laughed with the other students. Often she would slip away from the tour. She gave her blue jeans away to a boy in Agra. She discarded tennis shoes in favor of sandals. She bought richly designed cotton *kurtas* and wore them over flowing skirts. She wove her long brown hair into a braid that tumbled down her back. Beneath her *kurta* and skirt she wore nothing, and moved slowly, with the feel of her flesh heavy against her. Each morning she wrapped garlands of jasmine around her wrists.

The air was ripe with anticipation of the monsoon rains. Dogs panted, resting in the shade of the trees outside the hotel. The sun beat down on the empty and dusty road that ran between the hotel and the temple ruins at Khajuraho. Ellen, unable to nap, roused one of the bicycle rickshaw drivers from his afternoon rest. Reluctant and sleepy, he mounted his bicycle and began to pedal. Sitting behind him in the cart, Ellen passively watched the driver's stringy tendons pull hard against the weight of the cart and its passenger.

The bicyclist stopped on the outskirts of the marketplace outside the avenue of empty temples. Ellen paid him, then looked up at the nearest temple. When she had visited it earlier that day with the other students, she'd been entranced by the beauty of the sandstone carvings decorating the outer walls of the ancient temples. The carvings depicted couples sensuously entwined in the act of love.

The guide, who led the students through the temples, had dwelt long on the eroticism of some of the carvings, and told the students these represented the play of the divine. A tall boy with long, wispy hair asked the guide what he meant by the "divine." The guide had tilted his head to one side and then back again in that gentle Indian way of shrugging, and had replied that the divine could not be described; it was *neti, neti,* not this, not that.

Ellen had paused before one carving of a couple whose elongated eyes and knowing smiles suggested they knew the secret of the temples. The woman's high round breasts pressed against the man's chest as she pushed her full hip against his groin. She stood firm with one leg crossed over the other as if taking a step to draw closer to her lover. Her full thighs tightly squeezed the man's fingers as he dipped them into her yoni. He rested his palm on her mons, and pulled her closer to him with the arm he wrapped around her slender waist. Her delicately shaped arm clung to his shoulders. She held her other hand beneath her chin as she tilted her head in dreamy repose.

Ellen caressed the woman's outwardly thrust foot. It was warm and smooth beneath her fingers. As she gazed up at the couple, Ellen felt a slight movement beneath her hand. The man's full lips curled in a possessive smile. The woman sighed. Glistening drops of arousal trailed down the woman's thigh and over her lover's hand. Ellen stretched her hand to touch the inviting moisture.

"It is madness to touch the divine, Memsahib," the guide had whispered in her ear.

She thought of the guide's words now as she walked toward an open stall selling fruits. A young boy of about eight appeared at her side. He was dressed in khaki shorts and a striped, short-sleeved shirt. His dark brown eyes were very bright in his small face as he chattered at her. He offered her a necklace of dark beads and beckoned her to come with him. Without accepting the necklace, she smiled, and followed him.

He led her to a temple by the marketplace. It differed from the others in its simplicity. Beside the steps that led up to its inner sanctum sat a young holy man. Without a second glance at the *sadhu*, Ellen left her sandals where the young boy indicated, and followed him up the steps.

She stepped into the dark coolness of the round room, which was carved from stone. It was bare of any adornment. Some light flowed in through spaces left blank between the stones. A large black stone lingam took up most of the room. It rested on a trough filled with a white, milky substance. A garland of flowers adorned the tip of the lingam; other flowers floated in the milk, filling the yoni at its base. In the lingam's shadow sat an elderly priest.

The little boy handed Ellen the bead necklace. She closely looked at it and saw that the beads were made from dark brown seeds. She thought it must be some sort of a rosary. The child moved to the far side of the lingam, closer to the priest, and gestured for Ellen to stay where she was.

The priest chanted as he poured milk and *ghee* over the lingam. The air was dense from the smoke and the scent of sandalwood. The priest continued to chant to the god Shiva as he beat a gong. The sounds, echoing off the walls, filled the small room and charged the air with a dark electricity. Ellen focused on the milk as it flowed from the lingam into the yoni.

She felt a sharp bite of heat in the small of her back. The young *sadhu* stood behind her. She looked into His eyes. He had come for her. The *sadhu* silently walked out of the sanctuary. Ellen glanced over at the little boy, who smiled and nodded encouragingly. She turned to follow Him into the hot afternoon sun.

He led her across the deserted marketplace and into the avenue of ruined temples. He entered the tallest temple. She followed Him through the temple's porch and into its dark halls. The air felt cool against her skin. He began to climb the steps of the tower adjoining the temple's recessed inner sanctum. Keeping several paces behind Him, she followed. The air grew colder with each step she climbed. Snow drifted down and caressed her cheeks. They climbed until they reached the peak. There, He led her into a shadowed room.

He took off His *dhoti*, shook it out, and spread it on the floor. He was slender and muscular. His black hair hung in long, tangled locks down the hard planes of His back. He smiled at her while He removed the flower garlands she wore around her wrists. He scattered the flowers, and the scent of jasmine filled the air as the petals fluttered to the white cloth. He removed the seed rosary from her hand and placed it over her head to leave it dangling from her neck.

He stood waiting. She drew the *kurta* over her head and dropped it by her side. She untied her skirt and let it slide to her ankles. She stepped out of it. She stood naked before Him, as she'd done in her dreams. He placed His palm flat between her breasts. His heat seared her. She fell on her knees before Him, and rested her forehead on His feet.

Her hands caressed His ankles. She slowly moved them up His legs, testing each hidden muscle, and massaging it until she had memorized it. At the base of His lingam she paused, and cupped her hands beneath it. She looked up at Him in supplication. He briefly rested His hand on her head, and then removed the strip of cloth that bound her braid. Her hair floated free.

She brought her tongue close to taste His sweetness. Gently, she drew Him into her mouth, savoring His strength and His power. Her tongue wrapped around Him as she licked the length of Him. His hardness sawed and scraped across her soft lips as she tried to swallow Him. As she sucked, the ache between her legs increased. Whimpering, she fed on His nectar, and tightly clung to Him.

Roughly, He pulled her away from His lingam, and pushed her to the floor. His wild hair blazed as He leaned over her. Ashes fell in her eyes. She opened her legs wide to receive Him. He thrust into her, and she felt herself split open. Her yoni expanded and encompassed all the worlds of all the universes. She pushed against Him, trying to pull Him deep within her. He pushed hard, and established a rhythm to which she could only cling.

He moved with the force of lightning. She felt the thunder in her ears. Her smile ripped her face. Her flesh burned. He was everywhere — inside her, outside her, around her. There was neither a beginning nor an ending to their joining. She felt petals of jasmine brush her face.

Crying, she screamed her joy as He thrust harder into her. She mated with a god. She surrendered, and the air was rent with the touch of that which was not and could not be. She scraped her fingers down His back, and saw her own blood dripping from her hands. He took her into Him, and the dance they did was of violence and of gentleness. He destroyed that which was her. He made her His, and she opened more. He tore her heart from her. She knew it was safe within Him. She gave Him love and devotion. Not satisfied, He took more.

He held her wrists in His hands as she writhed beneath Him. Their bodies crashed against each other. They churned the white foam of the sea in the midst of a desert. She looked up into His eyes, and saw her world burning. He touched her parched lips with His tongue, and the ocean cascaded over her. When His mouth touched her breasts in gusts of breath and sweet tenderness, she knew what it was to live. When He blew His breath into her, she gave Him hers. He took His lips away, and she knew what it was to die a thousand times. She felt herself burning on the pyres through which He walked at dawn. Peacocks joined their call with vultures. She heard them cry.

His mouth touched the lips of her yoni. His tongue poured *ghee* into her fire. She blazed, lighting up the sky. Her substance became His. And He did not care. She was the dance He had danced throughout eternity. He took her. He stretched her. He

183

dismembered all that she was. He carelessly dropped her breasts and her yoni as He ranged across the world. She fell to earth in a crush of sorrow. She fell to earth in a crush of joy. His dance was wild as He pounded into her. Gentleness was denied by this ascetic, who took her body to use as an instrument for His wild dance. He knew no mercy. She was rushed to the extremes of the universe. She was drowned in His fire. She was lost in her love for Him. She wanted only to be His.

The naked ascetic, who owns nothing, would not take her. She died as His seed rushed into her. She was lost in the ache that covered a thousand worlds and a million years. To have given everything and to have lost everything.... This she knew as He closed her eyes and gently kissed her eyelids. This she knew as she felt Him leave her there in the dark. She felt the wet between her legs. Her body was no more. She was no more. She was *neti, neti*.

The little boy sat waiting on the steps of the temple. Ellen, naked except for a widow's white cloth draped over her shoulders and the rosary she wore around her neck, stumbled out of the temple and into the dusty, hot afternoon. Gently, the little boy took her hand and led her away. Her hair was wild with death and with love. She reeked of smoking fires and of sandalwood.

A little boy led the mad woman away from the holy temples. *"Neti, neti,"* the woman chanted, her eyes unseeing. The little boy tightly held the woman's hand, and led her away.

Triton Rising

ॐ

David Garnes

AFTER BARELY MORE THAN A DAY IN ATHENS, John knew he needed to get out of the city. The August heat, the awful snarls of traffic, the exhaust that hung heavy in the noxious air and—not least of all—his own shaky state of affairs: It was all too much.

Even the small hotel he remembered from before (Martin had insisted back then that they stay in the old Plaka district, within walking distance of the Acropolis) seemed changed, diminished in charm. His room was clean and pleasant enough, with whitewashed walls and a French door that opened to a wrap-around balcony connecting the outside rooms. If he leaned carefully over the edge of the wrought-iron railing, John could see a corner column of the Parthenon rising high above the jumble of open-fronted shops and taverna signs and rooftop umbrella tables.

But had it been this noisy, even in the early afternoon? Maybe he and Martin hadn't spent much time in their room, at least not during the day, he reflected wryly. At night, tired and eager for the tiny bed they shared, they wouldn't have noticed or minded the din of passersby in the narrow street below or the incessant sound of *bouzouki* music that lasted into the early hours.

John had headed straight for the Acropolis when he arrived from London the day before. To his surprise, he was feeling relatively relaxed, hopeful, even, for a good afternoon. He climbed the steep, winding street that led from his hotel to the entrance to the citadel, where he waited in line with a swarm of Japanese tourists taking photographs of everything in sight. A handsome Scandinavian or possibly German couple, healthy and blond and dressed in identical khaki shirts and skimpy shorts, asked if he'd take their picture.

He obliged, but replied, "No, I've no camera," when they asked if he'd like his taken too. Not this time, he thought, remembering the expensive Canon, complete with light meter and tripod, that Martin had insisted on lugging absolutely everywhere on their trips.

As John returned the camera, he noticed the large bulge at the young man's button fly. As if aware of John's glance, the man adjusted himself even further to one side with a quick hitch of his fingers. He smiled and walked away, his calves rounded and muscular, his buttocks two perfect mounds moving beneath the stretched cotton of his shorts.

Once past the ticket booth, John was disappointed to find that the Parthenon, rising before him and dominating the rocky terrain, was now chained off to visitors. On their earlier visit he and Martin had spent the whole morning on the Acropolis, wandering around the rocky expanse but repeatedly drawn back to the magnificent temple. They had roamed its vast open interior and later sat on the sun-baked steps under the east pediment, eating oranges and basking in the heat.

"You're right beneath where the horse would be, my dear," John had said, referring to that majestic head now sitting, incongruously, in the climate-controlled confines of the British Museum.

"No, no," Martin had replied, "We're under the chariot of Helios—remember, it's approaching on the left, for sunrise. I'm

Helios and you're sitting facing me—Dionysus, if I remember correctly. Actually, since you're the swimmer in the family, by rights you should be Poseidon, but he's over on the west pediment. Dionysus will do, but you must sit back and open your legs a bit and look at me with lust in your eyes."

John had dutifully obliged. Martin threw back his head and laughed, the narrow chain around his neck glinting in the noonday sun. His shirt was open in the front, and a line of brown hair peeked over the waistband of his jeans.

John had an urge to run his tongue up and down that wavy line of hair, but instead he watched the juice of the orange run down Martin's big-veined hand. Martin slowly licked his fingers before leaning back against one of the massive columns. That moment was a long time ago, but John could still see that hand so clearly, Martin's hand, warm and strong even when the rest of his body had diminished.

Now, after spending just a few minutes circling the exterior of the Parthenon, John headed back down the narrow street into the Plaka. He told himself he'd return the next morning, before the hordes of tourists descended. He stopped in a small café and ordered a Greek coffee, which he drank quickly. He sat for a while and watched a little black dog methodically clean scraps from under each of the café's tables. The coffee had made him jittery, and he decided he wanted a walk. He headed in the direction of Syntagma Square, in the center of the city.

John passed the Odeum of Herodes Atticus, the mammoth open theater where he and Martin had watched from an upper tier, enthralled as the Greek words of Sophocles rang out in the starry night. The stone slabs on which they sat still held the day's heat, though the evening air was chilly. Now, the glare of the late afternoon sun blinded him, and John's eyes began to tear from the exhaust-filled air, worse than he remembered from before. The din of the traffic was overwhelming, the horns of the cars and trucks and buses a dreadful cacophony of hoots and wails.

As he walked, John was reminded of the beauty of the Greek men, young and old alike, who passed him on the street.

He loved the blackness of their hair and the somewhat sinister allure of their thick moustaches and piercing eyes.

Did he imagine that a couple of them glanced at him with a certain interest? A handsome youth with curly dark ringlets walked toward him, definitely making eye contact as he passed. John turned to look back, but the boy had already disappeared in the crowd.

John reached the towering, rust-colored columns of the Temple of Zeus, rising unexpectedly amidst the asphalt and concrete on its tiny island of greenery. He negotiated, barely, the careening taxis on Olgas and walked along the border of the lush National Garden, near the Memorial to the Unknown Soldier.

From around a corner, two Greek soldiers approached, dressed in the uniform of the Euzones, the ceremonial military guard. Each wore a tasseled hat, a blousy white shirt, an embroidered vest, and a *foustanella* – a short pleated skirt that bounced mid-thigh around their white-hosed legs. Had these serious young men not been so swarthy and muscled, the effect would have been disconcerting or amusing, but somehow even the fluffy pompons on their hobnailed shoes were of a piece with the heavy brown rifles they held at rest against their shoulders.

By the time John reached Syntagma Square, he was drenched with sweat, a bit dizzy, and slightly out of breath. The air was really foul. So much for my tranquil state, he thought. He collapsed in a chair at an outdoor café near the edge of the square and ordered *retsina*. As he raised the narrow glass to his lips, John remembered the surprising jolt of the clear liquid with its bitter but not unpleasant taste of resin.

John was finishing his wine when he noticed a man leaning against a stone post further into the square, near a kiosk overflowing with newspapers and colorful magazines. The man was bearded and dressed in a very white loose shirt and white pants. Like the youth John had passed in the street, he too seemed to be smiling. Emboldened by the *retsina,* John smiled back.

The heat and the wine made the air seem to ripple in front of him, the effect not unlike the feeling John frequently experienced underwater, when everything before him was magically transformed into silence and shimmering movement. He fanned the air in a half-conscious gesture of beckoning, but this ambiguous effort got no response. The man continued to stare and smile. He took a long drag on the cigarette he was smoking, slowly exhaled, and then flicked the butt in John's direction.

No more, enough, I must get up and leave now, John thought. He motioned to the waiter and paid his bill. As he left the square, he glanced back and realized the man had moved from his station near the kiosk and appeared to be following him.

The walk back to the Plaka cleared John's head, and he tried to fix on a plan of some sort and not think about the man. What about tonight? Tomorrow? What *had* he come to Athens to do? This? He wondered if he was still being followed, but decided not to turn his head to see. He began to think of Martin and felt worse, although he knew that Martin would not be judging him. "Don't stop your life after me, John, promise. Stay alive," Martin had said many times, especially in those last weeks.

When John got to his room, he opened the door to the balcony and peered down cautiously into the narrow street. The man was standing at the corner. John stepped back quickly, not sure if he had been observed.

He closed the shutters, took off his clothes, splashed cold water on his face from the tiny sink in a corner of his room, and lay face-up on his bed. He was aware that his door was unlocked and that his balcony windows were open as well, offering entry from any of the outer doors or rooms on the floor. Glancing to his left, he could see himself in the framed mirror on the low dresser. The sight of his pale, naked body in the shaded room excited him and he began to fondle himself. He was surprised when he immediately became hard.

John heard a slight tap on his door. His heart began to pound but he did not lose his erection.

"Come in," he said.

The door quickly opened and the bearded man entered. Without a word, he approached John's bed and stood over him.

He loosened his shirt and raised it over his head, tossing it on the floor. His chest was heavily matted, and he was wearing a chain with a cross half-hidden in damp swirls of black hair.

John rose to a sitting position, unbuckled the man's belt, and tugged at his pants. As they slid to his feet, the man's erect cock bobbed up and down in front of John's face. John licked its warm, veined underside and drew the man down on top of him.

The fan above the bed did little to cool the steamy August air, and soon both John and the man were drenched. John's hands slid against the wet of the man's back as they probed each other's mouths with their tongues. The smell of the man's body, mixed with the tobacco smoke in his hair and beard, was intoxicating.

The man raised himself for a moment, and John was drawn to the glint of the golden cross reflected in the mirror as it dangled between their naked bodies. At that instant he thought of Martin's chain and how it had flashed in the sunlight that day on the Acropolis. Martin....

John couldn't take his eyes from the mirror. He tried to continue, but it was no use.

"I'm sorry," he said, gesturing downward.

"So...OK." The man shrugged. He straddled John and began to jerk off. Even in the shaded dusk of the room, John could see the shiny, purple head of the man's cock, a faint drop of moisture glistening at its tip, as the foreskin easily slid back and forth under the powerful thrust of his fist.

John grasped the man's heavy thighs and watched as his strokes became more urgent. The man played with John's nipples and slapped John's wet belly with his free hand.

Suddenly, the man arched his back and cried out. John could feel the hot liquid fall on his chest and stomach. The man remained motionless, his eyes closed and his weight heavy on John's thighs.

Finally, he swung his leg over John's body and moved off the bed. He washed himself in the sink and dressed quickly. With a quick tug of John's foot, he turned and walked to the door, and then he was gone.

John remained motionless on his back, his body gradually chilling under the silent fan circling above him. He was unsure of how he felt. He thought of Martin and of the heat and smell of the bearded man and again of Martin and the small bed they had occupied on another floor. He lay awake a long while listening to the music in the street below before drifting into a fitful sleep.

It was when he awoke very early the next morning that John knew he needed to get away from the noise and pollution of the city. Through the owner of the hotel he arranged for a car, and purchased the makings for a picnic lunch at a small grocery next door. After more than ample directions from the clerk at the nearby rental office and a tense fifteen minutes negotiating the rush-hour traffic, he found himself on the coastal road heading south to Sounion.

The day was clear and sunny and the breeze against John's face invigorating. Already he was feeling much improved. He followed the narrow highway as it wound in and out of rocky coves and past tiny sandy beaches. He considered stopping for a quick dip, since already he was missing his daily swim back home. John glanced at the sea only steps away from the road and thought ironically of his club's pool, whose venerable mosaics and faded seaside murals were meant to evoke some spa from classical antiquity.

Soon, however, he saw rising in the distance, outlined against the brilliant blue sky, the pillars of a temple. John immediately recognized this as the shrine of the god of the sea, Poseidon—for over two thousand years a lonely talisman for sailors heading out into the Aegean, and a welcoming beacon for those returning home.

John drove into a small parking lot near the foot of a hill leading to the temple. There was no one in attendance, so he carefully rolled up the window and locked the car. From a distance, the ruin had appeared small and insignificant, but as he walked up the sun-baked incline of scrub and sandstone, he became aware of its majestic proportions. A lone figure—perhaps another early riser, but without a car?—emerged briefly from behind a white column before disappearing on the other side of the rise.

John reached the top of the bluff and entered the exposed interior of the temple. He ran his hand along a pitted shaft of marble and gazed at the Aegean below...Homer's *wine-dark sea,* today an azure blue, motionless except for the slow movement of a boat far off to the south, sailing in the direction of distant Santorini and Crete.

John seated himself against a fallen stone slab at the edge of the temple. He was suddenly hungry for the feta cheese and olives and bread he had bought before leaving Athens. He was tempted to open the bottle of wine he had also purchased, but it was rather early, and he was still feeling a bit ragged from the day before. He decided to wait awhile.

A steady breeze blew in from the sea, tempering somewhat the heat of the summer morning. The sun beat down on the white marble, and the droning rhythm of cicadas underlay the faint rustling of the low brush. John closed his eyes and raised his face to the sky, conscious of the solid warmth of the stone under his bare legs. He thought again of that day with Martin at the Parthenon, and he imagined the taste of the orange that Martin had held in his hands.

Some minutes later, the gust of a stronger wind from the sea stirred him. When he adjusted his gaze, John became aware of someone at the opposite end of the ruin. It was the person he had spotted a while ago, but as his eyes became focused, John could see with a start that the man was not a tourist. He was barefoot and wore loose-fitting trousers and no shirt, and he was unusually tall. The two columns that framed him were massive, but they did not diminish him as he straddled the space between.

What was most astonishing was that, except for his exceptional height, he bore a striking resemblance to the anonymous man of the previous evening. John would have been somewhat afraid but for this man's incredible beauty and the serenity of his presence. He had a black beard and long hair that curled around his forehead and shoulders. He was not slim but his tanned body was perfectly proportioned, effortlessly graceful, as he stood motionless against the panorama of sky and temple. Like a

sculpture in an ancient frieze or the silhouetted figures in a terra-
cotta vase, he seemed of no particular age.

Eventually, the man turned away and began to make his
way down the hill on the opposite side of the temple. John slowly
rose and followed what seemed to be a path leading to the sea.

As they reached the bottom of the steep incline, John saw that
they had arrived at a small beach, a secluded inlet with a white
patch of sand no more than fifty or sixty feet wide. They were alone
except for a young man and woman stretched out on a blanket,
both very blond and tanned and naked. My picture-taking
couple from the Acropolis, thought John. How extraordinary.

The man passed the sunbathers but they seemed to take no
notice of him. He reached the edge of the sea and, without pausing, waded slowly into the water. When he was waist-deep he
began to swim and soon disappeared around an outcropping of
smooth boulders at the entrance to the inlet.

The light and the heat were intense. John shielded his eyes
and gazed from the glittering blue of the sea to the blinding
whiteness above. Helios riding his chariot across the heavens,
John thought. *Look, John, look, he's almost halfway there,* Martin
would have said.

John stripped to his shorts and walked over to the couple.
They were both on their stomachs, their bodies close together
and their faces touching.

"Well, hello there!" John said, before he realized that this
was not his blond pair at all. "Oh, sorry, excuse me...may I?" he
asked, pointing to his clothes and then to the sea.

As he turned over to acknowledge John, the man instinc-
tively made a motion to cover himself, but then he laughed and
raised his hand to his eyes to shield himself from the sun. He had
an erection, and as he moved, his pink cock slapped taut against
his stomach. His partner smiled sleepily and stroked the man's
chest with her fingers. "Ya, sure, please," he said, motioning to a
corner of the blanket. The man's teeth were very white against
his tanned face, and the pale hairs on his body gleamed in the
sunlight.

John placed his clothes near the man's upturned feet, and then he turned and walked into the warm water. The only sound in the still air was the soft and measured splash of tiny waves. The sea was very clear, and schools of little silverfish darted in every direction as John began to swim slowly from shore. He spotted a tiny sea horse floating upright near the sandy bottom, motionless as if waiting for its rider to return.

John reached the white boulders where the man had disappeared. He cupped their smoothness and made his way around to another small inlet that led, not to a beach, but to a sheer wall of rock. The man was about forty feet in front of him, swimming slowly in a wide circle. He had taken off his white trousers and tied them around his neck, where they billowed behind him like gauzy wings.

When the man saw John, he paused and appeared to stand. The water was up to his shoulders, which told John that it was way over his own head. The man leaned back and shook his mane of black curls. Drops of water exploded and evaporated in the sunlight. He looked toward John and inclined his head slightly — in greeting or invitation, John couldn't be sure.

John swam a bit closer and circled about the man. He dove underwater, where he could see the man clearly in front of him, arms bent on either side of his waist and legs spread wide apart, like some colossus of the deep. His cock, long and milky white in the pale aqua of the water, swayed slowly to the rhythm of his slightly moving body.

John surfaced, and this time the man smiled and then laughed. John dove again and swam underwater toward him. The man's hand rippled slowly through the water, beckoning. As John moved through his outstretched legs, the sides of his body brushed against the man's thighs. He felt the heaviness of the man's genitals softly grazing his back as they bobbed up and down in the still water.

John surfaced again and exhaled deeply. He took a deep breath and once again glided silently toward the man. This time, when he reached the man's massive legs, John grasped hold of them and kneeled on the fine-grained sand of the sea floor. The man lifted his cock with the palm of his hand and guided it to John's lips. He became hard as soon as John began moving back and forth. Despite its thickness, John was able to take the entire shaft of the man's cock. Soon he could feel its engorged head touching the back of his mouth. At each thrust, John's forehead brushed against the silky hair and knotted muscles of the man's lower body.

When he finally came up for air, John noticed a gap back against the rocks behind them. He took the man's hand firmly in his own and they began to swim toward the cliff, the man smiling enigmatically, as if amused by John's assertiveness.

Through the small arched opening, they swam into a little cave whose narrow roof was open to the sky. At the opposite end was a small strip of dry sand, hidden from the outside. John eased out of the water and lay back, raising his buttocks and stripping off his shorts. He beckoned the man to join him.

For a while they remained motionless, the sun quickly drying their bodies. John was excited, exhilarated even, yet at the same time strangely at ease.

The man gestured at John's cock, and he realized that he had become hard. He leaned over to take the man in his mouth again, but instead the man motioned John to move up to his face.

John leaned over and the man began to suck John's cock, his huge hands and fingers kneading John's ass. John knew he could not hold back for long, and he pulled away, motioning for the man to stop.

He moved down to the man's feet. He kissed and sucked the man's toes and rubbed them gently against his cheek. John moved past the man's legs, burying his face in the warmth of his inner thighs.

John then moved on top of the man, straddling his chest and rubbing his cock against his own. He thought of his hot and sweaty visitor from the night before, dimly silhouetted in the mirror. He thought of all the Greek men he had passed in the street, and the beautiful man on the beach with his big hard cock.

He thought of Martin, this time remembering with joy and passion the nights they had spent in that little room in the Plaka. And finally he thought of nothing but the feel of the man's body beneath his own, the hardness of his muscled thighs, and the damp warmth of his stomach and chest.

John came quickly, the sound of his cries echoing in the small cave. He opened his eyes and looked down at the man stretched under him, his face in profile, his body bathed in the light from the narrow opening above. The man slowly rubbed John's semen into his furry chest. John breathed deeply and rolled over and lay beside him. He watched the man's upturned foot make slow, lazy circles in the air, his arched toes circling around and around in the silence.

When John awoke the man was gone, and the rays of the sun had shifted. The cave was shadowed and peaceful, quiet except for the gentle lapping of waves. John slowly rose, put on his shorts, and paddled back out into the sunlight. As he made his way to the shore of the beach, he began to swim with increasing power and speed. He stopped midway to catch his breath and raised his head to the still-blazing afternoon sun—Helios more than halfway home, but still there, always there guiding me, he thought. John smiled to himself.

He yelled and dove deeply into the blue-green sea. As he resurfaced, the water exploding around him, he cried, "I'm alive, Martin. I'm alive, my dear. *I am alive.*"

The Beach Hut

༄

KIERON DEVLIN

MY MUM STILL BELIEVES IN THE GENERATION GAP, in traditions.

"Your father and I were married after we left school. We did everything the right way. We did what was expected of us. Not like nowadays," Mum says, toying with her straggly wet hair. As if how quickly you get hitched and sign the contract is what matters. She's never woken up to the fact that Dad has gone, that world has gone. She's refused to see anyone else since he left. I keep a picture of Dad too. He's standing on a beach in wet swimming togs. I keep it locked in my diary. If she found it, she'd be in a rage, or in tears. Her temper is like English weather—only without the benefit of a forecast.

She says this stuff about getting married all the time. I roll my eyes. I'm forced to switch on the morning news on the telly. I say "Oh, right," and she goes on, and I say, "Is that so?" or, "Well, I've got to go now. The bus'll be coming," and I stand at the door, waiting for the kiss she never lets me go without. To her, I'm a good boy, who just might have "tendencies." Hate the word. She thought I'd become one of those boys to get *anorexia nervosa*. But that's not me. I'm just a picky eater, and she doesn't want to see the difference. She worries because she loves to worry—she just picks on something to worry it to death. The focus is on me because I'm the only one there.

Yesterday, I overheard her in the hallway phoning Dr. Vashti. She was jotting something on a notepad. When I checked it later, it said "nocturnal emissions." She'd found a stain on my bed sheets and freaked out. She sulked all day, and in the evening demanded to know what was wrong with me. I turned away in disgust. She says loudly that all those Brighton perverts loitering in public gardens and on the seafront behind the rhododendrons should be hanged. She'd have a long line of executions if she could. And it's not just the pervs: She follows stories of killers, psychos, and weirdoes on TV. I think she's the one who's crazed, but what can I do?—she's my mum. You can't change them or send them back for repair.

"I'll be back home for practice," I say.

"Yes, you have to do your scales."

Mum is so proud of my piano playing, but it embarrasses me. My fingers are awkward.

"All right, darling. Off you go. Have a lovely day." And she folds her arms. I close the door neatly so as not to let it slam. She doesn't like noise. It reminds her of migraine days. She's got me trained to creep around the house on tiptoe.

• • •

I walk to the bus stop opposite the traffic lights. There's a light rain, a gray sky—nothing new in Brighton. The school is in Kemptown, up the hill. It's one of those red brick buildings built in the sixties: It looks like they skimped on decent materials. At least it hasn't had a demolition order placed on it yet. I never get to choose which school I go to. *She* always decides that. She claims it's one of the best in the area. They all claim to be "best." We've moved several times in the past few years. I sort of look forward to the disruptions now.

The English class is boring: *In Memoriam* by Tennyson, as if we haven't already had enough of eulogies to departed friends. By early afternoon, I begin to feel woozy and sick—maybe the salmon paste was off. Mum doesn't always remember to put the lid back on the jar. I put my hand up and ask if I can go home. The teacher has a high-pressure face, and his nose looks ironed flat. He looks at me suspiciously and murmurs something about it being irregular, but then he relents and lets me go. In the toilet I wash my face; it's pasty looking and I'm hollow eyed. On the wall some graffiti says: EAT MORE PUSSY. I wonder what they normally eat at this school then, that they have to be reminded.

Outside, the air is wet and salty. Once out of the gates, I begin to feel better and wonder whether I'm allergic to school. I just know I won't get on with the other boys or girls there. They all look arrogant pups, Xeroxes of their yuppie parents. Each time I arrive in a different school, no one's ever sure what to make of me. The first few weeks are agony—I don't make friends easily. When the boys find out that I play the classical piano, they look at me as if I'm a weirdo—not only precocious, but precious/precocious, a double freak. Add pretty and they're foaming at the mouth, it's so unpronounceable. They can't stand that. At this new school, the boys will strut and comb their greasy hair, have fringes that barely cover their pimples. They'll act like gangs of sixties' mods, pretended rock stars. Not one of them knows the first thing about real music. They'll all end up with jobs in the City, or as insurance salesmen, or renting cars.

• • •

Early afternoon, this town is quiet. Not many buses. I sit on the wall to wait. I watch every car that passes, as it lends movement to the scene. The sky is full of turbulent clouds. There'll be a downpour of rain any second, and I have no umbrella. The English Channel bears the worst of the wet, relentless Atlantic winds. There's supposed to be a warm current, but I think geographers have fooled us. The wind can howl, and sea freezes toes on the spot.

I'm distracted from my book. The wall feels cold and damp on my backside, so I step off. A girl is coming toward me. She pulls a long pink streak of chewed gum out of her mouth, then presses it onto the bus timetable on the side of the lamp post. She, oblivious to me, rummages in her bag, takes out a half-finished bottle of Lucozade, swigs it back, tosses the bottle into the waste bin, and disappears into the newsagent's. The bus draws up at the curb. Just as I'm snapping my ticket in the machine, I look back. The funny girl's sticking a magazine up her angora sweater when the Pakistani shop assistant isn't looking; she legs it for the bus. I tell the driver, a black man with white whiskers, to wait. He nods and the engine purrs. As I sit down, I hear a scream, and the side of the bus vibrates, "Tell him to stop. Stop that bus!" The doors are sliding shut; in two great athletic leaps, her foot is sandwiched between the rubber buffers and she's banging on the side of the bus. The driver, unfazed, reopens, and passengers turn to see who's made such a racket. She pops in a new stick of green gum, unconcerned by the stares she's getting. She's done something to her hair that looks savage, as if she used shearing scissors dipped in paint. It's all tufted and tussocked blue and green with a long, spider-leg fringe that drops over one side of her face, obscuring the eye. She has a series of rings on the lobe of her left ear, each one bigger than the next. I wonder if she sleeps in them. Yet she still wears the uniform colors on her jacket. She sits just behind me making great sighing, sucking noises. She pulls the magazines out but tosses them to one side.

"I'm so bored with school," she says, "I took the afternoon off." Then comes a smile, more of a smirk. "You got the same idea too?"

"I'm sick. I got permission," I say, looking round the bus to see who's listening. A couple of old men up front turn their heads.

"Yeah, right, " she says. Instead of annoying me, I start to see the funny side too. She makes me laugh—something I don't normally do. She's got my attention.

"Why are you bored?" I ask.

"Because I am," she says. "You don't have to have a reason." There's something weird and sour about this reflection, but I basically agree. "The place is fucking doolalley. And the teachers stink."

I don't say much until other people do. I open up gradually. This girl has speeded up that process. She's so outspoken. Her skin is white like bleached stone. She's taller than I am, too. I don't ask her why she's taking off from school as it's sure to be punishable, something I'd never dare to do. Or maybe she'll lie. She says the kind of things I never speak aloud. She folds her arms and taps her fingers on the rail on the back of the seat, never sitting still.

"I haven't seen you before," she says. "You're new."

"I've only been here a couple of months. We move around a lot."

"Things never go the way you want them to. Have you ever noticed that?"

"Yep," I say.

"School's a bitch. I hate it. They are just trying to socialize us, prepackage us fit for 'society.'" She says the word society in a mocking way. I like that.

"You never learn anything useful at school anyway, even a sixth-form college," I say. Although I had never uttered that before, I just know I believe it from this moment on.

"And the way everyone behaves is SOOOO Bad." She says this as if she is not a kid herself but totally grown up. She says I must come round. That quick. I believe I've been picked up already, that she's interested. I don't have to try. She shows me her house through the dirt-streaked bus window. She says I can phone her anytime.

"Here," she says, "give me your hand." She takes a green felt marker pen and scribbles a number on my skin. She stops to admire her work, and then adds a smiley face, only her version has a frown. Her joke, I suppose. But it's frisky. Is this the kind of girl my Mum wants for me? I don't think so. The idea of inviting her home does not seem promising. She looks like a punk, and

Mum would die. So for days I keep it quiet, and Mum doesn't guess what's on my mind.

• • •

I phone the girl; she sounds just as lively on the phone. We agree to meet; it feels important, like a big date. That makes me think hard: What am I supposed to do? I've never told anyone that I've never done it before. I tell myself that this time at least I won't run away. I did that once with a girl at another school. I saw her waiting but changed my mind. The whole thing left me cold, didn't know why—and we hadn't even kissed. She never spoke to me again.

Two weeks later, it's a Tuesday evening, I have no piano class, so I decide to call her again. There's no time to talk at school. She says to meet at the clock tower. First thing she says is that I mustn't call her Yvonne but "I've won," which is what she has painted on her torn-off T-shirt. She says she's busked in a skiffle group, and in the market square. She even got real money. My playing Chopin and Mozart impresses her, so I feel she might be all right, not stupid like the rest of them. She says that I could busk too if I bought a portable electric piano, ruffled up my hair a bit, tore a hole in my jacket or something. Maybe she could sing to my accompaniment. She talks fast; she has idea-flow, comes out with stuff I never thought of. We go down to the main pier. There's a show going on—kiddies doing ballroom dancing, look-ing like tiny, old-age pensioners. Yvonne says she's going to be a famous singer one day, she just needs a break. I think she may not have the patience, but the urge is without question. "But the police tend to move buskers on, they don't like musicians. We're not rich enough," I say. If I start to hang around with this group of punks, I might end up shaving my head too. I might start to look scabby. Or turn Mohican.

We sit down on a bench and look out toward the sea. This always makes me sad. Yvonne starts talking. I just listen. We do this a few times. Then, one day she tells me, "I got an offer from this dishy bloke. He saw me singing in the square and came up to me. He said he'd take me to London and I could stay at his place in Paddington, while he arranged a recording contract for me. Must've thought I was born yesterday, a Brighton yokel. He was a dirty rotten liar. I went with him, just 'cos I needed the free ride to London. Turned out he didn't have any links to the music business at all. He runs a mail order company, selling kinky lingerie. All he wanted was sex."

She offers me a cigarette. I'm afraid to tell her I don't smoke, in case she laughs and says I'm a wimp. Today's different, though, so I accept it straight away. Be cool, I think. Look cool, like Yvonne. I take a drag, holding it loosely between my index and second fingers. It tastes foul. I cough.

"I'm still ill. I had a chest infection," I say.

She nods. "Don't overdo it there, man. It's not even a joint."

I'm puzzled but sort of guess that she means marijuana. She must have tried everything. I can't remember knowing anyone else who talks this freely. We start walking toward the ramshackle west pier, pulling up collars against the wind. Then she looks at me and winks. "Let's go to this place I know."

"Where?"

"It's a beach hut. It's really nice. I broke into it. No one ever goes there, and we can hide out. Come on."

I've never broken into anywhere before, but decide this is a day of many firsts, and if Plato could do it in *Rebel Without a Cause*, so could I. Yvonne is my Natalie Wood. We don't have a James Dean with us, but I follow her anyway.

She can walk faster than I can. I tell her to slow down. We go all the way to the end of the promenade, past Hove, toward Portslade. We pass all the miniature golf courses, the tea shops, and the bowling greens. We come to a line of decrepit beach huts, some brightly painted yellow and pink, others warped, shabbier, more neglected. The one she points to is a dirty maroon; it has paint flaking and cracking off in large strips. It stands right at the very end, nudged in between a sheltering wall and the beach front. It has a huge padlock on it, just for show. She knocks it open without even getting rust on her black fingernails. We go inside. It's very sparse, like a monk's cell, the perfect hideaway. There's just a tiny fold-up bed that creaks, its chrome legs also rusted. There's a table splattered with candle wax, and a cupboard falling off its hinges, full of dried-up tea bags and sugar with black bits that could be mouse droppings. It smells of creosote and rotting wood. We decide to sit with the door open and look out at the scene before us, which is—how did I guess?—gray snot-green and ball-freezing cold. It goes quiet, she draws a breath, says she's meditating, intoning an OMMMM, so we can hear the waves licking the shore and drift into the rhythm of the sea. All I hear is my stomach telling me I'm hungry.

"Let's lie down on the floor, and let our heads hang out," she says.

"OK," I say, so we get down on our backs. I loll my head out of the window. She squeals. "It's a good way to get high without the drugs," she says. "I once took acid here and all the beach pebbles were my little friends." I look at them to check if they might speak. Then, my eyes look up. I see the total sky. I loll my head further back. I see the total sea. Yvonne makes me see things fresh. From this vantage point, the sea looks like a heavy sky weighing down on a beach of pebbles that is in fact the sky— it's in reverse. I'm getting into this. One star glimmers through the evening sky, and it seems it's winking at us. We stay quiet like this for a while. There's no one around on this part of the beach, not even anyone walking a dog. I notice she's stopped talking and has put her hand near mine.

"We need music," she says.

"Sing then," I say, thinking I want to hear anything that isn't classical. So she starts a song about two people sitting in a room who sound morbid. I listen, and think, *That's just how I'm feeling. How does she know?* When she's finished, I say, "That's great. It's really sad. I like sad songs."

"It's written by this band. Friends of mine. Nobody knows them yet, but they are going to be mega famous."

She gets up from the floor and pulls open the bed. She sits on it and lights a cigarette.

"What happened, then, with the man who promised you a contract?"

"Oh, that was chronic. He went off with this other girl. A fat cow. She sucks his cock and does anything he wants her to. That's not love."

"No, it's not," I say. I've never heard anyone utter the word *cock* so casually before, but I don't blanch. She seems strong where I'm weak. But I feel nervous that she's going to pounce. I just feel it. "What did you do with this man?"

"Oh, I don't know. Everything! He talked a lot. It was all rubbish. I don't know what I saw in him, really. He wasn't very good. When he made love it was all over in seconds."

I imagine this. He must have been in a hurry. Maybe he's the one who looks like James Dean. If it were James Dean, then I wouldn't mind. *He* could be as fast as he liked.

"Where is he now?"

"They're working in some casino on the French Riviera...but" — I wait for more to come — "I don't fucking care where they are."

I sit on the bed next to her. It creaks under my weight. Still she makes room. Yvonne has tried to make the place comfy, but she has no domestic skill. There are things all over the place. We just lie there smoking. I'm wondering, what's going to happen. She's got that look — her lips are moistening. I think she wants to kiss me and I'm not sure if I want to. She doesn't say anything, but I feel her thoughts are tangible, in the air. I don't even allow my Mum to get this near me. Yvonne then pushes me back so that my head is resting and I'm lying horizontal. I don't resist. With her leg she hooks into the cord that pulls the door, and it swings to a close, making the place go darker. She very gently starts to stroke my hair. I freeze — but it feels good, not freeze-dried. I don't want her to stop, but I don't want her to go further till I'm ready. It's like a trap. If I get up, she'll be upset. I don't want that. So I do nothing; I wait; I know I'm supposed to feel excited, as boys do, but I feel numb. She's biding her time, as if she knows my reserve might ruin it.

Then she starts groaning softly; she's pressing her lips against mine, all wet and sloppy. She opens her mouth and her tongue prods out, dipping into my mouth. I feel it at the top of my teeth, tasting of cherry gum, so I close my mouth. She tries pushing in again, but I'm firm, so she tries something else. She sits up and takes off her blouse; she's wearing a pink bra underneath. Her breasts are bigger than I thought; they hang round and low. She wants me to see them, so she puts her hands on them; they dangle like water balloons, one to the left and one to the right. I want to touch them too. I reach out, but then I stop. She'll just want more. I want to tell her to put her blouse back on. I like her, but wish she wouldn't do this.

"Come on. Take off your shirt," she says, eyes gleaming. She's already taking off her bra and I see her tits for real. So I unbutton my shirt so slowly that she gets impatient and helps me to take it off. My chest is pale and hairless, my shoulders hunched. But my flesh is warm and ticklish where her fingers are cold. She turns her back to me.

"Undo me," she says. And I undo the almost-invisible zipper on her gray skirt. She's wearing pink knickers with a lacy edge, like the bra. She lets it drop, then climbs on top of me and pulls my hands into hers from behind. She puts each of my hands on one breast. They feel strange and soft. They feel OK. Her skin is smooth. I think she's done this before; she has an advantage. It isn't fair. I begin to massage her breasts, but half-heartedly. She moans approvingly, as she must have heard them do in porn films. If I'm going to do it for the first time with anyone, it should be Yvonne. She won't be a cling-on. She won't make a fuss. She can act like a boy. She's only after a bit of fun. It won't go any further. She won't be stupid and get pregnant. I just wish she'd relax and maybe stop. It doesn't have to happen now. I turn my head away just as she's tugging at my flies.

"Is there anything to drink in here?" I say, touching my throat.

"No. We must bring some beer next time."

"Next time?" I say. She ignores my surprise.

I wriggle around and she tries to pull down my pants, but they only get half way. She lies on top of me. I don't help; I don't move. At first she just feels like a heavy lump. I feel there's a lot to say but don't know what it is. I don't have the words. I feel angry — as if I've been misled. Not by her, but by everyone as to what it's all about. Life, the ultimate: They never told me it would be this disappointing. I feel I might burst. Maybe it's my blood pressure again. I don't budge; I don't speak. Yvonne stops and stares at the ceiling. Her hands start to stroke my dick through my cotton jockey shorts. She's not about to give up. She fumbles around a bit. My hands are by my side, rigid. Her fingers are cold. She pulls one of my arms up and onto the small of her back. It rests there, and then falls away. She pulls my other arm up so that she can imagine she's locked in my embrace. I feel squashed. I have to stop. Hope she doesn't think I misled her. I just don't know how to say *stop*. She rolls to the side and starts kissing me all over again.

I move my hand up and down her back. She gives a look full of longing. She rubs her legs together and closes her eyes as she puts my hand down her crotch. It's already wet down there, around her clit. She's beginning to wriggle out of her panties. I remove my hand. She feels for my dick but it's limp. She stops; I stop; it all stops. Her eyes wake up. She kisses me on the forehead, a peck. Then she changes — she's thinking hard. We are silent for a long time, neither of us moving.

"It's cold," she says, pulling her panties back on. She reaches for her now-squashed cigarettes.

"I've never done this before," I say, but it sounds a lame excuse.

"It's OK," she says. It looks like she's thinking about me. I want to know what it is. How it will explain myself to me. I want her to tell me what's wrong.

"What are you thinking?"

"I was thinking what fun it was that night, on acid. My dad was bending over in the bathroom. I wanted to stick the vacuum attachment up my dad's arse. It was the funniest thing in the world. We stayed out all night until dawn and I was talking to the sea. I learned a lot. Every pebble on this beach is related to every other, you know."

I lie there and wonder what the dirty British Channel might have to say, were it able to speak to me. A family chorus. I hear a movement, soft and graceful, a faint melody of four notes, a key change—I have to capture that when I get home, get to the piano to play it out, or I'll lose it. It's slow and melancholy but grows in power. But I lose the connection to that new song. It fades out; I don't feel good; I feel stupid, ashamed.

. . .

Yvonne sits up, pulls her blouse and skirt back on, kicks at the door. It swings open. It's late evening, and a patch of sky has cleared, the sun straining through, all the gray tones turned warm tingly, all orange and blue. The sea is very still, calm monotonous, but with tiny white curls of surf that begin to glitter and twinkle.

"Let's swim," she says. "There's a towel here. We can dry off later."

How can I say *sorry*. I just can't.

"I've seen people do it naked. Shall we?"

"I don't know. I've never done that."

"Well, maybe it is too cold. It's better at night when no one can see you."

I don't know what to say anymore. She's full of life where I'm not. She walks out of the hut toward the sea's edge. The hut goes very quiet without her, as if only she filled the room. I put my jeans and shirt back on. I follow desultorily. I fear she might now want to be alone, or might be angry and upset. She squats at the sea's edge. She's gazing at the water as if she can see pictures loom from underneath—pictures of a narrative that's explaining her life. I wait and wait. I don't have anything to say.

"I'm going to go to France tomorrow. I've decided. Fuck school. I'm getting the ferry and then I'm going to hitch to Paris," she says finally, determined. It's the making of a decision she's hedged for months. It's what I'd do if I had the nerve.

"But what about your family? What will they think?" I say.

"Hunh," she shrugs. "They've never been any good to me."
Then she says, "And don't tell anybody about this hut."

"No, I won't," I promise. I'm good at secrets.

• • •

When I get home, my mother's laughing at a comedy show, but
she watches me, looking for signs of drink or some kind of
derangement. I go straight to my room and put on some loud
rock music. She taps on the door, always wanting to know, but I
say I'm tired and everything's OK. I have to say that so that she'll
go away. But she doesn't.

"Where have you been?"

"I just went for a long walk, that's all."

"Alone?"

"Ah, leave it out Mum, will you?"

"Be careful now."

"Oh, please."

I throw myself on the bed and touch my dick to see if it
really will get hard, and it's not defective, but I have to look
upward at my poster of James Dean and Sal Mineo to get any
lead. Something's not right down there, but it's not good to think
too much about it. I don't want to think too much, it hurts.

• • •

But I do think a lot—about Yvonne. That's so funny too after
what happened. Now a month's gone by, and she's not back.
Her parents went mental, but then they heard she was in Paris.
She's different. Unique and daring. People like this have to find
their own way of getting people to accept them, that's all. I'm
looking at the postcard she sent me. It's a Modigliani nude, dis-
torted and elongated. It could be her. I know that's why she sent
it. She's in Montmartre, living in an old loft near the Sacre Coeur.
She says she's found contentment with a French guy, an artist.
They are living together. He uses her as a model. She's found her
vocation, I think.

At school, it's just the same old stupidity. I'm sitting in the recreation room; when three girls pass, they see the postcard in my hand and figure out who it's from. They're such know-it-alls, these girls here. And really bossy.

"Oh, remember that girl. What was her name? From the English class. Said she wrote poetry?" The others sniggered.

"Oh, Ms. Slut, the punk poet," says the fat one, munching gum with a vengeance in the big folds of her mouth. Her friends all fall about cackling, but they've made sure I hear. First, rumors went around that I had pushed her off the cliffs, which I never did anything to discourage — it's good to have a reputation for danger. But then they heard she was in Paris, doing something Bohemian, so they started slagging her off, calling her *slut* and a *bitch*. But they are the sluts, the way they go on. They'll be in the pudding club and on the dole soon enough, with permanent sad faces. And Yvonne will be the one who did something she believes in.

• • •

God, how life goes on in this tedious little watering hole. I have no friends here. I go for walks alone now, much as I used to. I go near the beach hut and remember Yvonne. I like to wander about the promenade, sit on the beach, throw stones. Music is there, but only sometimes. It's getting hotter. More people are stripping off, straining to get meager tans. There seem to be more dog owners in this town than anywhere else in the world. When the weather is warm, my shoulders burn, but I never take off my top. But I do wear shorts and sandals. I have a white shirt on that's loose and open, but that's as far as I go. Sometimes, I read a book and doze off. Or I ride my bicycle as far as the pier, but there's never anything to see that's different. The same crazy stuff, noisy people letting loose, getting drunk and doing silly things. I've heard about the nudist beach much further up. But you'll never catch me there. I wouldn't mind looking but I'm not going to strip off. I did go one day. I spent hours trying to find it, but couldn't. I didn't dare ask anyone what I was looking for, so I gave up and came back home and paid homage to James and Sal.

It doesn't feel too good at home. Mum is sick all the time. She doesn't go out. She gets very tetchy when I don't run errands for her. She thinks I'm the one that needs to be watched, but she's a secret drinker, I'm sure of it. She has all these medications, and sometimes forgets which ones she's taken. Today she's sleeping from these new killer sleeping pills that knock her out. It gives me a break.

So I'm at the beach, near the hut, just sitting on the wall. The paint has flaked off even more, but it looks OK in the bright sunlight. I've been inside many times. I know how to work the fake padlock. No one ever goes there but me. My secret. I slip in when no one's looking. Yvonne's probably forgotten me completely. But it's funny—I don't wish she were back here. She's happier over there practicing her French, getting it fluent. And getting laid every night.

This is the kind of place too where there are a lot of lonely people. Men, mainly. They look at me and I never know what to do, what they want. One guy came up to me once, but he was horrible, old and crabby. He smelled of gin. Another one followed me for ages; he was younger and it was hard to shrug him off. It makes my flesh go funny, makes me nervous and gooey inside. I feel I must ignore them, and definitely not tell Mum. She'd throw a fit, go to the police, and get them into trouble, and I don't want that. They're no harm.

I look out to sea. A couple of kids are kicking a football around. I can hear them shouting. They decide to race each other, so they run a great distance away, but their voices still carry across the beach. I'm bored with my book now. I need something new to read, something wilder. Something French.

I feel tense suddenly and know someone's staring at me from behind, not saying a word. I hear a voice behind my shoulder—a man's.

"Can you go any further along here, or is that the end of it?"

I turn to see his face. He's about thirty and his shirtfront is open, revealing a hardened tanned chest. He's wearing sports shoes and has a quirky face. I think I saw him earlier on. I noticed his legs. He must play tennis or something. Looks fit. He walked up and down. He already knows the answer to the question. I feel I must be on guard.

I feel my head getting fuzzy. I'm overheating. I'm choked with half-formed words. There's something about this man. He's handsome — what can I do about it? It doesn't make me relaxed. He's not like photos of film stars, but almost. More real and alive, more animated. His face has a creamy look. He has wise eyes. Too wise. A couple of white hairs on his sideburns. I want to look more closely, but look out to sea instead. He doesn't go away, even though I don't speak. I feel his eyes on me. All over me. Eating into me. I take a quick look and there he is looking right back at me, strangely, his lips parted. God, it's bloody hot today.

"OK if I sit here too?" he says finally. I can hardly tell him to go away. Besides, I don't want him to. I nod without looking at his chest as he sits. He has a smell. Not ice cream, but joss, faintly patchouli and sweat. He doesn't have to say a word. I just know something's about to happen. It's inevitable. Why did Mum never prepare me for this? What good is all her advice? Why do I feel so weak? I feel tense, ready to detonate. My heart's going nonstop. But I'm gearing up. Nobody told me, but I just know I'm cranking up to fit my own niche. This is it. This is not Yvonne, and that's what was wrong. This feels right. Just right.

"So how's your day been so far?" he says.

"OK," I say, acting cool. I smile slightly. I'm going to laugh. Like being tipsy. His hair is in a special style — even the wind can't ruffle it. His eyes are instruments for saying things without words. They're warm, frightening, kind and cruel. It's weird. He must have been smoking recently, as I smell hints of tobacco and spice. I think he's foreign — Italian, or French maybe. I can't distinguish the accent at all.

"Where are you from?" the man says.

I point vaguely back in the direction of my house. But think, *obvious question*. This is leading me. To the point after which I can't go back.

"It's nice here."

"Yes," I say. How in-the-way all talk seems—I wish he'd shut up and get on with it.

"You're not very talkative, are you?"

I shake my head. I touch my bare legs, peeking at a spot over the knee. His eyes are drawn there too. It's as if I've always known to do this. To madden him. Then I scratch my shoulder, then my balls. I know I've got his eyes. This is fun, but I'm scared of what he might do. I think of Yvonne and her man in London, the lingerie salesman. She has balls, so it helps to think what she would think, to do what she'd do without hesitation. She'd probably say something hard and confident like, "So what do you do for fun, then, mate?"

"Have you got a cigarette?" I say. I'll just pretend to smoke it. I can't let him get away.

He hands me a cigarette, coming closer to light it. I feel his hot breath. I smile. He's not exactly a challenge. A mad impulse—I throw the cigarette away on the beach, and he looks dumfounded. I stand up. I nod my head in the direction of the beach hut. The man doesn't say anything. Then he laughs. He's learning. So am I. Just making it up.

"You're cute," he says. His hand is lightly touching his abdomen where the skin shows under his shirt. I can't help looking. His hand rests gently on his crotch, brushing the bulge, and then he pulls it away to his nose. But he's not doing the seducing here.

"I know a place," I say, not looking at him.

His blue eyes open wide from behind the sunglasses. He nods, he's ready. I notice his hands, which are big, long, and squarely shaped—they'd look very good stretched across piano keys, his muscular arms crisscrossing the keyboard. I could already see him sitting naked at the piano, the cheeks of his arse spread over the piano stool. I see the strings twang across flesh.

"Where?" He looks around, as if checking for a hotel. No one. Nothing to prevent us. He shrugs.

"Not far," I say, blinking slowly.

We move onto the beach, the pebbles crunching together underfoot. I wait for him to follow, but don't look at him. I know he's behind me. I shake open the padlock. I feel tense, as it smells musty inside. Hardly romantic, yet somehow it is urge that makes it seem daring, just lust, but fine for the occasion. I turn to see him come inside. He does so, shrugging his shoulders. I feel elated. I don't need wine if I have this, I'm thinking. My head is spinning, yet I'm acting so cool, like a professional whore. My face must be red. I feel like a conduit newly connected to a current of electricity, high voltage.

The man closes the door and immediately rips off his shirt. It falls gently. He runs his hands over his chest for me to admire, and I do. I touch his nipples. I move my mouth to them as if I'm sucking milk, licking each one in turn. He pushes his hands under my shirt, and I help him lift it off. The man pushes his hands under my shirt, brushing my chest. I see that under his tracksuit bottoms, he's already excited. I put my hand down and find he's got no shorts on underneath, not even a thong or G-string, it's all there, dick and balls at the ready to fondle, to grab and stuff into my mouth. He pushes his pants down, and sticks his hands into my zipper, ripping at it so that it jolts me forward and my whole body touches his. I'm shocked at his heat. He's giving off so much. And his dick is sticking straight out at me. He wants me to grab hold, so he pushes my hand onto it. He gives out an ecstatic gasp as I do so, moving my hand quickly up and down. Then I do it without his guidance. I'm staggering now. We are going to have to move onto the bed or my knees will give way. His hands are running into my underwear now, pushing furiously to get them off. I bend over to pull them off, and his hand touches my backside. He hums. He's in clover. Our hands are everywhere, and this feels great. Anywhere they want to go. Sliding up and down the contours of skin. I'm surging in this energy field. This is it. It, I think. IT. But I can't think anymore.

We fall onto the camp bed, which creaks under the strain. Its rusty hinges cannot take the weight of the man. I take his smooth dick into my mouth. Just the head of it, as I can't take it all. He kicks away his pants. He's completely naked now. I'm working up and down the dick, and it's melting, visibly, caving to my tongue. I allow my throat to open to take the entire shaft, but start to gag. I can't take it all. My nose is buried in his pubic hair and it's dark and furry. I don't want to move from there but my jaw gets tired, so he starts to do it to me. I'm going dizzy with pleasure. I hear the music from the sea, pouring into my ears, as he's working on my dick too, licking it. His mouth is big and sure, and takes it all—no problem. I hear the voice of Yvonne, and then of my mum calling me, but my mind is empty, clean. I'm off to another world where the pulse is different. He doesn't gag where I did, and soon I feel a surging force all over my body. Something's coming from deep, deep inside, latent all my life, dormant, and it's awakening. I'm shuddering. My knees tremble. He puts his finger into my hole and that does it. It breaks. Like a wave. But he holds it.

"No, not yet," he says. "Wait for me."

I pretend to know what he means. The surge feeling goes down, and I feel high. I don't even care that we are in this hut, with a broken lock so that anyone could come in. He licks my armpits. He swallows my nipples. I grab his dick. I want him to do things, anything, while he's so turned on. It will be good to try. But then he turns over onto his stomach, and he nods for me to do something. I'm getting instructions, but I don't know what he means, but I put my dick on his lower back and start rubbing anyway. I'll just do what he likes. He pulls me down on him harder, and positions himself more under me. Right, I think, that's enough of that. I get off and pull his shoulder. But he stops me—his first aggressive move. I stare at him.

"Fuck me," he says. "Go on. Do it, do it, now!"

I think: Is he joking or what? I'm not, what are they called?—the stud, I'm new to this, what does he expect? He's the older guy. He ought to know how to do it. I look down at his tanned back and his backside, which is now tilting upward, expectant.

I stand up, my hand on my dick. Something weird is happening. I come but in total shock. I'm shaking. What the hell is this? I'm groaning and it's spurting out in motions, regular, persistent.

He shouts, "I told you to wait!"

My dick, which was hard, is now falling and I'm arched over it looking at the stuff in my hand. More than ever before. Then I wipe it off on the hem of my shirt. I feel down. Then it happens—I start to cry.

"What's the matter?" the man says, turning his head. He was just lying there annoyed before but now he's concerned, as if I might be a mental case.

"No, I can't see you," I shout loudly.

"Shussh," he says, getting up and reaching for his pants.

I never shouted at anyone before, but I feel I want to hurt him. I want to make him feel my pain, my confusion. I'm angry because it's all different, dark. Nothing will ever be the same. I just know it. I'm crying. He gets angry.

"Stop crying. It's nothing."

"You're not my father," I say. "You can't tell me what to do."

"I'm not your *what?*" he says. His eyes harden toward me. "So you're looking for a daddy, huh? That's not good. I believe I'm going. Thank you very much." He starts putting on his shirt. He looks like he's in a hurry to get away, as if I might pull a knife.

"You're not him. You don't look like him."

"Of course I'm not. What are you talking about?" Then I hear his accent. Not Italian but German.

His eyes flare open. The kind of anger I would not have believed existed in such a kind, mild-mannered person, if I had provoked it myself. I think, in a flash: My God, he really does look like my father, why did I say he didn't? I will always want him. So I lunge at him. I have to hurt him somehow or I will be the first to die of pain. He pushes toward the door and screams, "Dumb little shit. You need psychiatric help."

I pick up the rusted can opener and hold it high, staring at him.

He rushes out and the door slams shut, the hinges flapping. I lie down on the bed. It creaks and groans like my naked body. I think I've burst a blood vessel or something. I feel scared, empowered, lost, in need of care. Then I start to smile. A big smile. I see how funny it is. How stupid. It's a big, daft joke. I want to run into the sea naked, screaming. But I screw up my eyes, caress my own shoulders, smell my hands, inhale, and float off up into the sky over the sea, carried on a wind swipe, like a kite, dipping and bobbing, darting across the bay, the Channel, over to France, a seagull's plaintive cry just echoing. I think about my father trying to reach me. When I play the piano, I will think the keys are his bones and teeth. Now I know who he is, how he has made me.

The Red convertible

࿋

NALIN KANT

WILL SHE COME?

I am at the Princess Caravan Park, an old, unused parking lot on the top of a hill near Princetown, overlooking a lush green valley. At the bottom of the valley, a stream of clear blue water stretches quietly among the eucalyptus trees. Occasional chirping of birds is the only sound punctuating the tranquility — no human beings, no cars, and no worries.

Morning sun casts elongated shadows under the trees, and a light sea breeze brings in a whiff of the salty sea air.

Dressed in my beige woven T-shirt and loose khaki cotton shorts I am sipping herbal tea. Delicate aroma of chamomile reminds me of her perfume. Hot, smooth surface of the round-bottomed Mikasa mug feels like her skin. Sitting on a low beach chair, atop a picnic blanket, I am lost in delicious daydreams of our previous rendezvous. My longing to touch her is so intense, it hurts.

To take my mind off her, I start reviewing my plan for the day.

"I know where you want to take her," the Little-I in my head challenges me. "To the cave in the Loch Ard Gorge."

"Yes! She will then remember everything, and never leave me again." The thought of her becoming mine forever puts me in a trance. I lie down flat on the blanket, the sun penetrating every pore in my body. I take a few deep breaths and exhale slowly to relieve the pressure building in my groin.

Just then, I hear a car arrive on the driveway behind me. I know, without looking, it's her. I knew she would come. I get up and walk toward her. "Don't rush, she is here now," the Li'l-I tries to calm my thumping heart.

I notice that she is wearing the same light blue dress—thin shoulder straps, deep V neck, and the hem touching her thighs— etched in my memory. A year did nothing to fade these memories and the memories of all the curves it tried, but failed, to hide.

Her hair is ruffled. She still drives her "Red." That is what she calls her red Mercedes convertible. I look at my Ford Econovan next to her Red, and smile at the Freudian metaphor conjured up in my mind.

She smiles back and extends her hands. I kiss one, then the other, and then both together.

"I missed you," I babble.

"Shh." She puts a finger on my lips, and points at the picnic blanket with her eyes.

I move backward, looking at her, devouring every inch of her body. The light breeze is pushing her dress against her curves. With the sun almost behind her, a silhouette of her slender hips and thighs is clearly visible through its delicate material. The tri- angular gap at the junction of thighs and pubis glows like a jewel. Tops of her firm and round breasts peek through the deep V-neck.

A pair of birds sits ogling us. They look at us and then at each other.

"I am starving. No breakfast, I had just a cup of coffee before I started," she says, making herself comfortable on one of the low beach chairs. As she sits, knees folded between her arms, her dress falls, revealing the clear pale skin of her smooth thighs and a glimpse of her black silk panty — small as a G-string.

As I hand her a cup of herbal tea and a piece of cake, she gives me a light kiss on my lips — a sample of goodies to follow.

My hands glide from her thighs to her feet as she takes the last bite of her cake. I kneel down in front of her and slowly pull off her golden sandals. Sandal straps have made grooves on her feet. I move my fingers through these grooves as she takes the last few sips of her tea.

"What about you? Aren't you hungry?"

"I ate just before you arrived. Now all I want to eat is *you*." My mouth jerks toward her and bites the air.

"Hold on just a few more moments," says her smile.

"I have waited so long, now, a few moments is all I can wait," murmurs my Li'l-I.

She places the cup aside and leans back on the beach chair, stretching her legs slightly apart. As she slides down, her dress is gathered under her hips, exposing her thighs fully.

I am ready to be devoured, says the black triangle of her panty.

Her head is thrown back and her slender arms hang on either side.

Before mixing fluids, I want to mingle my air, my spirit, with her. I move my mouth to her parted lips. They rise to meet their soul mates. Our lips acquire a life of their own, they suck each other in every possible way: her lower, mine upper; her upper, mine lower; hers together between mine....

Beep beep. Oh God! Who is this? I sit up, looking for ways to hide the bulge in my shorts. She straightens her dress and sits demurely on the beach chair. A car appears in the parking lot.

That pair of birds flies away. They must know of a more secluded spot.

• • •

We met exactly a year ago.

She was standing next to her Red on the side of a desolated dirt track off Winchelsea, heading toward the Great Ocean Road.

She was pointing at the flat tire with her left hand, her right hand forming a stop sign. The look on her face clearly said, "Please stop."

By the time I hit my brake and skidded on the loose gravel, I had already passed her. I could see her in the rear-view mirror, waving frantically. I started reversing my van. She stopped waving, touched her hands to her lips, and blew a kiss. As the left window of my van came in line with her, she started talking at a hundred kilometers per hour. I leaned toward the window and noticed the blue dress straight away—and its cut, perfect for her petite, curvaceous body.

I could not hear what she was saying; all my sensual energy was concentrated on her vision—her face exuding venerability and her body emitting sensuality. For a few moments I was mesmerized. I had a sense of déjà vu. I knew that I had never seen her before, still I felt that I knew her.

All I could do was keep staring at her, and her light blue dress fluttering in the breeze. Her hands desperately tried to keep the dress from rising. She noticed that I was staring at her. She raised her hands to point at the rear wheel. Whirling wind floated the dress up, up above her thighs. Her sheer black panty shone in the brilliant sunshine of a True Blue Australian summer.

She stopped talking and smiled; there was no need to say anything any more.

As I got out of my van she handed me her car keys. Now *she* was staring at me. I could feel the heat of her eyes on my face, neck, back, biceps, torso, and all over. I felt being watched, as I often did in the gym mirror. I opened her car boot, removed the spare tire and the jack. She watched my every move—putting the jack, removing the flat tire, putting on the spare, removing the jack, replacing it in the boot—in perfect silence.

"Shall we take it for a test drive?" I asked.

"Don't call it an *It, please*," she complained, putting on the look of an unhappy little girl. "I call it Red."

"Sorry, shall we take your *Red* for a test drive?" I said with a mock apology, and a little pat on Red's rear fender.

"That will be good." Her lips stretched in a cheeky asymmetric smile—the left side of her lips went higher than the right side. "What about your van?"

"Don't worry, she'll be all right. No one will touch this junk." I parked my van off the road and locked it.

As we started the test drive she began telling her story—not that I asked. She had intentionally bypassed the Surf Coast Highway to Torquay, and taken this dirt track to be close to Nature. How close she got to Nature I am not sure. But Nature, for sure, was drawing us close. She had to lean closer to be heard in the open convertible. I just drove on. Every time she started saying something, I had to tilt and turn my head toward her—and our heads touched lightly. At one point Red bumped in a ditch just when our heads were close. They banged like two coconuts. We looked at each other and laughed. I rubbed her injured spot. "That's nice," she said.

Her shoulder-length red hair fluttered in the wind, revealing her long neck tilted slightly forward. Her clear pale skin, visible in the deep V-neck, was glowing in the morning sun. The loose hem of her dress kept dancing on her thighs.

Herds of cows grazed, roamed, or rested under shady trees in meadows on either side of the track. Clouds of dust bellowed behind Red.

"I am thirsty," she said, putting her hands on my left thigh and leaning toward me, coming so close to my ear as to kiss my left cheek. I knew where to find water. A track through a paddock led us to a shed with a mix of new and old farm machinery. The door was open, but no one was in. Dodging oily rags and their earthly smells, I took her behind the shed to an open tap over a cement trough.

She drank in big gulps, splashed her face, and let lots of water run on the front of her dress. It became nearly transparent. Her nipples became hard, pointing at me. As I straightened after having a sip myself, she gave a quick kiss on my lips.

"Thanks for stopping, repairing my car, and for the drive."

I kissed her hand. "With pleasure."

"How did you know about this tap?"

"I installed it last year. I know this area well."

"Oh, I see. I wondered about the van. Shall we go back?"

"If you like, I can drive you along the Great Ocean Road till dusk, and then we can come back to my van via the Princess Highway."

"You sure?"

"Positive."

"Let's go!" She jumped, put her arms around my neck, and took her feet off the ground. I had no choice but to support her with my hands under her buttocks. She stole a sip of my lower lip. Her kiss, the touch of her silken bottom, her pubis pressed hard against me, and her hard nipples poking my chest, shot a bolt of electricity through my body. My manhood woke up and I could hardly breathe. My fingers dug into her baby-smooth bottom and my penis pushed into her. She winked.

I took a deep breath and tried to return her kiss. But she was off, as quickly as she came on. Holding my hand, she pulled me to the car. "Let's not waste any time here. We'll have to find a better spot."

I knew a better spot — in fact, a perfect spot.

I took the track heading for Aireys Inlet. From there I would take her to Lorne for lunch, Apollo Bay for siesta, Lavers Hill for evening tea, and then to the perfect spot in Princetown for the sweetest sweet-dish.

"Wow," she said as we hit the Great Ocean Road. "Wwow... wooaw," she said at least a hundred times in a hundred different ways. Every time we took a new turn she went, "Wow!"

Majestic green hills on the right, sparkling Southern Ocean on the left, and clear blue skies can make even gods drunk with beauty. We were mere mortals floating in a dream-like trance.

The café at Lorne, overlooking the span of a wide golden beach, smelled of olive oil and oregano. Her Greek salad and my toasted focaccia were washed down with half a bottle of Pinot Noir as our legs played hockey under the table.

The sloping grassy area at Apollo Bay provided the perfect spot for snuggling. Kids ran past, parents chasing, shouting, "Be careful!"

By the time we reached Lavers Hill tearooms, the sky had assumed a crimson hue. As we walked, my hands caressed her back and occasionally wandered under her dress to caress her almost bare buttocks. She hung onto my arm. A pot of English Breakfast tea and chocolate chip cookies injected some energy that we would soon need.

We were on the final approach to the unused Caravan Park at Princetown. In the paddocks around us cows were returning dutifully to their masters for unloading their swaying udders. The sun played hide-and-seek behind undulating hills.

As Red caressed the curves on the hills, so did I hers. By the time we reached our destination it was getting dark — dark enough to provide a shroud of privacy, and lit enough to use it well.

The sun emitted a burst of rays and dipped into the Southern Ocean. Now only faint sunlight reflected off the sky. Crickets chirped around us, a kookaburra laughed somewhere, as the aroma of eucalyptus rose from the valley. She asked me to spread the picnic blanket from her car boot.

The brightest of stars became the audience for our *Romeo and Juliet*. Balmy air invited us to discard our outer clothes and relish the sensual delights of body-to-body touch.

As she lay fully stretched on her picnic blanket I began by kissing her knees, then thighs, and moved toward the silken black triangle of her panty. I dug my lips into the outline of the thick, juicy lips of her vulva, clearly visible under the light material. As I pulled it off, a light musk aroma of sex rose from the curly red triangle of her pubis. As I moved my tongue inside her juicy slit, she moaned. My lips moved up and kissed her belly button; as I sucked, her belly reverberated. She giggled.

She undid the front hook of her bra, and two cherry-red nipples appeared atop her firm and full breasts. I slid up to cover these cherries with my lips, tickled them with my tongue, and sucked them. I could hear her gasping for breath. She slid her hand inside my jock and encircled the length of my fully aroused cock. Now our need for closure was urgent. As she guided it in, my cock almost drowned in the hot and thick juice oozing inside her. A tingling sensation ran down my spine.

Our movements started slowly. We savored the pleasure of every stroke. Her whole body trembled every time I pushed in. As I pulled out, her pelvis rose and her vagina muscles grabbed at me, as if she didn't want to let go.

Slowly but steadily the tempo hastened, till it matched our heartbeats. Our final tremors came with full abandon: Hoarse cries echoed in the valley; bodies pounded together, and exploded.

Stars applauded with their twinkling, as we lay gazing with languid eyes, touching each other's bodies, slippery with sweat.

The test drive, and its sequel, must have been as rapturous for her as they were for me.

We promised to meet next year, same day, same time, and same place. Not on the roadside, but at the secluded Princess Caravan Park, where we came together, in a desperate rush to finish what started from the moment we saw each other.

On the return journey she sat very close, leaning on my left shoulder, as if we had been lovers for a long time. Tall eucalyptus trees lined the roads through the Otways hinterland. We were engulfed in complete darkness, but for the two beacons guiding our path. Occasional flashing headlights of a car coming from the opposite direction, and dim lights of a few houses in the distance, added to the magic of the 110 kph drive in the open convertible.

"Are you sleepy?" "No," were the only words exchanged on the road from Colac to Winchelsea.

"Your van is still here," she said as we approached our starting point.

I bent over and kissed her on the lips. Her face glowed in the vanity light of her Red.

"Hey, aren't you gonna tell me your name?" she asked, ready to leave.

"Tom." Then I remained silent.

"Aren't you gonna ask mine?" She gave me that asymmetric smile.

I didn't have to. I just smiled back, my eyes exploring her face.

"Eva. My name is Eva." She told me what I already knew.

"Can I have your phone number?" I pleaded.

"Nope."

"Why not?"

"Because." And she laughed like a naughty little girl.

"I'll follow you and find out your address," I challenged.

"Do try, *please*," she said softly, looking into my eyes, and slowly extending her right hand.

I cupped her hand between mine and kissed it for a long time. I wanted to hold it forever. Slowly, she pulled her hand away and drove off. Total darkness added to my feeling of loss.

I quickly started my van and followed Red's taillights right up to Geelong. To keep up with her in Geelong I had to endure rude horns and upturned fingers from crazed footy fans hanging out of car windows. Then, just when I thought that she could not elude me, she did. At the junction where the Princess Highway becomes a freeway heading toward Melbourne, she just vanished. One moment she was in my sight, and the next she was gone.

Why did she do that again?, I have thought a million times over, the last year. Just when I thought I had found her, I lost her, *again*. I had been waiting for her for at least ten years in this life, and over a hundred in all.

· · ·

On my eighteenth birthday I had visited the Loch Ard Gorge on the Great Ocean Road.

My search for her started (in this life) when I read the story of the Loch Ard clipper, which came to grief on the 1st of June 1878. As I read the story I knew that I was the Tom Pearce who had rescued her—Eva Carmichael. And she, she married another man! How could she? We were the only two survivors bound by a celestial bond.

It was 4 A.M. on a bleak Saturday morning. The sea was calm, but the fog had reduced visibility to less than a hundred feet. I had been on duty all night. My shift was over. If I wanted I could have gone down to my hammock in the iron womb of the ship. Something told me to stay on the deck. Suddenly we heard a big crack; the ship jolted and came to a halt. I knew that it had hit a reef near the Mutton Bird Island. We were aware of the dangers on this coast — called the Ship Wreck Coast for a reason.

I had seen her on the deck many times. I knew that she had been watching me as I worked the ropes; her neck always craned to look at me, perched on one of the three masts.

She must have been asleep comfortably in her cabin when we struck the reef. I wanted to rush down and look for her. But the ship sank within seconds, and the current carried me against my will.

All around, water looked as if it was boiling, when in reality it was freezing. I clung to an overturned lifeboat. Pushed by the swell, I reached the only beach around, deep inside a gorge.

For some time I lay exhausted on the narrow beach. But I could think of only her — imagining her drifting on a life buoy.

I heard faint cries for help. *It's she,* I thought. It was still dark, but I could see a faint outline of the opening to the gorge. With my thoughts I pulled her through this narrow opening. Guided by her cries I waded through the freezing water, groping, hoping to find her. I did, and dragged her toward the beach for what seemed like an eternity. Once my feet touched the ground, I carried her in my arms as far from the water as I could.

She was shuddering violently. I held her tight, trying to warm her with my body heat. I lay her on the beach and covered her body with mine. Finally, her shuddering subsided. When the dawn broke I saw that she was wearing just her nightgown. Her light blue eyes looked so sad.

She lay exhausted on the beach, her white silk gown clinging to her body — accentuating its every contour. We noticed a small cave on the other side of the cove. I implored her to move to the cave. She put her left arm around my neck, and I encircled her waist with my right arm. As she walked, her body slumped and slid down till her breasts rested over my arm. She looked at me with soft, tired eyes.

As we took turns sipping on a bottle of brandy washed up with other wreckage, our bodies warmed. With a pile of foliage I made a sort of blanket against the cave wall. After some hesitation she sat next to me. As we discussed our predicament, her head slumped on my shoulder.

When I told her that the sheer cliffs surrounding the gorge were impossible to climb, she started crying in my arms. As teardrops spilled from her eyes I drank them before they could touch the ground. She held me tight. I kissed her eyes, her cheeks, her lips as she sat curled in my lap. Cuddled together, we saw a glimmer of hope in this hopeless situation and felt a sense of calm amidst tempestuous waters.

My lips traversed down to her neck and then to her chest as my hands brushed all over her body. The touch of her silk gown, and my lips on her translucent skin, aroused me. I kissed the pink nipples on her demure breasts—pushed against the gown, as if trying to break free. She closed her eyes and bit her lower lip. As I pulled her over my body, she began returning my kisses. My hands traveled along her spine and reached the valley between her petite buttocks. The cave suddenly felt hot and humid. Her palms were burning, as she held my face in her hands and pressed the full length of her body on mine. Our lips came together, and stayed together, almost motionless, for a long time.

The gurgling sound of waves lapping against the shore provided the rhythm to our ensuing love dance. Tattered clothes provided no protection against our young bodies, rolling and grinding together.

A massive rock stood like an apostle protecting the entry to our cove from huge waves forming in the sea. A loud thunder shook me and broke my trance. She was dozing peacefully: so close, yet so far. I was filled with the desire to make her mine forever and be able to do all that I had just imagined.

I kissed her hand and told her that I *will* get help. Full of bravado, I climbed the sheer cliffs surrounding the gorge. Sharp rocks and thorny shrubs made innumerable cuts in my hands and feet, but I got out. After many hours I came across two drovers from Glenample station, and their manager organized a rescue.

We survived together, for we were meant to be together. Why did she leave for Ireland without telling me? Why? Why? *Why?*

I admit, I could not gather the courage to ask her to marry me. She should have understood. I was a poor apprentice sailor and she the daughter of a wealthy doctor. I was waiting to become something. She should have waited for me.

· · ·

Now, in this life, I had to find her.

All these years I had not dated, despite all the girls at my Brimbank College, and in my neighborhood in Yarraville, being quite willing. Some of my friends looked at me suspiciously. Others teased me. They said that because I looked like Gregory Peck, I expected an Audrey Hepburn as my girlfriend. I didn't care. I was waiting for her.

Since then, I have gone to the Loch Ard Gorge hundreds of times — looking for her. Every summer I take my plumber's van and camp around the Great Ocean Road.

The moment I saw her I knew that it was she. But then I lost her, and had to wait for a full year, hoping that she would keep her promise. This time I did not want us to part at the Princess Caravan Park. In fact, I did not want us to part ever again. I was ready with a solitaire diamond ring, having booked a suite at the Lighthouse Bed & Breakfast, with panoramic views of the ocean.

At the end of our last rendezvous, she had threatened that she would not come again, if I did not slow down on the curves. Which curves? I didn't ask. She didn't tell. Why would I slow down? The fast ride on the curves had raised her to a feverish pitch that brought us closer.

· · ·

I am not unhappy with the earlier interruption to our love serenade.

I want the entire theater to ourselves when the music plays. I want to savor the sensual delights of her touch to the fullest before partaking in a feast of sexual pleasures. I will build her fever higher than ever before, capture that elusive moment, and make it last forever.

I have carefully chosen the milestones that lead to the Perfumed Garden.

First milestone is Beauchamp Falls. She is *wowed* by the majestic falls crashing over a ledge into a pool of crystal clear water. We set up camp behind a big boulder. She takes off her dress and wraps a hot-pink Turkish towel over her silken panty and sheer bra. At the edge of the pool she removes the towel and enters the water quickly to hide her body from the ogling eyes of a group of teenage boys. She screams immediately, struck by the chilly water. The boys laugh.

"You should have warned me," she complains as I enter. I placate her with a delicate kiss. We find a secluded nook, away from the prying eyes of the boys. I rub her body. She comes closer. Underwater, our hands explore each other as our lips join above. I take her to a little ledge behind the sheet of water. Sunrays shimmer through it as she sits in my lap. Now it's impossible to hold back the urge to merge; we have to get out.

A warm rock beneath us and sunshine filtering through Douglas firs dry our clothes and outer bodies, but make amorous juices flow inside.

Meandering through a beautiful fern garden, we reach the 300-year-old Big Tree at the Maits Rest. I push her against the tree and try to embrace her, along with the tree. A little boy laughs, she smiles, he comes closer and peeps up her dress.

By the time we finish our picnic lunch under the rainforest canopy, it's late afternoon. We head back toward the ocean, following the curves of the Great Ocean Road. Curves are the journey, not the destination. Lighthouse B&B is Red's destination; she is mine.

Every time I take a sharp curve at high speed, she screams. Her screams are full of laughter. She is laughing even with her light blue eyes. Her whole body is laughing.

"Look at the bloody road," she shouts at me—still laughing—pushing on my left cheek. "I don't want this to be our last drive together. Understood?"

"Yes, ma'am," I shout back.

"One day we'll go flying together. Can you fly?" she asks me out of the blue.

"No," I say, taken aback. "But I'd love to fly with you. Can *you* fly?" I ask.

"That's for me to know and for you to find out." Her cheeky, asymmetric smile appears again. I hope I find out soon.

Twelve Apostles is my next milestone. We have to retrace our path and go past the Princess Caravan Park. She waves *bye-bye* as we approach it. The car that disturbed us in the morning is still parked next to my van.

"Shall I blow my horn?" I ask.

"Yes," she says, waving her fists.

Beep, beep. She laughs. I wish she would keep laughing like this forever.

At the Twelve Apostles we stand on the walkway overlooking the row of "apostles" at the edge of the sea. All along the coast sheer cliffs drop down to the sea. One such apostle guards the entrance to our gorge. I am longing to go there now. She looks as if she could read my thoughts. Her arms around my neck, she gives me a lingering kiss. I hold her tight, our bodies squashed together. A newlywed Indian couple looks at us as they pass. The young *sari*-clad woman, loaded with gold ornaments, smiles and nudges her husband. He winks.

The final milestone: Loch Ard Gorge. Long, winding steps take us down to the beach inside the gorge surrounded by imposing cliffs. My heart beats faster with every step we take. As we reach the bottom I head for the cave. She comes with me as if she knows where exactly we have to go. The cave is dark, humid, and desolated. Hundreds of people are moving about, but luckily on the other side. As soon as we enter I have the feeling of going into another era. She stares at me for a long time, and then her tears start rolling, followed by muffled sobs. I drink her tears, kiss her eyes, and caress her all over. Her sobbing subsides. We lock our mouths. She guides my hands to her breasts. As I touch them, her nipples become hard. I take one between my thumb and forefinger. She cries out with pain and pleasure. I move my hand down to her belly and insert my finger in the belly button. She giggles. I slide it lower, inside her panty. Her vulva is smooth all over. I insert a finger in the slit. It is moist. She moans lightly.

Suddenly she pushes me away, and says, "Let's go from here." She starts rushing toward the stairs. I have to adjust my shorts before I can follow her.

As we enter the car we're both quiet. I take the road heading toward Port Campbell. This is the way to our heavenly abode for the night: the Lighthouse B&B, perched on the edge of a cliff.

The sun is diving toward the ocean, near the edge of that cliff. Her light dress is no protection against the emerging chill. I can see goose pimples on her chest and thighs.

"It'll be dark soon. We should be returning to the caravan park, shouldn't we?" she asks in a subdued voice.

"No...ma'am, not...this...time." I slowly shake my head, tilt it to the left, and strain my eyeballs to watch her reaction.

"Then where?" Her eyes widen, lips part, as she turns her head toward me. "A motel?"

"Better than that." I move my head to kiss her parted lips.

"Looook," she shouts, as she covers her face with both hands.

"Oh, shiiiit!" I swerve left to miss the car on my right, going in the opposite direction. "Sorry for the language…. Everything is under control now…. You can open your eyes."

She's still got her face covered with both hands.

"Sorry, baby—I am really, really sorry." It's the first time I've called her *Baby*.

She opens her eyes, looks at me with anger and then relief, slumps into her seat, throws her head on my left shoulder, and lets out a big sigh. She is trembling.

"We are almost there. Can you see that lighthouse?" I point out the tall white structure barely visible with the setting sun in the background. My waving left hand is almost in front of her face. "That's where we are bunking."

That left hand of mine, it has a mind of its own. It does not return to the steering wheel. Why would it? The skin wrapped around the steering wheel is dead. Hers is alive and imploring.

She presses a button to close the convertible roof. It rises like a cobra and latches onto the windscreen as the cobra lashes out its tongue. I get the hint. We drive in silence, letting our fingers do the talking.

My left hand explores her breasts, popped out of her dress of their own accord. Her face is contorted with fever. I ask her to remove her seat belt, lower the backrest, and relax. My left hand travels down and enters her panty, and tries to pull it off; she twists and turns to help me.

We are now approaching the lighthouse cliff. My left hand still refuses to return to the steering wheel. In fact, it can't. It would be rude to refuse such imploring. It keeps exploring. So does Red.

Between the explorer and the destination remain a smooth curve to the left, and a hairpin bend to the right. The smooth curve is on a steep rise, the hairpin bend on a plateau at the edge of the cliff. This path I have explored before, and been to the destination too. I can do the curve with one hand.

I take the smooth left curve without reducing speed. Red hugs the perfectly banked road as it rises like the segment of a spiral highway to heaven. My heart beats faster, and I can hear her breathing deeper. She presses hard on my left hand, her nails digging in, hurting me.

Slow down on the hairpin bend, the Li'l-I warns me. It had noticed the sheer drop on the other side when we had come to check out the Lighthouse B&B.

Her pelvis is now moving with my hand. I twist my index and middle finger to caress her G-spot, her inside is full of hot and sweet juices. She sings loud, high-pitched tones. My hand is playing the notes, and her throat is producing a symphony of love, sex, pleasure, and rapture.

To raise the temperature I pull out my fingers, and glide my hand all over her burning body: thighs, buttocks, and breasts.... Goose pimples come alive wherever I take my hand.

My right foot comes off the accelerator and slowly presses the brake. *Take it easy, don't spoil her mood again with rash driving. But not too slow either, keep the motor revved up,* the Li'l-I keeps saying.

With her left hand she opens the lips of her vulva and exposes its pink interior. She pushes my left hand to her palpitating clitoris. I oscillate my palm over it, lightly, like the bow of a violin barely touching the strings. Her hips push in and out of the seat. Her hand commands mine: in, out, harder, faster. It obeys.

The tempo of our symphony rises. The entire orchestra goes crazy, playing multiple tunes at the same time. Her aria reaches its crescendo. I feel waves of silver and golden lights shimmering up my spine.

Red eases onto the plateau, and suddenly the setting sun becomes visible in its full glory: Direct rays blind me. My left hand is now massaging her inside. My right hand can either shield my eyes, or hold the steering wheel — one, or the other. It tries to do both; ends up doing neither.

She cries out her final orgasmic notes as we start flying in her Red convertible. Her body floats up from the seat, my fingers still inside her. Her mouth slightly open, eyes partly closed, head thrown back, lower legs hanging down, upper legs and body horizontal, arms hanging on either side, and hard nipples standing proud on firm breasts, she looks like an angel floating on ether.

I remember, she wanted us to fly together.

But, without wings and propeller?

All I care is, she came — and now forever.

Historical Note:
The Red Convertible is a work of fiction. The events depicted at the Loch Ard Gorge are based on a real-life shipwreck. Nonetheless, specific actions and dialogue used in the story are figments of the author's own imagination.

Lilly's Loulou

MICHÈLE LARUE

(STORY TRANSLATED FROM THE FRENCH BY NOËL BURCH)

MY MISTRESS ABANDONED ME over a Chinese restaurant. There are at least twelve on *la calle Cuchillo,* a busy street in Havana's *barrio chino.* The Cuban Chinese chefs threw thick Mexican spaghetti in their soups instead of rice noodles, which always riled my Lilly. When I heard that eight chefs were due in from Canton to teach the locals how to make genuine sharks' fin soup, I was frightened: I myself am pink—the color of flesh, in fact—and I look a bit like a sausage. When my mistress said melted condoms had been known to replace the mozzarella on Cuban pizzas, I thought to myself that the contents of a condom, i.e. yours truly, might make tasty meatballs in their soup.

I'm ten inches long and an inch and a half in diameter. I'm veined and flexible like a *paupiette de veau.* Two alkaline batteries set me to twitching, with a choice of three speeds. For years I was Lilly's favorite dildo. Nestled in a red velvet zip-bag next to a round-tipped candle, I toured the world in her trunk. She always flew during the off-season so that she could negotiate a whole row just for the two of us. She took me out of my case when the movie began. In the darkness, she slipped me under her panties where I started buzzing in low gear like a fly caught in a lace curtain. Lilly began to pant as she slid me sidewise under her panties and pressed me to her flesh. My hum became muffled as I drilled into the zones she chose around her clitoris, then over the little bridge of flesh to the anus. There, I skated around in circles…. After a while, my mistress would heave a little sigh and drop me under the seat. She rarely reached climax in the air. When the plane landed, she would pick me up with a fistful of crumpled newspapers.

On the infrequent evenings when Lilly was at home alone, I played stand-in, alternating with a black, cone-shaped competitor called Plug. I never knew much about Plug's capabilities, but they must have been far inferior to mine. One morning, as I emerged from the bag where Lilly had forsaken me all night long, I noticed him lying on the bed. Whenever she chose me for her evening bodyguard, she told all her boyfriends she would be getting her beauty sleep at home that night. I was delighted to count among the treatments meant to make her even more desirable. As she stepped out of her bath and slipped into a slinky Chinese negligée and mules trimmed with black swan feathers, my mistress would already be planning an orgasm. Pulling back the blankets, she would stretch out on the cool percale sheets. I could feel her finger applying a male-scented gel, then the touch of her clitoris as I swung into action. She would put me down and caress herself with her fingers. Pick me up again. Arch her back to see me standing between her thighs. Her pleasure came in moans that made me feel proud. The next morning, her hand would come looking for me under the sheets. She'd give me a few licks with her tongue, spit on my tip, and back to work!

When Lilly had a man in her bed, she would let me watch the lovemaking that I had, in a way, initiated. She would bring the man into the bedroom and take me out of my case. I heard the usual "it sure is big" or "just like the real thing." Wearing the string she never removed with any partner, and for which she was known as "Lilly-string," she rubbed me against her pink lips to make them moist. When the man tired of my collaboration, she would throw me on the carpet. But sometimes she quietly picked me up again while the man was in the shower. To finish herself off. To drench me with her juices. The mechanism would stop just in time for me to feel her spasms, and it would be my turn to feel the throbbing of my mistress's body. Her little squeals were more audible and attractive without the sound of my motor. When the man came out of the shower, kissed her cheek, and asked, "Was it good for you, too?" it was as if he were talking to me.

My role was usually restricted to surface-work. Except for that one time in Africa, when we ran out of batteries. I had a whale of a time! My mistress took me firmly in her hand and slowly drove me nearly halfway inside of her. Never before had she thrust me thus into the sheath of her flesh. It was in Zimbabwe that I realized what Plug was for. Actually, Lilly's cavity wasn't my size. Her eyes had been bigger than her stomach when she picked me out in her favorite sex-shop on the Rue de la Gaîté in Paris. Was she trying to talk the price down when she told the salesmen I was too big to be of use to anyone? It was under a tent in the African bush that I first experienced confinement inside my mistress, and every night I wanted more. It was soft and maternal in there...I still have fond memories of that expedition, although, without my vibratory powers, never once during the long safari did I manage to bring her off.

And so now I don't belong to Lilly any more. She sold me — traded me, rather — for two boxes of Robusto cigars, scarcely thicker than a little finger. How's she going to manage with those, unless she ties them in a bunch?

The tall black man who bought me puts on a silk fuchsia vest every evening. He claims that anyone who lives for any length of time in Chinatown (where he was born forty years ago) will inevitably turn tradesman. Orestes — for such is his name — has ignored this year's big craze in Havana: going in for a barman's job on a Caribbean cruise ship. He devotes himself solely to managing my activities, an occupation well suited to his tropical indolence. Any effort to entrust him with something other than coaching my depraved little body — keeping an eye on the workers painting the family *terrassa*, for example, or having sex with a woman — makes him terribly nervous. He's often so stressed that his body ceases to function and he has to lie down. If it were in my power, I'd rebel against this boss of mine, who thinks the exhalations of an expensive scent should fill the street where he walks. Fortunately, I have little contact with the man. I change condoms several times a day and pass from hand to hand: I'm a dildo for hire. When I'm squeezed into a Chinese rubber, it reminds me of Lilly's tender sex. Her tight vagina. Between jobs, my manager takes me back and washes me clean. When I'm dry, he pours white rum all over me. "She" never washed me at all. I've never seen so many black men and women at close range before. The rum has so blurred my memories of Lilly that I can scarcely recall her scent. Some days, I feel homesick.

About the Authors

M. CHRISTIAN, a Bay Area author, has published more than one hundred short stories in *Friction, Best Gay Erotica, Best Lesbian Erotica, Best Transgendered Erotica, Best American Erotica, The Mammoth Books of Erotica*, and many other books and magazines. He is the editor of seven anthologies, including *The Burning Pen, Best S/M Erotica, Guilty Pleasures*, and *Rough Stuff* (with Simon Sheppard). He is the author of *Dirty Words*, a collection of gay men's erotic short stories, and *Speaking Parts*, a collection of lesbian erotica, both from Alyson Books. He teaches writing classes for a variety of venues and thinks *way* too much about sex.

KIERON DEVLIN's fiction, reviews, and features have appeared in *PIF: Prose in Fiction* (www.pifmagazine.com), *The New Writer,* and *Tattoo Highway*. His was the winning flash-fiction story for the Hayward Fault Competition at *Doorknobs and Bodypaint* (www.iceflow.com). He is also associate fiction editor for *LIT* magazine at the New School. He is originally from the United Kingdom, where his poetry was published by Oscar's Press. A traveler and expatriate for more years than he can remember, he is writing a novel set in Saudi Arabia, where he lived during the Gulf War, and completing a study called *Imaginative Geographies: Teachers Abroad in Fiction*. He lives in New York City, where he's currently completing his M.F.A. in creative writing.

ANN DULANEY is at work on a volume of erotic short stories, as well as a biographical novel. Her writing has been published at *Sexilicious.com*. A former editor from Chicago, she lives and writes in Copenhagen.

TABITHA FLYTE is no stranger to erotic travel tales. Her second novel, *The Hottest Place,* concerns a British woman's (mis)adventures in Thailand, while her third and most recent book, *Full Steam Ahead*, is about a sexy, scam-pulling croupier on a Caribbean cruise ship. Both these, and her first novel, *Tongue in Cheek,* are published by Black Lace. Her work has been included in *Best Women's Erotica 2001, Aqua Erotica,* and *Herotica 7*. She lives and writes in London, after spending four years traveling in Asia and honeymooning in Nepal.

DAVID GARNES' work has appeared in *Latin Lovers: True Stories of Latin Men in Love, Quickies, Quickies 2, The Isherwood Century, Connecticut Poets on AIDS,* and numerous reference volumes on gay and lesbian literature. He is working on a book of poems about a boy's childhood. A longtime academic reference librarian, he lives in Manchester, Connecticut.

MICHAEL GOUDA was born and raised in London. After a "midlife crisis," he left the world of commerce and entered that of education and is now a teacher at a comprehensive school in Worcestershire, England, teaching English and information technology. He lives in a limestone cottage in the Cotswolds with two Border Collies and a cat. His short stories have been published by Idol Press and Blithe House Quarterly. At the moment he's writing a novel set in London during the 1940s.

CHRISTOPHER HART was born in 1965, and educated in Cheltenham, Oxford, and London, where he completed a Ph.D. on W. B. Yeats. He now works as a novelist and journalist. He has published two novels, *The Harvest* (Faber and Faber, 1999) and *Rescue Me* (Faber and Faber, 2001). His newest, entitled *Julia*, is a historical novel set in the dying days of the Roman Empire. He is the literary editor of the *Erotic Review*, contributes to a wide range of English newspapers and magazines, and lives in London, but escapes to Italy whenever possible:

DEBRA HYDE caught wanderlust early when her parents uprooted her from the English countryside at the tender age of ten months and moved to the Nevada desert. Today, she lives in New England, with her wanderlust in remission. There, she tracks sexuality news at her web-log *Pursed Lips* and writes erotica. Her most recent work appears in *Herotica 7*, *Zaftig: Well Rounded Erotica*, and *Strange Bedfellows*, which she coedited. Although she misses visiting places both plain and exotic, she does not miss sitting in crowded airports.

MAXIM JAKUBOWSKI toils in the galleys of erotica wearing various prophylactic hats: writer, editor, broadcaster, publisher, reviewer, and other functions he dare not reveal. He is responsible for the best-selling series of *Mammoth Books of Erotica*, now into six volumes, a handful of novels that have earned him the sobriquet of "king of the erotic thriller," and anthologies in other areas, including mystery fiction, film, science fiction and fantasy, humor, and most recently photography (with *The Mammoth Book of Erotic Photography* coedited with Marilyn Jaye Lewis). Previously a publisher, he now owns London's famous Murder One bookstore, where he impersonates the enquiries counter behind his perennial Apple—when not traveling in Europe, the U.S.A., or the Caribbean for nefarious reasons, some of which actually include pleasure. His last novel was *On Tenderness Express,* and if Eros grants him time, the next one will be called *Kiss Me Sadly.*

NALIN KANT was born in New Delhi on a hot summer day in 1952. He took B.Tech. and Ph.D. degrees from the Indian Institute of Technology, Delhi, and migrated to Australia in 1984. He lives in Melbourne with his wife, Hema; son, Ankur; and daughter, Pallavi. A professor of computer science, he has published in the area of computer communications. *The Red Convertible* is his first short story. He is at work on several short stories and a screenplay for *The Red Convertible*. On the back burner simmers his first novel, *The Cyber Guru*, which kindled his interest in fiction writing.

MICHÈLE LARUE studied six languages that she has used around the world as a freelance journalist, based in Paris. Today her signature prose is familiar to readers of the Parisian erotic press. She has shot two documentaries in Cuba and a third dealing with the European S/M scene. At a recent Cannes Film Festival, she shot an adaptation of one of her short stories, starring Deborah Twiss.

S. F. MAYFAIR lives with her teenaged son, an impossible dog, and a demanding cat in the Puget Sound area of Washington. As a student of Indic folklore, she has traveled extensively in India. She earned degrees from Victoria University of Wellington, New Zealand, and the University of Chicago. Her stories have appeared in *Prometheus*, *Venus or Vixen?*, and *Amoret Journal*, and on the websites *Erotica Readers Association* and *MyErotica.net*.

MARY ANNE MOHANRAJ (www.mamohanraj.com) is the author of *Torn Shapes of Desire*, editor of *Aqua Erotica*, and consulting editor for *Herotica 7*. She has been published in *Herotica 6*, *Best American Erotica 1999*, and *Best Women's Erotica 2000* and *2001*. She founded the erotic webzine *Clean Sheets* (www.cleansheets.com) and serves as editor-in-chief for the speculative fiction webzine *Strange Horizons* (www.strangehorizons.com). She also moderates the EROS Workshop and is a graduate of Clarion West '97. She has received degrees in writing and English from Mills College and the University of Chicago, teaches writing at the University of Utah, and is currently enrolled in a fiction Ph.D. program at the U of U. She is now reading for the sequel to *Aqua Erotica — Bodies of Water*.

JILL NAGLE (www.jillnagle.com) most recently associate-edited *Male Lust: Pleasure, Power and Transformation* (Haworth, 2000, Kerwin Kay, ed.). She also edited *Whores and Other Feminists* (Routledge, 1997). Her erotica has appeared in *Best Lesbian Erotica 2000*, *Best Bisexual Erotica 2000*, *Black Sheets*, and *First Person Sexual*. Her essays, articles, and reviews have appeared in *American Book Review*, *Girlfriends*, and *On Our Backs*. She is working on several collections of writings and a few screenplays. She lives in the San Francisco Bay Area.

JIM PROVENZANO is the author of *PINS*, an acclaimed novel about gay wrestlers (Myrmidude Press, www.myrmidude.com). He is the weekly "Sports Complex" columnist for San Francisco's *Bay Area Reporter* (sportscomplex.org), and a contributor to nearly every gay magazine in the past ten years. His other short fiction is included in *Best American Gay Fiction 1996*; *Waves*; *Queer View Mirror*; *Hey, Paesan!*; *Contra/Diction*; *The Mammoth Book of Gay Erotica*; *Swords of the Rainbow*; and *Men on Men 2000*. He lives in San Francisco, but often brags about being born in New York City.

NATASHA ROSTOVA (www.hyperlinx.net/~blue) is the author of four Black Lace novels, including the best-selling *Captivation*, as well as *Tea and Spices* (Carroll and Graf, 2000). Her work has appeared in several erotica anthologies, and she is working on a compilation of short stories. She lives in Montreal, where she is studying art history.

HELENA SETTIMANA trained as an art historian and later became a potter, poet, and short-fiction author. Her work has appeared in various web publications, including *Clean Sheets, The Erotica Readers Association,* and *Scarlet Letters,* as well as in print in *Best Women's Erotica 2001* (Cleis Press, Marcy Sheiner, ed.) and *Prometheus, Volume 36.* She lives with her husband and family of cats in Toronto.

SIMON SHEPPARD is the author of *Hotter Than Hell and Other Stories* (Alyson Books). He is coeditor, with M. Christian, of *Rough Stuff: Tales of Gay Men, Sex, and Power* and the forthcoming *Rough Stuff 2.* His work has appeared in well over fifty anthologies, including *Best Gay Erotica 2001* and *Best American Erotica 2002.* He's now hard at work on his next book, *Kinkorama.* He lives in San Francisco.

ALISON TYLER is the author of thirteen erotic novels, including *Learning to Love It* and *Strictly Confidential* (both published by Black Lace). Her short stories have appeared in *Wicked Words 4, Guilty Pleasures, Noirotica 3, Midsummer Night's Dreams, Sex Toy Tales,* and *The Unmade Bed,* and on the website www.goodvibes.com. She lives in the San Francisco Bay Area.

GERARD WOZEK is the author of *Dervish,* which won the Gival Press 2000 Poetry Book Award. His poetry and erotic fiction have appeared in *Reclaiming the Heartland* (University of Minnesota Press), *The Road Within* (Traveler's Tales), *Best Gay Erotica 1998* (Cleis Press), and *Rebel Yell 2* (Haworth Press). His award-winning poetry videos have been screened both nationally and internationally. He teaches creative writing at Robert Morris College in Chicago.

About the Editor

MITZI SZERETO is the author of *Erotic Fairy Tales; A Romp Through the Classics* (Cleis Press). Her work has appeared in *Wicked Words 4* (Black Lace), *Joyful Desires* (Masquerade Books), the *Erotic Review*, the online creative writing journal *Proof*, and the *Shiny* magazines. She is also known as M. S. Valentine, author of erotica titles *The Martinet* (Chimera Publishing, 2002), *The Captivity of Celia, Elysian Days and Nights, The Governess,* and *The Possession of Celia.* An itinerant spirit herself, she has lived in Miami, Los Angeles, Seattle, and the San Francisco Bay area. At present she divides her time between California and Yorkshire, England, where she is working on a master's degree.